THE CATSPAW OF PIPEROCK
and Other Tales from the Pulps

THE CATSPAW OF PIPEROCK
and Other Tales from the Pulps

W.C. TUTTLE

"Derelicts of the Hills" was originally published in *Adventure*, June, 1916.

"His Brother's Keeper" was originally published in *Short Stories*, Jan. 25, 1928.

"The Catspaw of Piperock" was originally published in *Adventure,* Feb. 1, 1929.

"Injuneered" was originally published in *Adventure*, July 15, 1929.

"Henry Goes Prehistoric" was originally published in *Short Stories*, January 25, 1948.

"Dancing Devil Range" was originally published in *Short Stories*, Oct. 25, 1948.

Contents

Contents

DERELICTS OF THE HILLS

"Now, I RECKON YUH had to come clear up here to tell me that th' grub is on th' table, eh? Of all th' gol dinged—"

The grumbler turned from his inspection of the three split fuses in the gopher hole and cast a baleful glance in my direction. He spat against the side of the cut and smiled after looking me over from new sombrero to riding boots.

"Ex—cuse me, stranger," he grunted, climbing out of the hole and wiping the day off his hands on his weather-beaten overalls. "I shore thought yuh was Magpie. Yuh see we ain't used to havin' strangers hereabouts. Magpie's my pardner and he's supposed to be down at th' cabin gittin' dinner."

"I saw a man sitting on a log down the trail a ways as I rode up," I remarked. "Seemed like a curious kind of a person. Wouldn't talk at all. Just sat there and gazed off across the hills."

"'Bout six feet long and ten inches wide—sort of uh roan with sparsely settled whiskers?" asked the prospector.

"Exactly," I agreed. "I noticed particularly the moth-eaten hirsute gathering and also the immense distance from the lobe of his right ear to his rear suspender buttons."

"Haw, haw!" exploded the prospector. "Suspender buttons! Haw, haw! Dog-gone good thing yuh didn't mention suspender buttons to him, 'cause he's sort a sensitive over such trifles. Uh-hu," he grunted reflectively, "that was Magpie Simpkins, shore was. Did yuh say he didn't seem to be lookin' at anything particular—jist sorta lookin'?"

I assured him that as far as I was able to discern there was nothing about those mesquite-covered hills to cause a man to focus on one certain spot for an indefinite period of time, oblivious to all material matters.

"There's one or two words in th' American langwidge I ain't never been introduced to," he replied, "and jist now yuh used 'em all in uh heap, but I gits th' drift. Magpie's trancin'."

"He's what?" I asked.

"Trancin'," he repeated, with a wide smile. "Anyway, I reckon that's what it's called. Yuh see, this pardner uh mine yuh gazes on down there has got th' idea he can commune with th' speerits, and I reckon he's down there tryin' to raise uh ghost."

"Go ahead and laugh," he continued, when I smiled. "Mebby it sounds funny to you, but, dog-gone it, you ain't never been partners to uh scientific loco human or yuh would jist shed uh tear and wish me well. Jist lemme tell yuh something now. I been— Say, I plumb forgot to ask yuh if yuh was lookin' fer some one up here, stranger. My name is Harper—christened when I was young and plumb helpless with th' appellation of Wellington Alexander, which same ain't no title fer uh sourdough. Th' first pardner I had rubbed it all out and called me Ike."

"My name is Frederick Norwood," I replied, and smiled with Harper. "My family are of the old English stock, and believed in saddling a child with all the names in the family record, and as names were dirt cheap at the time of my christening they never stopped at one little old middle name."

"Jist lookin' over th' mineral wealth of this great and glorious country, eh?" reflected Harper, as if I had made that statement but corrected his presumption by adding, "That's all there is to ever bring uh feller north uh Piperock."

"I'm looking for a fellow by the name of Woods," I stated.

"Tellurium Woods?" asked Harper.

"I believe that is what he's called. I stopped at the Empire Hotel at Piperock and the proprietor, a Mr. Jones, directed me up here. It's a queer thing, but the description he gave me seems to cover the man I saw down the trail—your partner, Mr. Simpkins."

"Uh-ha," he agreed. "I reckon it would. Yuh see, this Cobalt Jones thinks he's funny. He expected yuh to spring it on Magpie. Mebby you'd have got past with it, bein' as Magpie's in uh trance, but I'd shore hate to try it. Yes, sir, I reckon it would have laid the ghost."

"Would you mind explaining?" I asked. "I come up here to look over a copper prospect for some Eastern parties—property belonging to one Tellurium Woods, whose description fully covers the party you assure me is Magpie Simpkins, an embryo spiritualist. Also, that he's sensitive to suspender buttons."

"Mister Norwood," said Harper, biting off a fresh chew, "I sent Magpie down to th' cabin to cook uh pot uh beans about two hours ago, and knowin' th' animile as I do I'll bet uh dobie dollar that he'll start that fire in about two hours more. Also, bein' as I ain't in no hurry to shoot them three measly blasts, which won't uncover nothin' but shovel work, I'll tell yuh what and why fore.

"Yore time ain't worth no more than mine, I figure cause yuh won't find Tellurium Woods in this country no ways, so lets me and you mosey over under that big mesquite and I'll wau-wau yuh th' hull thing."

We reached the comfortable spot indicated, and he began:

Uh course Magpie ain't his right name. He got that name 'cause one time he gits lost in th' Bitter Roots and near starves to death. Shot all his ca'tridges away tryin' to kill uh magpie—th' same bein' classed with coyotes and buzzards as eatables—in uh country where blue grouse is thicker than fleas on uh pet coon.

I been pardners with Magpie for ten years now and I knows that jasper jist like I knows astronomy. Th' milk uh human kindness jist plumb bogs him down at times, and as a pardner he assays big; but when it comes to doin' useful things he don't show uh trace.

First he tries hypnotism. Tried it on uh wildcat in uh spruce-tree, but somehow th' cat didn't sabe th' play. If yuh ask him he'll show yuh where he was boloed down in th' Philippines. That was ten year ago that I met him in th' hospital in Helena and we went to Nome together.

Man, that human string-bean has dabbled in all kinds of scientific stuff. He took up Christian Science and played her four ways from th' jack, but one time he gits an ulcerated tooth and shifts his affections to psychology.

That shore was an affliction. He suffered from that fer uh year. Psychology goes bust when he salts uh feller's mine with copper to make said miner work harder, and some sucker come along and buys th' mine on th' strength of th' "salt" for five thousand—said mine-owner bein' that same Tellurium Woods yuh pilgrims up here to see. I know this is stringin' th' what and whyfore out pretty long, but I wants yuh to git an idea of this pardner uh mine.

I'm sittin' in front of our cabin uh couple uh months ago and watchin' th' sun set behind th' Medicine Men peaks and keepin' one eye on th' trail. Magpie's been down to Piperock fer seven days—which same trip after grub don't take more than two days. I'm down to greasin' th' fry-pan with uh ragged bacon rind, and th' coffee has been boiled so darn much it tastes like stewed gunnysack. In other words there ain't enough grub in th' shack to feed uh hummin'bird's offspring.

Long about that time I hears uh jackass brayin' down th' trail and 'long comes Magpie and them three pack-jacks and all four uh them animiles is singin'. Th' jacks is singin' 'cause they knows th' packs is soon to come off, but

I ain't hep to what makes Magpie so care-free—him usually bein' too deep in thought to sing above a whisper.

"Top uh th' evenin' to yuh!" yells Magpie, as they gits in range of th' wick-iup.

I jist grumbles somethin' about starvin' to death and workin' my fool head off while others take singin' lessons, but Magpie jist sighs deep and helps take th' packs off. I don't see no new books in th' packs, and I'm uh heap relieved.

"Feels sort a lonesome like up here," states Magpie, while I'm busy linin' my spare-ribs with good bacon and beans.

"Uh-ha," I agrees between mouthfuls, "especially after sojournin' in th' city fer quite uh spell." Piperock bein' all of uh hundred souls, six Chinks and uh small Greaser settlement.

"Ike," sez he, after uh long spell uh silence, "did yuh ever think what uh lot uh life we miss livin' thisaway?"

I'm too busy eatin', so he continues!

"Sort a shut off from th' society uh wimmen, and all that. Th' more I think about it th' more it appals me. No place to go, nothin' to do. Dog-gone it, Ike, we're jist uh pair uh deerylicks on th' hills uh life, you and me. Jist driftin' and driftin'—"

"Well, gol dang it, Magpie," sez I, "that's th' only reasonable way fer uh poor man to git depth. Uh course if yuh think we'll hit it any sooner by sinkin' uh shaft, why—"

"Ike Harper," states Magpie, sort uh lofty like, "yuh got uh soul like uh packburrow. All yuh knows is to eat and work. Yore thoughts don't soar higher than th' top of th' table. I'm sorry fer yuh, Ike, 'cause uh feller uh yore plebian tastes can't appreciate life. This life we're follerin' leads but to an unmarked grave. Don't yuh ever git th' soul hunger a-tall, Ike?"

"Mebby not soul hunger," I replies, "but I've been out of beans and bacon fer two days now."

Magpie plumb ignores this last, and ruminates deep.

"Ike," sez he after while, "there ain't much use askin', but did yuh ever figger any on th' wimmen question?"

I replies sort a offhand-like that I oncet knowed uh squaw down Yuma way, but I never finished th' romantic discourse 'cause Magpie looks me over with th' same look in his eyes that he had jist before I starts wearin' fresh meat on my right eye once.

"Mr. Harper, I asked yuh that question thinkin' that perhaps yuh had uh tiny spark uh mentality on top of yore neck, but I finds that I'm all wrong. I grieves for yuh, Ike."

I swallers my chew tryin' to make uh snigger sound like uh yawn, but Magpie don't notice and keeps on ramblin' in th' same vein.

"Ike, didn't yuh ever think about comin' home at night and find uh pretty wife waitin' supper fer yuh. One with eyes th' color of th' deep places in Sawtooth Lake and hair like th' sunset on th' Medicine peaks. Some one to love yuh, Ike, and clean up th' cabin and make yuh quit wearin' nails to connect yore suspenders to yore pants."

Magpie sighs clear down to th' bottoms of his boots and fumbles fer th' makin's after deliverin' this oration.

I takes uh fresh chew and asks friendly-like—

"When did she come to Piperock, Magpie?"

"Week ago last—say, who yuh talkin about?"

"That new blue-eyed, yaller-haired waitress at Cobalt Jones' hashery."

"Yuh danged old sourdough sleuth!" yells Magpie, but seems tickled uh heap to think I done guessed it. "How did yuh ever figger it out, Ike?"

"Magpie," sez I, sort uh patronizin'ly like, "I may be of uh low order of intelligence and never suffer none from th' soul hunger, but by golly, I'm kumtux on this here love stuff. Th' little jasper with his bow and arrer shore beat yuh on th' draw, old-timer."

Magpie don't deny it none. Jist set there and grins and rubs his hands over his boots like they hurt his feet.

"Bein' as there ain't much to do around here," he opines after while, "I reckon I'd sort a like to go down to Piperock in th' mornin'. Yuh can make out uh list uh what yuh wants and—"

"Say, what's th' idea?" I cuts in. "Yuh jist gits in with enough to last uh month or more."

Magpie gits up sorta weary like and as he shuffles into th' cabin he makes th' following statement:

"I reckon that's right, pardner, but I gotta go back right away. Yuh see I'm goin' to marry her, and I plumb forgot to ask her—sorta forgot it, I reckon."

The next mornin' Ike lights out down th' trail with th' rest of th' pack-jacks and I don't see him for four days. When he comes driftin' in about sundown on th' fourth day he's smilin' all over his face as he comes up th' trail to th' cabin. He shakes my hand sorta excited-like and tells me I'm lookin' skookum.

"Ike," sez he, "I went and done it."

"Got married?" I asks.

"Not yet, but soon. I'm goin' to enter th' solemn and holy bonds uh matrimony and wedlock next Tuesday."

"Uh course," sez I, "not havin' been uh pardner uh yours fer more than ten years and not havin' saved yore worthless life more than once uh year, it would be presumptuous I suppose to inquire what name this unsuspectin' female person answers to."

"Her name is Minnie," he replies.

"I read about uh female named Minne Haha oncet," I states, sorta off-hand-like.

"This one answers to Summers," he tells me, "and she's some girl! Uh danged old sourdough like me ain't noways fit fer her, Ike, but dog-goned if she didn't tell me she loved me."

He does uh portion of th' Piegan wardance on th' wood-pile and then chases th' burrows clear down to th' crick. I reckon love must be worse than loco weed, 'cause he's already pilgrimed over twenty-five miles uh rough trail that day.

"Git uh ring?" I asks when he comes back.

"Did I!" he yells. "Well, yuh better believe I did. Paid uh hundred and fifty fer uh diamond as big as uh pants button and she's set in uh gold ring she can't wear out in uh lifetime. Bought it off Slim Jackson, th' faro dealer at th' Mint.

"I wanted to tie up right away, Ike, but she said next Tuesday. Yuh see she wanted to buy uh troosoo and all that kinda stuff. She was uh little shy on money, so I lends her uh couple a hundred—gives it to her, I mean. By golly, Ike, she can have all I got! Why don't you git married, too, and then we'll all live in th' same wickiup, Ike?"

"See anybody else down there?" I asks, ignorin' his foolish question.

"Let's see—uh-ha, I seen that danged ol' woodchuck, Tellurium Woods. He's back again and was all dressed up like uh plush horse. Even had them cloth things over his shoes and smokin' uh seegar. Darn old misfit's sailin' high with th' money I made for him by saltin' his old copper prospect. I meets him on th' street, but him and me don't wau-wau none a-tall. Honest, Ike, I gotta plumb sit on my gun hand every time I sees his onery ol' face."

Well, sir, from that time Magpie don't exhibit no more brains than uh fool-hen. When he ain't sighin' way down in his boots he's singin'—that is, he's yellin' th' words uh two songs and th' tune uh neither. And when he ain't doin' that he's oratin' about bungaloos, geeraniums and chiny dishes. I'm plumb disgusted with him. When uh feller uh Magpie's type gits in love it's worse than uh floatin' kidney—yuh kin anchor th' kidney.

On Sunday night he can't seem to sleep none, and finally gits up and leaves th' cabin, and don't come back until I'm jist about finished eatin' breakfast.

"Beautiful night, Ike," sez he. "Finest moonlight I ever seen."

"Magpie Simpkins," sez I, "yore as crazy as uh shepherd, and if yuh don't shake yourself it will only be uh few moons until yuh will be drillin' fer soap in th' asylum at Warm Springs. Far be it from me to laugh at love, pardner, but I'll be hanged if I'll stand fer yuh kissin' that old he burrow. He's half mine and—"

"Ike," sez he, reachin' absent-mindedly fer th' ax, "that's uh danged lie. I never kissed uh jackass in my life."

"Then yuh shore got th' edge on Minnie," I returns, and beat th' ax to th' corner of th' cabin by uh hair.

One nice thing about Magpie is th' fact that he don't hold uh grudge and I'm safe to come back in an hour.

Uh course I'm elected to be th' best man at this weddin', which means I'll have to git my boots greased, buy uh new necktie and keep reasonably sober. Also, I've got to stand in front of th' Gospel Peddler alongside uh Mrs. Cobalt Jones—th' same bein' several degrees worse to look at than th' squaw I knowed down at Yuma.

The day before th' happenin', that bein' uh Monday, me and Magpie packs th' burrows and hits th' trail fer Piperock. Magpie drills along uh mile or two in front until we gits almost in sight uh town and then he drops back and sits down on uh boulder.

"Ike," sez he, wipin' his face on his sleeve, "I'm gittin' plumb nervous. Sorta gun-shy, I reckon. Th' more I thinks about it th' worse it seems. I wants to git married, Ike, but every time I thinks about me bein' up there in front uh that preacher feller and sayin' 'I do,' dog-gone it, I gits buck fever."

"Well, old-timer," I remarks, "here's uh good place to turn th' outfit around and make uh getaway."

"Not any a-tall!" sez he. "I don't buy diamonds and loosen up my roll fer uh troosoo and then stampede. Lead on, McDuffy, and danged be he who first yells I gotta plenty!" Which is uh favorite sayin' of Magpie's.

I prods th' leadin' jack and we pilgrims on down th' trail toward town.

We're almost into Piperock when we sees uh little feller comin' ploddin' up th' trail toward us. He's sort of uh runty little party with rusty whiskers and most awfully bowlegged, and when he gits closer we sees that he's packin' uh sawed-off ten gage shotgun.

He stops uh few feet in front of us and shifts th' hardware to cover our hull outfit.

"Say," sez he, "which one uh you specimans is Tellurium Woods?"

"Yuh danged little imitation of uh crokay wicket!" yells Magpie, droppin' th' lead rope and startin' forward, but th' riot gun covers him and he stops sudden like. "What do yuh mean by that question?" he roars.

"Hurry up and answer!" roars bowlegs right back at him.

"Neither of us is that polecat!" snaps Magpie. "And what is more and conclusive, I kin lick you and th' funny party or parties that sent yuh out here to ask it."

I sees that th' little feller is sorta overcome like, and not knowin' how easy that scatter gun is on th' trigger, I steps in sorta soothin' like and tells him who we are.

"What do yuh want of Tellurium?" I asks.

"Dang his measly hide!" wails th' feller. "I aims to shoot his old hide into shoestrings. I'm plannin' to pulverize his system with buckshot and I'm hopin' this here gun don't scatter so much that he will miss any of th' contents."

"And th' reason fer his demise?" I asks.

"Dang him, he done stole my wife!" yells th' little feller.

"Tellurium Woods stoled yore wife?" parroted Magpie, reachin' over and appropriatin' th' hardware. "Well, well, don't cry, little feller. Any danged woman that would run away with that old hedgehog ain't worth cryin' over a-tall. Come on back and have uh drink. Uh drink uh hooch will make th' world seem brighter."

"I know I'm foolish," he agrees, "but it ain't a square deal. We been married over five year now and she's been uh kind, lovin', thoughtful wife until now. We was in business down to Curlew, and when th' mines shut down our business went busted and so did we. She gits uh job up here and I stays there to settle up th' business, and when I comes up here she's gone. Dang it all,' I sez to her when she was leavin', 'Minnie,' sez I. 'when yuh gits——'"

"What name?" interrupts Magpie.

"Minnie," sez th' little one. "My name is Summers, Gus Summers, and I sez to her—"

Magpie shoves th' gun back into th' little feller's hands and pats him on top of his rusty old derby hat.

"Good huntin' and good luck to you, Summers, old scout," sez Magpie, who is jist uh little white around th' gills. And then he kicks th' lead burrow in th' wind and turns him around toward th' back trail.

We gits about half-way back to th' cabin when Magpie stops to fill his pipe.

"Ike," sez he, "that Tellurium Woods is uh—"

"Friend in need," sez I. "Fifteen buckshot to uh shell, and two shells, make thirty holes."

Magpie is silent fer quite some spell and then he sticks out his hand with uh smile.

"Ike, old pardner, shake. We may be deerylicks uh th' hills, me and you, but—say, did yuh notice her husband was wearin' bailin' wire instead uh pants buttons?"

"Say, I been noticin' smoke comin' out of th' stovepipe for quite uh spell, Mister Norwood, so I reckon Magpie's normal once more. Come on down and taste beans cooked scientifically."

HIS BROTHER'S KEEPER

IT WAS ALWAYS HOT in the Bitter Water Valley, and the hills were like rumpled yellow and gray blankets, shimmering in the summer sun. Folks didn't tan there—they simply charred. The winds were hot, even in the shade—when there was any wind.

The old dirt road, inches deep in dust, wound in and out among the old lava beds, like a long, yellow worm, with its head in the town of Calor, its few tails ending at the scattered ranches. The valley was not a summer resort, and those who were financially able went into the far mountains, to escape the heat.

Along this winding, yellow road came a team and wagon, almost hidden in a cloud of dust, which drifted up from wheel and hoof like the smoke from a foundry stack. On the seat were a man and a woman, and in the back of the wagon was a single trunk, already dust covered.

The woman had a scarf twisted about her mouth and nose, while the man's face to his eyes was covered with a bandana handkerchief; two masked figures, their dusty eyes blinking, red-rimmed. Their conversation was limited; had been limited for several weary miles, but now they struck a slight raise, where the dust was less deep.

"I had to do it, Joe," said the woman, as though picking up the conversation of an hour gone. "I just had to."

"I know it, Mrs. Deming," said the man nodding slowly. "I seen it comin'."

He spat dryly, still nodding. "I told Jim. I told him he was a fool. But," resignedly, "yuh can't tell him nothin'. Bull-headed as hell, Jim is. He read me the riot act. Said fer me to mind my own business."

"And he'll fire you, Joe."

The man turned slowly and looked at the woman. She had removed the scarf now. Mrs. Jim Deming, wife of Jim Deming, sheriff of Calor, had been a pretty girl in her youth. She was still pretty, except that her hair was gray and her once smooth face was creased with deep lines. Her gray eyes were clouded with sadness, as she looked at Joe Mills, her husband's deputy.

Joe was tall, thin, harsh-faced, burned to the color of a dark Indian. Joe Mills was as hard as the lava beds, but he had found a man harder than he. Jim Deming, known as "Duty" Deming, was so hard that he rather appalled even Joe Mills.

"Yeah, he'll fire me," agreed Joe slowly. "But that's fine, ma'am. I'm kinda sour on this county, anyway. Seems to me that I'd kinda like to go somewhere else, where there's green grass and lakes. I've allus lived here, yuh see. Don't you worry about me, ma'am; you've got a-plenty to worry about for yourself."

"Thank you, Joe. I'm glad you don't blame me. It had to come. He—he wasn't so bad until they elected him sheriff. We got along, yuh know. Goin' onto three years now. I—I hoped they'd defeat him last election."

"Shore. Prob'ly been better if they had. But they say he's the best sheriff they ever had—I dunno."

"Because he sent my son to prison," she said painfully.

"Yeah. It was his son, too."

"Joe, you know Harry wasn't a thief, don't yuh?"

"I don't reckon he was. The JB outfit started out to git Harry—and they got him."

"His own father got him, you mean!" exclaimed Mrs. Deming. "Jim was alone when he found that evidence at Harry's place. It was nothing but a JB hide. Jim could have buried it and warned Harry. That hide was planted there by the JB. But Jim took the evidence and arrested Harry. Ten years! It was Jim's evidence that sent my boy to the penitentiary."

"Yes, ma'am."

"And he sent Al Seymour up for stealing a horse, which he didn't steal. Al was drunk that night and got the wrong one. It was wrong for him to get drunk, I know; but he didn't intend to take the wrong horse. Jim knew it. Oh, yes, he did. But he went straight out and arrested Al, instead of bringing the horse back. He could have explained it all. Al was no thief."

"He was going to marry Jane, wasn't he, Mrs. Deming?"

"Yes. It broke her heart, Joe. I'm going to her now. Oh, I've pleaded with Jim; talked and pleaded until my throat was raw. But what's the use? He defends himself by saying that he swore to uphold the law, and both Harry and Al broke the law. His duty to the law! He sits in judgment on this whole desert; brags about his iron hand. Oh, it's iron, all right. It smashed his home; it will smash him, too."

"I dunno; he's pretty hard, ma'am. I never knowed a man as hard as Jim, and I've knowed a lot of hard ones. His job is a religion with him."

"And some day it will raise up and kill him."

"His star is his god," said the deputy slowly.

"And don't the Bible say something about thou shalt have no other gods before me?"

"Mebbe. I dunno much about the Bible. I don't reckon that God operates much around here—it's too hot."

"I've wondered about it," she said, wearily. "I've prayed a lot, Joe; but nothing came of it."

"Too hot, Mrs. Deming. I don't reckon a fried prayer ever got any further than a fried aig. Mebbe not as far, because yuh can eat the aig. Well, there's the town. Yuh've got plenty time, 'cause the train ain't never on time. Lotsa folks would miss the train if it ever came on time."

———————◦———————

The train was of the mixed variety, half passenger, half freight; a branch line train, using something like seven hours to complete the sixty mile run from Santa Leone to Levering, which was twenty miles south of Calor.

Calor was the usual desert type of town. Perhaps a little larger, due to the fact that it was a county seat, but the buildings were unpainted, scourged by wind and sand, until they blended nicely with the gray of the desert. Two huge water tanks, thrusting their ungainly bulk upward on their scaffolding, like huge, rotund giants, with spindling legs, supplied the town with water, which was always warm.

The depot had once been painted a bright red, but time had dimmed its luster until it was a sickly pink, where any color yet remained.

The team came up to the depot platform, guided in close to the high platform. The deputy helped the woman down, and unloaded the trunk. He tied both horses securely to the platform, because they were unused to trains, and then began twisting the trunk around to the front, the woman following him.

The telegraph wires hummed in the hot wind, and there was a strong odor of pitch frying up from the planks of the platform. A man stood near the doorway to the waiting room; a tall, lean figure of a man, harsh of feature, his gray eyes deep set under beetling brows, and separated with a high-arched nose. His mouth was wide and thin lipped.

In raiment he was practically the same as ninety-nine per cent of the desert men; well-worn sombrero, colorless shirt, stringy vest, overalls, from which the color had long since fled, tucked in the tops of high-heeled boots. Around his lean waist hung a belt and holstered gun, and on the lapel of his vest gleamed the insignia of office. Such was Duty Deming, sheriff of Calor.

He shot one sharp glance at his deputy, who handled the trunk awkwardly as he rolled it out near the edge of the platform. The woman stopped short and studied the face of her husband.

"You didn't think I'd come, did you?" she asked.

"If I hadn't, I wouldn't be up here," he said slowly.

The deputy walked from the trunk to the waiting room. He had Mrs. Deming's ticket, and was going to check the trunk. The sheriff's eyes followed him.

"You don't need to blame Joe," she said.

His eyes shifted from the doorway and came back to her.

"You're not sorry?" she asked.

"What for? I've got nothing to be sorry about."

"After thirty years, Jim?"

"No. You said you'd go away. I've provided for yuh all these years, and——"

"And sent my son to prison; drove my daughter away."

His jaw set grimly for a moment. "Well?"

"I guess that's all, Jim."

They were silent now. Came the soft humming of the rails, as the train came creeping through the desert. The telegraph instrument in the office clanked spasmodically.

"They call you Duty," she said bitterly. "And you're proud of it. You think more of that than you do of your family. Your evidence ruined the happiness of your daughter; your evidence ruined my happiness."

"I swore to do my duty," he said slowly. "I raised my right hand and swore to uphold the law. It doesn't mean that an officer can be lenient to *anybody*. I've been the best sheriff this county ever had, and I'll keep on bein' the best sheriff. The voters put their trust——"

"I've heard all that, Jim. I'm going away now; going to be gone forever. I'll never come back to the desert—to you. You've made a god of your job, Jim. Maybe they'll put up a monument to you some day."

The train whistled shrilly, as it came into view. The deputy came out and gave Mrs. Deming her ticket and her trunk check.

"Thank you, Joe," she said, holding out her hand. They shook hands, and she turned her back on her husband, watching the train come in. There were only a few people at the station. The engine clanked past and the train ground to a stop. The sheriff's eyes were looking down the train, and without a word he walked away from his wife and strode down the platform.

She looked curiously after him, but he did not look back. So this was his good-by. Stifling a sob she climbed up the steps of the coach and went inside, while the agent's helper threw her trunk in the baggage car.

Duty Deming walked down to a box-car and hunched on his heels, speaking to a man who clung to the rods beneath the car.

"Come out of that," he ordered gruffly.

The man slowly edged off the rods and almost fell headlong. His legs were cramped from the uncomfortable position, and he was black with dirt and sand; his clothes driven full of it.

"Stealin' a ride, eh?" grunted the sheriff.

The hobo straightened up, looked around through bloodshot eyes, which finally came back to the sheriff. The train was moving again.

"What's the big idea?" asked the hobo hoarsely. "What right have you to drag me off here? You're just a hick sheriff and this is a little town. I was just travelin'."

"Stealin' a ride," said the sheriff grimly. He did not look up as the coaches passed him. "You know it's agin the law, young man."

"That's up to the railroad company. Or do you own this particular branch?"

"No, I don't own the railroad," replied the sheriff harshly, "but I do represent the law around here."

"Represent it, eh?"

The hobo sighed deeply and looked at the passing coaches. The sheriff did not look at them.

"Hot ridin' under there," said the hobo. "I was just heading out of this country. Tough riding, I'll tell you; but they had all them box-cars sealed. Still, I could have made it to Levering."

"Well, yuh didn't!" snapped the sheriff.

"That's true. Still, you haven't any rock pile. All you can do is to put me in jail and feed me. That's not a profitable thing. Better let me sit here in the shade, until the next train comes along."

"And let you steal another ride, eh?"

"What do you care, as long as you don't own the railroad?"

"I'm paid to uphold the law," said the sheriff stiffly.

The hobo sighed wearily, as he scraped his heel against the cinders.

"Do you always uphold the law?"

"Always—that's what I'm here for."

"A little authority has made you your brother's keeper, eh?"

"I'm the sheriff."

"Oh, I can see that. But what right have you to haul me off that train? It isn't your train. You're not paid to guard that train, are you? Don't shove me. Can't you see I'm a sick man?"

"Sick man!" sneered the sheriff. "Sick because I'm goin' to lock yuh up for a few days. Don't play 'possum with me."

"I'm not playing 'possum, as you say; I'm sick."

The man really looked sick, in spite of his grimy face, but the sheriff twisted him around by the shoulder and started him toward the jail. Several persons, including the deputy, waited on the depot platform to see what the sheriff was going to do, and as the sheriff marched his prisoner past them he told the deputy to come with him.

The deputy followed down to the jail, where the hobo was locked behind the bars. The deputy made no comment, but followed the sheriff back to the office, where they sat down.

"Said he was sick," remarked the sheriff disgustedly.

"Looked sick," said the deputy wearily, fanning himself with his sombrero.

The sheriff studied the lean face of his deputy for a length of time. "How did you happen to bring the old lady in today, Joe?" he asked.

"She asked me to. I came past the ranch. I told her I'd take the team back and get my horse. She was comin', anyway," as though to defend his position in the matter.

"She was, eh? You never stopped to think that you were workin' for me, did yuh? You waste a day, bringin' her in, and waste another day in goin' back with that team. Do you think I'm payin' you to use up time that way?"

The deputy flushed slightly and his lips tightened.

"I didn't know that *you* paid me anythin', Deming. Ain't I paid by the county?"

"I'm part of that county, Joe; the sheriff part of it. I hired yuh, didn't I?"

The deputy got slowly from his chair and put on his hat.

"You hired me, Deming, but I'll be damned if you fire me; I quit right now."

"All right; suit yourself."

"I intend to, Deming. In fact, I intended to quit yuh when I came down here. You never even told yore wife good-by; just walked away to arrest a hobo, who wasn't doin' you any harm. Yo're plumb loco over duty, ain't yuh? I'm scared of yuh, Jim; honest, I am. Yore wife said you was worshippin' that tin god on yore vest; that sheriff's star. I reckon yuh are.

"She said somethin' about it raisin' up and killin' yuh. Said somethin' about what the Bible said about not havin' wrong gods. I don't sabe just what she meant. But I do sabe how she feels toward yuh. Deming, you've gone crazy over duty to the law. It's all right to enforce the law, but yo're just a damn' fool over it. I knowed you was crazy when yuh sent Harry to the pen. You didn't need to do it, and you know yuh didn't. Oh, I'm glad I quit yuh."

Deming's face flushed hotly and he started to rise from his chair, but sank back heavily, a queer expression in his hard gray eyes.

"What did she mean by sayin' that it would rise up and kill me?" he demanded. "That's fool talk; women's talk. Nobody can scare me. I'm glad yuh quit, if yuh feel the way yuh do about me—and yore job. You didn't always fulfill yore oath, Joe. Mebbe it's best that yuh did quit. I'm goin' to be more particular in the next deputy I hire."

"They'll probably be, too," said Joe. "You'll have a hell of a time, hirin' a new man, 'cause everybody knows how hard yuh are, Deming. Well, I'll pack my stuff and get out."

"All right, Joe; give me your star. And them ca'tridges in yore belt belong to the county."

Several days passed in which Deming was obliged to run the office alone, which meant that twice a day he must carry food to his prisoner, against whom no formal complaint had been made. But the hobo was far too ill to care whether he had food or freedom. He spent most of the time on his cot, talking deliriously, and in the dim light of the little cell the sheriff could see nothing wrong with the man, except a fever.

But finally he called in the doctor, who was also the coroner, and he immediately pronounced it a malignant case of smallpox; quarantining the jail. He was minded to quarantine the sheriff, but while he was making up his mind just what to do a cowboy, Slim Delong, fairly tore up the street of Calor, bringing news of a murder.

Delong was fairly incoherent. Red Cowan, another cowboy working for the JB outfit, had murdered Al Mitchell, owner of the outfit, and had headed for the lava beds. Delong, riding in at the ranch, had seen Red Cowan riding away swiftly toward the lava bed country, and a few minutes later he had found Mitchell lying on the front porch, shot through the heart.

———◆———

Mitchell was a big cattleman in that part of the country, and the sheriff's son had been sent to the penitentiary for stealing Mitchell's cattle. The town was rather in an uproar over the murder, but the sheriff did not ask any of the cowboys to ride with him.

He saddled his roan horse, tied a quantity of food to his saddle, filled a canteen and headed for the lava bed country. He did not need help. He knew every inch of the lava bed country, although he did not know Red Cowan. Red had only been there a short time and he had heard Joe speak of meeting him at the JB.

Shortly after Delong had delivered his message to the sheriff, Delong imbibed a few drinks before starting back to the JB ranch with the coroner and several others, who were going out there to bring the body to town. He happened to be riding a half-broke bronco, and in the flurry at the hitchrack, as they were starting out, Delong's horse bucked wickedly, throwing Delong against one of the hitchrack posts.

In the parlance of the range, it knocked Delong flatter than a snake's belly, and he was unable to get on his horse; so they half carried, half led him back to the saloon, where they left him propped up in a chair.

The sheriff did not hurry his horse. He swung in west of the JB ranch and headed for the lava bed country, making no attempt to pick up the tracks of Red's horse. He knew that Red would cut straight through the lava beds and head for the Mesquite River country, sixty miles away; sixty miles of waterless waste, a broken mass of twisted lava, which seemed never to have cooled since those prehistoric days, when it had been poured indiscriminately over the landscape.

The sheriff felt reasonably certain that Red Cowan had started without any preparations for food or water, and would probably expect, at least, to find water. But there was no water in that part of the country. And a man must ride slowly, because the sharp lava would soon ruin the feet of his horse, unless the animal was allowed to make its own pace.

Mile after mile he plodded along, squinting his eyes against the glare of the sun, until he developed a queer sort of a headache; a dull throb in the back of his head, which caused him to wince at times. It bothered his eyes. He drank from his canteen, but the water did not seem to quench his thirst.

His mouth felt dry a moment later; so he took another drink, which caused him a slight nausea. Must be the sun, he decided. Still, the idea did not seem so good, because he was used to the sun. It made him angry. After a while he filled and lighted his pipe, but after the first few puffs of the pungent weed, he put the pipe in his pocket.

Ahead of him stretched the interminable wastes of the lava beds, where the heat devils danced before his eyes, and he cursed them aloud, as though they could heed his voice. Then it seemed as though he realized the utter absurdity of such things, and cursed himself.

The setting sun found the sheriff riding aimlessly. His eyes ached continuously now, and he had lost all desire to scan the country. But he was not going to turn back. He was following a murderer, a cold-blooded killer, and the law must be avenged.

He felt a little better when the sun went down and the short desert twilight had blended with the night; a time in which the temperature drops swiftly from a hundred and fifteen in the shade to sixty in the dark. The sheriff had ridden away without any blankets, and now he shivered in a sudden chill, which seemed to crinkle his vertebrae.

Queer thing, that chill. It rattled his teeth like castanets and increased his headache until every movement of the horse brought him fresh misery. So he dismounted, uncoiled his lariat and picketed his horse. It was only after several minutes that he was able to summon enough energy to remove the saddle.

Duty Deming was a sick man—and knew it. He thought of saddling his horse and heading for Calor, but he had lost all sense of direction. The stars blurred in his eyes, and he flopped down beside his saddle, burying his aching head in his arms.

—◇—

It was possibly two hours later that the sheriff's horse nickered softly in the darkness, but the sheriff did not lift his head. Came the sound of a horse walking, and the bulky form of a horse and rider came in through the broken rocks, plainly visible by the light of the stars.

The rider drew rein near the picketed horse, as though rather surprised to find a horse there. He dismounted and discovered the rope, speaking softly to the horse. He turned away and soon discovered the sheriff.

"Sleepin' kinda heavy, ain't yuh, pardner?" he asked in a soft, drawling voice; but the sheriff did not move.

Coming in closer, the man scratched a match. He was of medium height, thin-faced, blue-eyed, dressed in a faded blue shirt, well-worn bat-wing chaps, black Stetson. The light of the match glistened on the butt of a big Colt in the holster swinging at his thigh. As he removed his hat to shield the match the light glistened on his copper-colored hair.

He was Red Cowan, the murderer. He knelt down beside the sheriff and shook him by the shoulder.

"Wake up, pardner," he said softly, but the sheriff merely grunted and began mumbling deliriously.

"Sick, eh?" muttered the red headed one. "Funny. Got a bad fever and he's plumb loco. And it's a long ways to a doctor. Jist what'll I do next?"

He squatted on his heels and rolled a cigarette. After due deliberation and another cigarette he saddled the sheriff's horse. The sheriff was not easy to arouse but he talked steadily, mumbling his words, swearing and laughing foolishly, while Red Cowan swung him into the saddle and roped him on. He swayed forward, both arms dangling loosely, while Cowan mounted his own horse and picked up the lead-rope.

Cowan took his bearings from the North Star and started out, looking back at the humped figure of the sheriff, swaying in the saddle.

"Stay with her, pardner," he grunted. "We'll make the old Alkali Spring ranch by mornin', and mebbe we'll find somebody there."

And all through the night they wended their way through the lava beds, and it was just about daybreak when they came out at an old tumbledown ranch house. The old buildings seemed about to fall down, the corrals were in bad repair, and only one fan was left on the old windmill, which creaked in the morning breeze.

Down by the old stable was an alkali spring, where a few cattle, drifters from the herds in the Mesquite River ranges, came to drink. Red Cowan looked them over appraisingly. They meant fresh meat.

He unroped the sheriff and lifted him to the ground, propping him against the wall while he went inside. The inside of the house was not as bad as the exterior, as it had been used by some cattlemen during a recent roundup. There was a roll of blankets, tightly wrapped in a tarpaulin, swinging from a rafter, while from a tightly closed box he took flour, baking powder, salt, sugar, beans and some cans of vegetables and fruit.

"Thought there might be a cache here," he said, as he removed the provisions.

He took down the bed-roll and spread it out on one of the bunks, before going out after the sheriff, whom he dragged in and put to bed. He looped the sheriff's belt around a bunk post, removed his clothes, and prepared a breakfast, before attending to the horses.

—◇—

The sheriff was burning with fever, tossing his arms, mumbling incoherently all the while.

After a breakfast, in which the sheriff did not join him, Cowan brought a pail of the cold water to the house and proceeded to give the sheriff a sponge bath. This treatment seemed to sooth the sick man, and he dropped into a slumber.

Cowan found an old pair of hopples, which he put on the sheriff's horse, and turned his own mount loose to forage. There was little to be done. Cowan did not want to leave the sick man long enough to go after a doctor, which would take at least two days; so there was only one thing for him to do, and that was to stay and see it through, hoping that someone might come along and lend them a hand.

For the next three days and nights he worked with the sheriff. There were no medicines of any kind, and it seemed to be a losing battle. He killed a steer and made beef broth, which the sheriff could not eat, gave him both cold and hot baths, worked over him like a mother over a child, and on the evening of the third day the sheriff awoke—conscious for the first time.

After a period of deliberation he remembered starting out after Red Cowan. Seated near the bed, his head in his hands, snoring loudly, was a red-headed man. The sheriff did not know any red-headed men. He was very weak; so he shut his eyes and tried to think. After a while he heard the man move, and opened his eyes.

"That's better," said the red-head wearily.

"Who are you?" asked the sheriff, and was surprised that his voice was so weak.

"I'm Red Cowan."

The sheriff closed his eyes quickly.

"I guess I don't know yuh," he said slowly.

"Mebbe not. I was with the JB a while. What's the matter with yuh, anyway? You've been here three days."

"Three days?" The sheriff's eyes popped open.

Red told him all about it.

"Didn't have no medicine," he explained. "Had to do the best I could."

"Know who I was?"

"Saw yore star. Yo're Deming of Calor, ain't yuh? Yeah, I thought yuh was. I've heard of yuh. How'd yuh happen to be out there in the lava beds?"

The sheriff closed his eyes, thinking swiftly. Cowan must not know why he was out there.

"I dunno," he said. "Took sick. Must have ridden a long ways."

"You picketed yore horse."

"Oh, I wasn't plumb out until after—just awful sick."

"You shore know how to be sick," grinned Cowan. "Do you feel like some eats?"

The sheriff shook his head.

"Better not talk any more, pardner. You've been pretty sick, and it might fever yuh up, if yuh talked much."

That suited the sheriff. He didn't want to talk; he wanted to think. His eyes shifted to his belt and gun on the bunk-post at the head of his bed, and he wondered if the gun was loaded.

When Cowan went outside he lifted a hand toward the gun, and as he did so he glanced at his hand. He felt of his stubby face, and a look of horror spread over his face.

"Smallpox!" he exclaimed to himself. "That's what it is—all them little red specks. I got it from that damn' hobo!"

***

Cowan came back into the house, but the sheriff did not tell him. He was afraid that Cowan might leave him in fear of the disease. Not exactly that he felt an immediate need of Cowan, but he wanted to take Cowan back a prisoner.

"Still feelin' pretty good?" asked Cowan as he busied himself around the stove.

"I don't feel so good, Cowan."

"Probably not. Can't expect to. But I reckon I've busted the fever. How about a little broth, eh?"

"Not now."

"Uh-huh. Tomorrow mornin', if yo're feeling pretty good, I think I'll head for Mesquite River and send some folks in to take care of yuh. You need a doctor pretty bad, and you'll need the right kinda food."

That was not so good. The sheriff huddled down in bed, trying to think of some way to prevent Cowan from leaving. Just now his thoughts ran in circles, because his head ached again. Ten minutes later he was delirious again.

And all that night Cowan had to use force to keep him in bed. He babbled of murderers, horse thieves and of his own prowess as a sheriff. And in the light of the candle Cowan saw the rash on the sheriff's hands and face.

"Smallpox!" grunted Cowan. "So that's what's the matter, eh? Lucky I've had a good dose of it. Tomorrow I'll tie him down and head for a doctor."

It was daylight again before the sheriff became conscious. The fever had abated enough to allow him to realize and recognize again. Cowan's face was drawn and tired, his eyes red from lack of sleep.

"Sane again, eh?" he grunted. "Well, you've shore been off yore nut a-plenty, pardner. Listen to me and get this straight. I'm goin' out and round up my bronc. You've got a sweet case of smallpox, which means yo're goin' to be here mebbe a couple weeks. I can't stay all that time; so I'm headin' for Mesquite River to get yuh a doctor and a nurse.

"Yuh take her easy while I get my horse. Mebbe I better tie yuh down, 'cause you might go wanderin' around and die out in the desert. Anyway, yo're all right for a while, and I'll see yuh before I pull out. I'll leave plenty water, such as it is, where yuh can reach it. But you've got to have plenty nursin' and the right kinda food."

Red Cowan picked up his rope and went out, leaving the sheriff staring at the rafters, trying to force his mind to function properly. He didn't want Red Cowan to leave him. He had never failed to bring in his man, and if Red Cowan ever left that ranch——

His hand reached up weakly and drew the heavy Colt from the holster. It was fully loaded. The weight of it quickly tired his wrist, and he stared at his bloodless hand. The fever had sapped his strength badly, and he lay back wearily, cursing himself for a quitter.

He was no match for Red Cowan now. Hadn't Cowan said something about tying him down? The sheriff tried to sit up. If Red Cowan tied him down——

"Get up, you fool!" he told himself. "Yo're all right. Are you goin' to lie here and let a murderer escape? You are Duty Deming, sheriff of Calor!"

With a superhuman effort he managed to swing around on the bunk and get his feet over the edge; but toppled back, where he lay breathing heavily, gripping the gun in his right hand.

He could feel the fever coming back, but he would not let that stop him. It was now or never. No thought of the future—only the present. The law must be served.

He managed to reach the doorway, where he went to his knees, blinking out at the sunlight. It dazzled his eyes, until the tears ran down his cheeks, and he dropped his head to one knee, covering his eyes with his arm.

"No other gods before Me," he muttered. "What did she mean? What would rise up and kill me?"

His fumbling fingers tried to locate his star, not realizing that he wore nothing but his underclothes. He laughed foolishly in the crook of his elbow. His mind was clouding again.

"I can't die," he told himself. "It's my duty to live. I've got to live!"

He got slowly to his feet, fighting hard. "They'll hang him—hang Red Cowan. Eye for an eye. The law demands that. I'm the law of Calor, ain't I? Don't the law demand his life?"

The sheriff sagged wearily, gripping the side of the door with his left hand.

"I'm the law," he muttered drunkenly. "I demand——"

The fever cloud was enveloping him again, and the little blue devils with their sledges were beating on his brain, trying to batter him into insensibility.

Where was Red Cowan, he wondered? Where had he gone? He was obliged to use both hands to cock the Colt. Red Cowan. That was what he wanted. The man with the flame-colored hair. There was no gratitude for what Red had done for him. No thought of the days and nights of nursing. The law must be satisfied, and Duty Deming was the law.

He went stumbling across the uneven ground, sagging at the knees, his head swinging from side to side, almost trailing the cocked revolver in his right hand; fighting, fighting all the while.

Then he saw his quarry just at the corner of the old stable. It was Red Cowan, looking at him. The big Colt swung up and his finger tightened on the trigger. The recoil jerked the gun from his hands and he almost fell.

He did not look for the gun. One shot had been enough. He hunched one shoulder against the old stable wall, gasping for breath. The law had been satisfied. He closed his eyes for a moment. The devils were still hammering on his brain, but above it all he could hear another sound; a thump, thump, thump of horses walking.

Slowly he opened his eyes and tried to see what the blurred thing was. He knew it was a man on a horse, although his eyes did not register the figures.

"Jim Deming!" said a voice. "For God's sake, Jim!"

It was Joe Mills, the ex-deputy.

"Don't yuh know me, Jim?" he asked.

"This is Joe Mills."

"I know," whispered Deming. "Yuh quit me."

"Aw, forget that. We've been huntin' all over the country for you, Jim; and I——"

"I had to do my duty," whispered Deming. He lifted his right hand with a supreme effort and pointed a finger waveringly.

"That's Red Cowan," he said.

"Yo're crazy!" blurted the deputy. "That ain't Red Cowan."

For several moments the sheriff did not move. His face twisted strangely. "You say that ain't Red Cowan?" he whispered hoarsely.

"Of course not, you danged fool."

"Don't lie to me, Joe! My God, don't lie."

"I ain't lyin', Jim. Yo're crazy, I tell yuh. Of course this ain't Red Cowan. I know Red."

For a moment the sheriff's head sagged heavily, but he swung himself away from the stable, started toward the house on uncertain legs, but collapsed, falling flat on his face.

"Now, wouldn't that rasp yuh!" snorted the deputy, as he swung off his horse and walked over to the prostrate sheriff. He picked him up and took him to the shade, where he laid him on the ground.

Something about the sheriff caused the deputy to make a quick examination.

"I'll be totally darned!" he said slowly.

Then he turned his head and saw Red Cowan, riding in from beyond the stable; riding a bareback horse and leading another.

"Hello, Mills!" yelled Cowan. "Where'd you come from?"

"C'mere," said the ex-deputy, and Cowan rode up to him.

"By golly, I thought I should have tied him down," said Cowan.

"He's dead," said Mills slowly.

"Dead? Whatcha know about that? I found him several nights ago, plumb flat over there in the lava beds. He was too sick to talk; so I brought him here. I've had one hell of a time, nursin' him, Joe. Got smallpox, I reckon."

"Measles," said Joe. "Must 'a' got 'em from a hobo he had in jail at Calor. Hobo almost died, too. Didn't Deming tell yuh what he was doin' in the lava beds?"

"Too sick, I guess."

"He was lookin' for you, Red. Wanted yuh for the murder of Mitchell."

"What?"

"Fact. Delong brought the news of it, and Deming started on yore trail. But Delong got throwed against a hitchrack post that mornin', and it hurt him so bad he died that same afternoon. But before he died he confessed to murderin' old Mitchell himself. He just thought he'd put the deadwood on you, 'cause you quarreled with Mitchell before yuh quit."

Red Cowan laughed shortly. "So that was it, eh? Deming didn't mention it to me. Mebbe he was too sick."

"Prob'ly. Too bad he didn't live longer, Red. Delong confessed that Mitchell hired him to plant evidence that sent Harry Deming to the pen. We'll have Harry out in a few days."

"Well, I'll be danged!"

"Queer, ain't it?" mused Joe, looking down at the body of the sheriff. "His wife said that some day his star would rise up and kill him. She said he was makin' a god out of his star. I dunno, Red. Things have a queer way of workin' out. If he hadn't been so strong on duty he'd never have taken that sick hobo off that train. Deming always had the idea of bein' his brother's keeper, yuh know."

"That's what I've heard. Duty they called him, didn't they?"

"Yeah. Awful set in his ways. I suppose we might as well start back with him."

"Sure; might as well. Sorry I didn't rope him down. But he seemed to be all right when I left. Fever made his heart weak, I suppose. But he never told me he was after me, Joe."

"He wouldn't. I can figure out where he got the measles and I can figure out why he didn't tell yuh what he was doin' in the lava beds, but I'll be damned if I can figure out why he killed the red bull calf and said it was you."

"I didn't know about that, Joe. He must have been crazy."

"Mm-m-m-m," said Joe slowly. "I s'pose he was. Red, do yuh believe in them Ten Commandments?"

"Never read any of 'em. What are they about?"

"Everythin'."

"Must be good, eh?"

"Worth readin'. Git a rope and we'll take him home."

THE CATSPAW OF PIPEROCK

DIRTY SHIRT JONES AND Scenery Sims got religion. That in itself ain't of much interest, unless you knew these two. I've knowed lots of men who got religion jist like Dirty Shirt and Scenery got it. Remorse, that's what she was—not religion. Too much liquor on an empty stummick. I've felt the error of my ways from the same cause.

Dirty Shirt Jones wasn't very big. His face was kinda antegodlin', and one eye sorta roamed around indefinite-like, usually comin' to rest with the pupil lookin' down the length of his nose, as though amazed at the crookedness of said organ. Dirty Shirt had some quaint ideas of humor, and as far back as I can remember, he's harbored a deadly hatred against the towns of Yaller Horse and Paradise. Bein' a loyal Piperocker he couldn't do otherwise.

Scenery Sims is smaller than Dirty Shirt. He's a hard little devil, this here Scenery Sims, almost bald, square above the ears, with eyes like a pair of faded shoe buttons, one flarin' ear—and a sense of loyalty to Piperock.

It's December in Piperock. There's only one tree between Piperock and the North Pole, which don't noways temper the wind to the shorn lamb. Piperock ain't no metropolis—but, gentlemen, she's a town. We sink or swim, live or die, survive or perish together. As Magpie Simpkins says, "We're one and indigestible."

Me and Dirty Shirt have been tryin' to wrest some wealth from the bosom of Mother Nature on the headwaters of Plenty Stone Creek, but the weather drove us back to the fleshpots, where we're doomed to spend the rest of the winter. I've been spendin' two days against a stove, tryin' to git some heat inside my frozen carcass. When I does pilgrim uptown, I finds old Dirty Shirt settin' on the sidewalk in front of Buck Masterson's saloon. He's humped up there, with his old mackinaw collar above his ears, hands shoved down inside his old yaller angora chaps, settin' there in the snow, the thermometer below zero—and right behind him is the saloon, where boot heels are sizzlin' against the old base burner, and water gittin' hot for the next round of drinks.

Magpie had told me that Dirty and Scenery were paralyzed drunk the day before, and I had a hunch that Dirty had froze to death. But he wasn't dead. His active eye does a few loops, steadies down to a strained contemplation of that crooked nose, and he says to me—

"The way of the transgressor is pretty damn' tough, Ike Harper."

"All depends on how heavy your underclothes are," says I. "How about a shot of hot liquor?"

"Strong drink is ragin', Ike."

"So's the thermometer."

"I'm repentin' of my sins."

"Well, you've shore got a long hard season ahead of you, Dirty Shirt. Where does it hurt you worst? You ain't done got religion, have you?"

"My sins are heavy among me, Ike. I've shot and slashed and cut and cussed pretty much all m' life."

"Not countin' horse and cattle stealin', card markin' and other forms of malignant sins," I reminds him. "But freezin' to death ain't goin' to wipe 'em out none to speak about. Why not try goin' to the penitentiary for life?"

"Wouldn't pay me out, Ike; I'm half through livin' right now. Me and Scenery got it together. He's repentin' in sackcloth and ashes right now."

"Yea-a-ah—but I'll bet he ain't sucker enough to freeze along with 'em."

"Old Testament Tilton told us—"

"You ain't takin' his word for it, are you, Dirty?"

"He's our preacher, ain't he? Me and Scenery went to church."

"How in hell did anybody ever git you two in church?"

Dirty's eye wobbles a lot, but pretty soon she jerks back to attention.

"They ain't got no bell," he says kinda sad-like. "No bell on the church. Don'tcha know it's a shame—no bell on the church. Fact of the matter is, it don't look like no church. It's a shame for a place to not even look like a church. I tell you I'm goin' to do somethin' for that church. I'm goin' to fix her up so she'll look and sound like a church."

"What'll you use for money?" I asks.

"I'll sell my horseless carriage to the highest bidder."

I laughs through my chatterin' teeth.

"Scenery might sell his camel," says I, merely as a suggestion.

That camel was always a sore spot with Dirty Shirt. Him and Scenery owned a placer mine back on Dog Town Creek, and they cleaned up about fifteen hundred dollars, before the little pay streak played out. Durin' that time, Dirty discovered a stretch of pretty good lookin' quartz, and him and Scenery decides to work it. They needed machinery; so Scenery takes his share of the money and heads for Butte to buy the machinery.

In about a week he shows up, half drunk, leadin' a moth-eaten camel. It seems that he got drunk in Butte, got in an argument with a feller over how long a camel could go without drinkin', bought a camel from a travelin' carnival and came back to prove he was right.

Naturally, Dirty Shirt got awful mad. He busted up his partnership with poor Scenery, bought Scenery out for fifty dollars, and went to Butte himself to get the machinery. And then he came back, trailin' an old automobile behind a pair of misbegotten mules. He had got drunk, bought six hundred dollars' worth of chances on a raffle—and won the danged thing.

It was the second automobile to ever come to Piperock, and a vigilance committee waited on Dirty Shirt right away; so Dirty stored it in the Piperock Livery Stable, where it couldn't scare anythin'. Scenery kept his camel out at his shack, and put a warnin' on the gate, which read:

BEWAIR THE CAMUEL
THE DAMN THING BIGHTS.

Scenery called it Araby. The danged thing smelt like a street in Frisco Chinatown, and it would bite. Acted most of the time as though it had a bad bellyache. The vigilance committee also warned Scenery to keep his menagerie off the main roads, 'cause every bronc that saw it throwed a fit and its rider at the same time.

Anyway, Dirty Shirt wouldn't come in out of the cold; so I left him there and went into Buck's place, where I finds Magpie Simpkins, Buck Masterson, Wick Smith and Old Testament Tilton, all settin' around the old stove. While Old Testament is our minister, he's broad minded, six feet six inches tall, and no man ever had a more "if I die right now you won't hear a squawk out of me" expression on his face. Accordin' to him, there ain't no livin' man knows more about hell. Magpie says Old Testament will prob'ly git a job as a guide down there, after he's dead.

————◇————

Magpie Simpkins is and has been my pardner for years. He's as tall as Testament, wears a flowin' mustache, and is a livin' example of a man who never did mind his own business. He thinks his mission in life is to elevate humanity. His brain is filled with wonderful ideas, but each and every one is shy some sort of a dingus that makes 'em tick. But he'll back any of his ideas with a six-gun or a neck yoke, when all else fails.

Wick Smith is a retired killer. He still retains the disposition, plus a walrus mustache and some bunions. He runs the Piperock Merchandise Company, and agrees with his wife, who scales two hundred and sixty. Buck Masterson was suspected of many things, before he settled down to runnin' a saloon. He ain't so tall, but he's got plenty waist, big shoulders and skinny legs. On the Fourth of July he wears a collar, and on Christmas he adds a necktie to same.

Them four pelicans is plannin' somethin', I can see that right away; so I backed out and went home. I'm scared of them fellers, and when they git to plannin' anythin' I want to be outside their plans. Magpie didn't say nothin' when he came home, but he's got somethin' on his mind, and I seen him sneakin' a few peeks at a little black book.

"Whatcha got there?" I asks, but he don't answer.

But I sneaked it out of his overalls pocket that night, and it's a Bible. I've knowed Magpie to have most everything else, but this is his first time to pack a Bible. I didn't say anythin', but I got all set to listen to mornin' prayers. Mebbe he wasn't that far gone, 'cause he didn't pray, but he did mention that fact that Dirty Shirt Jones had turned over a new leaf and bid fair to become a valuable citizen of Piperock.

It was the followin' mornin' after that, when I went up to Buck's place. I knowed I had twenty dollars in my pocket; so I invited those present to partake with me, which they did with cold weather alacrity, as you might say. Magpie was one of the elect. But when I dug deep for my twenty, my gropin' hand encounters a lot of hunks of cardboard.

I took out a handful and looked 'em over. They're about two inches square, with a pen and ink number on one side, and on the other is written:

Good for one chance.

I dug once more, but there ain't no money in my pocket. Buck looks at me kinda dumb-like, and I says softly—

"Charge this up to me, Buck—until after the funeral."

"No hurry," says he.

I counted them tickets, and I've got twenty. Magpie smoothes his mustache and watches me in the back bar mirror. Then he clears his throat and says—

"It'll be somethin' we'll all date time from, gents."

"To me," says I, "it'll be jist a justified killin', you long geared pickpocket. You took that twenty out of my pocket and put in them numbered cards."

"Blessed be the meek," says Old Testament.

"Meek be damned! I want my money. What are these chances on, anyway?"

"Scenery Sims' autymobile," says Buck. "It cost a thousand, new. If you can win it for twenty dollars—"

I blowed right up, but Wick Smith cramped my gun hand and tried to explain:

"It's to build a new church and buy a bell. It means advancement for Pipe-rock. Here's Old Testament, grown as gray as a jackrabbit, tryin' to chase the devil away from us. He's been a long laborer in the vineyard of the Lord, and we've got to show our appreciation. Our church don't look like a church. There ain't no bell. Your twenty will do more good where it is right now than over Buck's bar."

"You don't need to git so damn' enthusiastic," growled Buck. "I've gotta live, ain't I?"

"That's all fine," says I, "but I don't never go to church. I'm master of my own soul, and I don't need no sky pilotin'. I wouldn't give twenty dollars to that church, even if they'd give me Testament's hide and taller as a bonus. And that was the only twenty dollars I had left."

"It is better to give than to receive," says Testament. "Just remember that Dirty Shirt is donatin' that autymobile, free gratis for nothin'. There's a lot of tickets bein' sold in Paradise and Yaller Horse, and the grand drawin' is to be held at the Mint Hall on Christmas Eve. We're goin' to give the best entertainment that's ever been given in this country."

"I don't care," says I. "I won't be here."

"You'll be here," says Magpie. "As one of the local donators, you'll be here to see that it's a success."

———◇———

I walked out of there and went down to Dirty's shack, where I found Dirty and Scenery. They've got a bottle and a warm fire.

"How's religion?" I asks, as I imbibes about the full of a mule's ear.

"To'able," says Scenery. "Day after t'morrow is Christmas, usually spelled with an X. Know why they spell it thataway, Ike? The X marks where the body fell. Me and Dirty Shirt are gettin' organized."

"I thought you fellers had religion."

"We did have," nods Dirty.

"Oh, we need a reg'lar church," says Scenery. "We need one that you can see and recognize. That danged church we've got now looks like a saloon. I'll leave it to you, if it don't. We need one with a belfry."

"We do," agrees Dirty. "Oh, we shore do. The present one is a shame and a disgrace. I'm doin' my part, ain't I? They're rafflin' off my autymobile."

"Will the danged thing run?" I asks.

"Shore will. It's got gas'line in her, and all you've got to do is twist the crank. Run? My Gawd, that thing'll rear right up and paw the sky. Stands me five hundred on the hoof right now. They're goin' to put planks on the Mint Hall stairs and run her into the hall, where all may gaze upon same."

"And I've donated Araby," says Scenery, grabbin' for the bottle.

"They ain't goin' to raffle that thing, are they?"

"They shore ain't! Raffle Araby? Huh! Nossir, they ain't. I dunno what they want Araby for, but I've done made the loan to Magpie and Testament. I reckon the camule is part of the entertainment. I hope he don't eat an arm off somebody—unless they're from Yaller Horse or Paradise."

I stayed all night with them two public spirited men, and the next day I'm so filled with remorse that I almost got religion. Along about midnight Dirty went out to git some wood, forgot to shut the door, when he came back, and when I woke up in the mornin' I had one frozen ear.

I asked Magpie what the performance was to be, and he asked me if I knew what Christmas was all about. I said it was a time when folks traded shirts, as far as I could understand. He said for me to attend, and I'd learn what it was about. I told him I thought I would, bein' as it had already cost me twenty dollars. I went down to Paradise that afternoon, and almost froze my other ear. Paradise town is about the same size as Piperock, but if all their morals were laid end to end you'd have to use calipers and a magnifyin' glass to measure 'em.

I finds Tombstone Todd, Hair Oil Heppner and Hip Shot Harris over from Yaller Horse, and if there ever was an unholy trinity, these are it. Tombstone tries to question me a lot about our festivities, but I don't respond very much, 'cause I don't know enough about it myself.

"Peace on earth!" snorts Hip Shot. "Good will toward men! Does that mean men from Piperock? I'd crave to know about it, that's what I'd crave?"

"It means *men*," says Hair Oil. "That natcherally cuts out critters from Piperock. I heard the same thing, Hip Shot. Magpie Simpkins and his misguided cohorts aim to kinda soft soap us fellers. I know him of old. His dove of peace usually turns out to be a chicken hawk. I won't go up there at no danged Christmas time."

"Piperock will be glad about that," says I. "They sent me down here to find out how many of you ain't comin'. I'll mark Hair Oil off my list."

"Mark me off, too," says Hip Shot.

"You're off. How about you, Tombstone?"

"I'm comin'. Like a danged fool I bought ten tickets on that raffle, and I attends to see that no skulduggery is practiced."

"If you ain't there, your tickets ain't legal."

"Mark me back on," says Hair Oil and Hip Shot together.

"There's bound to be skulduggery," adds Hair Oil. "I p'tects my dollar."

Over at Hank Padden's saloon I finds 'em playin' poker, usin' tickets as legal tender, and only bein' discounted fifty per cent. I got into that game and lost nineteen tickets on the first jackpot. I'd have lost twenty, but I'd misplaced one of 'em, and didn't find it until I was halfway home. Old Tombstone Todd won 'em all from me.

Paradise has always wanted that autymobile, and as far as I can see, most of the town are comin' up to our shindig. Paradise can't get along together well enough to ever pull off a celebration; so they've got to git outside their own limits, if they ever want entertainment.

———◇———

I didn't go uptown that evenin', but stayed at our shack. Magpie wasn't at home, and I knew he was as busy as a rat-tail bronc in fly time. He's always the movin' spirit in Piperock, and up to the present time, I'm the sacrificial goat that you read about in the Bible. But not this time. For once in his life Ike Harper, Esquire, is goin' to set back and let somebody else be the burnt offerin'.

About nine o'clock that night Dirty Shirt comes down to my cabin.

"Do you want to re'lize on them tickets you got, Ike?" he asks. "We've plumb run out of cardboard, and the market is good in Paradise. I can git you jist what you paid."

"I'll ride on what I've got," says I, kickin' myself for that poker game. "I may win that machine myself."

"Don't be a danged fool, Ike. It ain't got no brakes. Why, the whole thing is loose. Anyway, you can't run it around here. Let Paradise or Yaller Horse have it. They won't live long enough to enjoy it much."

Then I told him about the poker game. I'd found the other ticket, but one ticket wasn't worth botherin' about.

"You're the only person in Piperock who has a ticket; so I reckon the town is safe for democracy. We've done collected enough to build the new church, and the admission fees will hang a bell on her."

"Why are you and Scenery Sims so interested in havin' a new church?"

"The other one is a disgrace, Ike; it looks like a saloon. Well, I've got to go back and rehearse."

"Rehearse?"

"Shore. I'm one of the Three Wise Men."

"Who'r the other two?"

"Magpie and Tellurium Woods."

"Yeah, you better go back and rehearse, Dirty Shirt. You three jiggers will shore need a lot of rehearsin' for a job like that."

"The Cross J quartette will sing. And Bill Thatcher's orchestry will render plenty."

"Well, that isn't anythin' to git excited about. There's a lot of things I'd rather hear than Telescope Tolliver, Muley Bowles, Chuck Warner and Henry Clay Peck singin'. They're awful, but they ain't as bad as Thatcher's orchestra, accordion, bull fiddle and a jew's-harp, playin' 'Sweet Marie'. I ain't finicky about m' music either."

"The rest of it'll be good, Ike. It's a specktickle. Livin' pitchers, as you might say. Well, I've got to go back. We're puttin' the autymobile up into the Mint Hall, and we've got to cut out the side of the wall at the top of the stairs. We'll elevate the machine up on a couple saw horses, where everybody can look her over. Goin' to run her up on planks, with a block and fall."

It shore was a good lookin' machine, all fancy with shiny paint and brass dinguses. We never had but one other machine in Piperock, and somebody put dynamite under that one. Yaller Rock County is a horse country.

I don't reckon that machine would do very well in Paradise. But them Paradise and Yaller Horse folks will buy raffle chances on anythin'. They are so danged crooked themselves that they think Piperock is goin' to pull a crooked deal on the raffle. And me with the only ticket in Piperock! I don't know what the odds are against me, but if they've already got enough money to build the new church, them Paradisers and Yaller Horses has shore dug deep in the old sock. But it's all right with me—I'm lookin' for competition. I don't want the danged machine. I've got a horse and a burro, and that's plenty rollin' stock for one man in my position. I ain't even goin' to the entertainment. I'm goin' to stand Buck off for a couple quarts and spend a quiet evenin' beside my own fire.

Well, I got the couple quarts all right, and I packed plenty wood into the old shack for the evenin'. Then I put my gun on the table beside me, declared plenty peace on earth, good will toward all men, and settled down to enjoy life. Once in a while I can hear a few shots fired uptown, but nothin' to speak about. Christmas is usually quiet thataway, and mostly always it's so danged bitter cold that it freezes up the grease in a six-gun so badly that you can't shoot it outdoors. Most of our killin's are done indoors durin' the winter months.

I'm setting there by the fire, kinda dreamin', when all to once the door flies open and there is Magpie and Tellurium.

"Merry Christmas," says Tellurium. "Git on your hat, Ike."

"I don't wear no hat in the house," says I, reachin' for my gun, but Magpie beat me to it. Without that gun, I'm outnumbered.

"Here's the whole thing in a nutshell, Ike," says Magpie. "Wick Smith fell down the chimbley durin' rehearsal a while ago, and he busted his collarbone. You're the only man who can take his place on short notice. Git your hat."

"Nothin' less than murder will git me up in that hall," says I. "Right now I'm filled with the milk of human kindness, but don't agitate me. All I crave is to be left alone."

Well, they both talked with me plenty, and like a fool I let 'em lead me uptown. I don't know what they want of me, but what chance have I got against two men, both bigger'n I am, and three guns? If Wick Smith, sober, fell down and busted his collarbone, what'll happen to me? Gravity is somethin' I ain't never found out how to defy, and if there's any rubber in my system, it shore crawls to the upper side every time I fall off anythin'. I pleads a plenty, but it falls on deaf ears; so I resigns myself to fate, reservin' the right to kill both of 'em as soon as I git around to an even break.

They leads me up to the Mint Hall, where everybody in the world is congregated, and takes me around to the rear of the big platform, across the front of which is stretched a big black curtain. They've shore cut a big hole in the side of the wall to git that autymobile through, and there she sets on a couple saw horses and some heavy planks. They've got the old hall decorated with green branches, and the orchestra is already murderin' "Sweet Marie", playin' it in jig time. After while they'll play it for a march, play it for the openin' hymn, and then change the time for the first waltz. I looks over the assemblage with fear and tremblin'. There ain't a paid murderer in the whole gang— They do their stuff for nothin'.

"Thank Gawd, there ain't no Piperocker ownin' any tickets on that raffle," says Magpie. "If Paradise or Yaller Horse don't win that autymobile, it's 'cause they've lost the right ticket."

I reckon Dirty Shirt has told Magpie about me losin' mine in that poker game—that is, all except one. I'm wonderin' if they know the money is to be used to uplift Piperock. Prob'ly not. There ain't no church in Paradise or

Yaller Horse, and if they thought for a minute that Piperock was goin' to have somethin' they ain't got, they'd never bought them chances.

------◆------

We climbed in at the back of that big platform, and I fell over a ladder. There was more danged carpenter stuff around, and it seemed as though most everybody in Piperock was in there.

"Oh, I'm glad you came, Ike," says Mrs. Smith. "Poor Wickie had a ter'ble fall."

"You'll do fine in his place," says Mrs. Dugout Dulin, who is six feet six inches tall, and will weigh about a hundred and ten. They ain't got no bathtub in their house—they use a shotgun barrel.

I'm too full of Christmas cheer to pay much attention, and like a fool I let 'em dress me in a buffalo robe coat, string me with sleigh bells, and try to tell me all about it at the same time.

"No time to rehearse," pants Magpie, cinchin' up my belt. "Anyway, you'll know what to do, Ike. That's fine! Where's the whiskers?"

There's an apparition holdin' the lantern, and it gradually dawns on me that this is Dirty Shirt. He's got a white cloth wound around his head, and his figure is draped with one of Mrs. Smith's front room curtains. And there's old Tellurium Woods, naked to the waist, with a homemade horsehair wig on his bald head. From his waistline to his boot tops he's wearin' a Navaho rug. I begin to see things a little plainer, and my eyes focus on somethin' that's hangin' from the ceilin'.

"Whazzat?" I asks.

"That," says Dirty Shirt, "is the star of—of—where was it, Tellurium?"

"I dunno the exact location. Pete Gonyer made it for us. Iron star, with a glass front. Put a candle in her, and she looks like somethin'."

They started to tell me more about it, but jist about that time Magpie and Scenery hooks some sort of a doodad around my chin, ties it off tight in a few places, and I looks down at about three feet of chin whiskers. They kinda shoot out from jist below my lower lip like a waterfall, and they shore smell awful horsey.

"There!" says Magpie. "You look more like Santa Claus than Wick did."

I try to say somethin', but I'm whisker bound. I talk through my nose, but I can't even understand what I'm sayin'. Magpie explains what I've got to do. They've got a chimbley all built. It's about ten feet tall, and about three feet square. At the bottom is what looks kinda like a fireplace.

"Here's your chore," says Magpie. "You climb that ladder to the top of the chimbley. There's a ladder built inside for you to come down. Your act is the last on the bill. Up to that time, your chimbley is part of the stable. When we git everythin' cleared after the next to the last act, we make this up to look like a room in the house. Mrs. Smith will recite a poem entitled 'It Was The Night Before Christmas', and while she's recitin', you come down the chimbley. There'll be a Christmas tree, and you'll have some doojinguses to hang on it, while she speaks. And that's about all. We aims to show the folks jist why Christmas started; sabe? Kinda show the modern way of celebratin', jist as a—a extra act, as you might say. Mebbe you better git up there jist before the show starts; so as to be all set. Now, I've got to see that the raffle is all pulled off right."

I got up out of that chair, kinda gropin' in the dark. I wanted to git that horse's tail off my chin, so I could talk a little, but that heavy coat and all them sets of sleigh bells prevents me from liftin' my arms. I'm jinglin' around, grabbin' for somethin' or somebody to support me, when all to once, somethin' grabbed me by the whiskers and gave an awful yank.

It knocked my feet from under me, but I didn't fall down, 'cause I was still suspended by the whiskers, and I looked up at the flarin' nose of Araby, the Scenery Sims camel. The damn' thing has got me by the whiskers, kinda holdin' me up at arm's length, as it were. And then the blamed thing began to swing me around. My neck is jist about to break, when all to once the toggle busts, and I went end over end out through the black curtain, hit the edge of the platform on the seat of my pants, where I ricocheted straight out and landed with both legs around Bill Thatcher's neck.

There's a lot of yellin', but it don't mean much to me and Bill and his bull fiddle. Willin' hands separated us, and somebody hauled me back onto the platform, where they yanked me back behind the curtain.

"I'm through Santa Clausin'," says I. "No damn' camel is goin' to use me for a sling shot."

"Swaller your gorge," says Magpie. "You ain't hurt."

"You take that camel home, or I won't play with you."

"We've got to have that camel, Ike."

There's so much yellin' out in front that you can't hear anythin'.

"C'mon with that raffle!"

"Throw Ike out again!"

"Start your show, before we freeze to death!"

Old Judge Steele and Old Testament Tilton went out on the platform. The judge has a sawed off shotgun and Testament has a Bible.

"Peace!" says Testament, holdin' up his right hand.

"Or-r-rder in the house!" snaps the judge, and cocks both barrels.

"We'll open with a prayer," says Testament.

"Show your openers," snorts Tombstone Todd. "And what's a lot more, we never came up here to listen to prayers. If you've got any prayers to offer, go behind that curtain and offer 'em to Piperock. Ain't that right, folks?"

"Yea verily," says Dog Rib Davidson, of Yaller Horse, standin' up. "I'd like to say a few words. I've got ten tickets on that raffle—"

"I've got eighty!" snaps Tombstone. "Set down, Dog Rib. I've done promised Mrs. Todd that autymobile."

"You've got a lot of nerve," growls Hank Padden. "Better wait'll you win it."

<hr />

Magpie went out on the platform. He's got a basket with all the numbers in it.

"We'll pull off the raffle, Testament," he says. "No use prayin' to or for that bunch of horsethieves. No use wastin' your breath, 'cause the Lord would discount anythin' you could say good about 'em, anyway.

"I've got all the numbers in this basket, folks. I'll select somebody to draw a number, which will designate the winner. Judge, will you do the drawin'?"

"Not for mine, he don't!" yelps Tombstone. "Not for mine. You've got to deal off the top of the deck to us this time, Magpie. I suggests that my wife draw the number."

That seemed to suit everybody; so Mrs. Todd waddled up and drew out a number.

It was number eighteen, and you never seen such a scramble to look over tickets. One after another, I hear 'em cussin' their luck. Tombstone and his wife are talkin' their numbers out loud, and they ain't hittin' nowhere near the right number. The room is kinda still after the countin' is all done, and when Testament clears his throat, it sounds like somebody tearin' a horse blanket.

"Who has the lucky number?" he asks. "Who has eighteen?"

Nobody speaks, and I suddenly realize that I've got that number in my pocket. It's the one I couldn't find when I was in that poker game. I manage to unhook that big coat, and I got the ticket out. It's number eighteen.

I stepped out on the platform and handed it to Testament, who squints at it over his glasses.

"Ike Harper wins," he says.

The crowd is kinda dumb over it all. Magpie grabs me by the arm and hustles me back through the curtain.

"I've won me a horseless carriage," says I. "One ticket was all I had."

"Jist enough to start a killin'," says Magpie. "Why didn't you keep that ticket out of sight. Now, they'll swear it was a brace game, and instead of peace on earth, it'll be pieces of Piperock scattered over the earth. Scenery, git Testament off the platform, and let's start the show before they git time to start anythin'. Ike, you danged fool, we swore to Paradise that there wasn't a ticket held in Piperock. That's why they spent all their money. Somebody git that quartette to sing. Dirty Shirt, you do it. Tell Muley Bowles to start it. Where's your whiskers, Ike?"

"The camel done et 'em."

"Hell! Well, you'll have to be Santa Claus without the whiskers. No way out of it now. Somebody light the star, will you, Scenery. Will you git Araby set for this scene? Everybody clear off the stage, except Araby and the Three Wise Men. There they go!"

"Ho-oh-lee-e-e-e ni-i-i-i-ight," wails the quartette.

Blunk!

"Si-eye-lent ni-i-i-i-ight," wails the trio.

Whap!

"In the good old sum-mer-r-r-r ti-i-ime," sings the duet, and then quits.

"Who hit Telescope and Henry Peck?" asks Muley, who sings tenor.

Comes the click of a gun, and then Tombstone Todd's voice:

"I did! Whatcha goin' to do about it, you hunk of leaf lard?"

"I'm goin' to do the best I can without 'em, Tombstone."

"That's the spirit," says Judge Steele. "And I want to warn all of you; this gun scatters pretty bad at fifty feet, but as far as that's concerned, I don't expect to hit any *innocent* folks, no matter who I shoot at."

"We've been lied to," wails Dog Rib. "They told me that nobody in Piperock owned any chances. I tell you, we've been gypped. It don't stand to reason that one lone ticket—"

"Don'tcha worry, Dog Rib," says Tombstone. "This ain't over yet. The Todd fambly never quits! I had eighty tickets, and any old time I spend eighty dollars, I hang around pretty close."

"You ain't got no more right to it than I have. Numbers don't—"

"Ladies and gentlemen, the show is about to begin," says the judge. "As far as Piperock is concerned, the raffle was on the square, and Ike Harper wins."

Old Testament steps outside the curtain.

"The first scene," says he, "is the Three Wise Men in the desert. They see the star of Bethlehem, which is brighter than all the stars. It is so bright that it leads them on. And so they arise and foller the star."

"Do they ever ketch it?" asks somebody.

But jist then the curtain is drawed back, showing Magpie Simpkins, Tellurium Woods and Dirty Shirt Jones standin' in single file, with Araby back of 'em. And there's the iron star, with the candle inside it, hanging up in front of a black cloth.

"And the Wise Men saw the star," says Old Testament piously. "And they—"

"*Um-m-m-m-m—a-a-a-a-ahhhh-oo-o-o-o—o-a-a-a-ah!*" grunts Araby.

"And they looked and were much amazed, and they—"

"*Hoo-o-o-o-o-a-a-a-a-aw-w-w-w-oo-o-o-o-o-a-a-a-ah!*"

"Shut up, you moth-eaten, hump-backed old bum!" snorts Dirty Shirt.

"*A-a-a-a-a-ah-a-a-a-a-a-aw-hoo-o-o-o-o-oah!*"

Araby's voice was almost a wail now. I feel shore that he ate and swallered my whiskers, and it's done give him a bellyache.

"And they were much amazed," repeated Testament, tryin' to make himself heard.

"*Wah-hoo-o-o-o-o-o!*" wails Araby.

"They shore sound amazed!" yells somebody in the audience.

"Who in hell said I didn't win?" yells Tombstone. "That wasn't eighteen at all—it was eighty-one. I've got her right here, boys. My wife's drawed my number! Here she is! By grab, I win that prize! Yah-hoo-o-o-o-o-o! Ike Harper never won nothin', the bow-legged sheepherder!"

Well, I never let none of that gang call me names, even when I'm sober; so I steps right out on that platform, with all my bells ringin', and I grabbed the shotgun out of the judge's hands.

"Who's a bow-legged sheepherder, you cross between a tarantler and a polecat?" I yelps.

The only light in the place is that big iron star; and that's behind me, so I didn't know where to shoot—but they did.

Wham! A bullet fanned my ear, and down came the star—*ker-plank!*

I ducked down and rolled in behind a corner of the curtain.

"My Gawd!" says an awed voice in the audience. "You shot his head off, Tombstone; I heard it hit the floor!"

Somebody yanked the curtains, and they began turnin' on the lamps. Magpie took the shotgun away from me and shoved me into a corner.

"This is one of the best shows I ever did see," declares Hair Oil Heppner. "Two singers done got knocked out, one bull fiddle busted, and a Piperocker minus his head—and this is only the first act."

"I've won that prize," declared Tombstone. "Jist somebody try to stop me from claimin' it. Eighty-one wins."

"I've got ten tickets," says Dog Rib. "If eighteen was the number, I've got as much right to have it as you have, Tombstone. I'm from Yaller Horse the same as you and I—"

"You're *from* Yaller Horse," admits Tombstone, "but if you don't shut up, you won't never go back there, Dog Rib."

Dog Rib is settin' right behind Tombstone. Comes a dull thud, a sort of a scramblin' noise, and then Mrs. Todd's voice:

"Git up and take to him, Tombstone. Git up, can'tcha? He hit you with a boot. Did he hurt you, honey?"

"Honey's in the comb," says Hair Oil. "You shore do lift and drop a wicked boot, Dog Rib. But you ort to have removed the spur. Common etikette will tell you that it ain't ethical to pet a man over the head with a loose boot and not remove the spur first. I'll betcha he'll part his hair in the middle for a long time to come. Well, the show gits better as we go along, don't it, folks?"

"The danged murderer's got some of Tombstone's tickets!" wails Mrs. Todd.

"You had that boot off all the time, didn't you?" asked Hank Padden.

"Shore did. How'd you know it?"

"You wouldn't appreciate my reply, 'cause you live with 'em all the time. Well, let's go on with the show. What's holdin' us back? I paid four bits to see a show, and all I've seen yet is small arguments. If all we're goin' to do is fight—let's build up a good one, and then go home." Magpie hauled me off the floor and led me back, where they're fixin' up that stable scene.

"They're about to do battle out there," says I.

"That's fine. If they fight among themselves, they won't have time to start trouble with us. Climb right up the ladder, Ike. I'll tell you when to come down, but it won't be until the next act."

———◦———

I started to climb up the ladder, when all at once I seen the rear end of an old red steer below me. The lower part of my chimbley is fixed up like a stall, and they've got a mean lookin' old steer, with jist his head showin'. The rear end is in the clear, but his head is locked tight. On the other side of the scene is that danged whisker eatin' camel, also caught by the head. They've got lanterns to light this scene. I'm pretty sore and stiff, but I climbs up my ladder and sets down on the edge of my chimbley. Anyway, I'm too high up for anybody to bother me, which ain't such a bad position, but I didn't realize that I stuck up above the top of the curtain.

Out in front, they're still quarrelin', but I ain't interested. I've made up my mind to buy Dog Rib a drink for hittin' Tombstone Todd. That old steer kinda starts weavin' back and forth, tryin' to git his head out, and I'm doin' a balancin' act on the top of that chimbley.

"You better calm that cow down there," says I. "I'm no damn' canary."

"So-o-o-o, boss," says Magpie. "Somebody git behind that damn' steer with a hunk of two-by-four, will you? Go out and explain this part of the show to them ignorant sheepherders, will you, Testament. They won't know what it's all about, unless you diagram it for 'em."

"Go ahead with your prep'rations," says Dugout Dulin. "I'll calm this steer. Whoa, you bald-faced hunk of rawhide. Stop weavin' or I'll knock your rear end out of line with your ears. How're you comin', Ike?"

"Feet first, if I have m' choice," says I, hangin' on tight.

Testament Tilton's voice comes to my ears, and he's shore exortin' somethin' about somebody bein' born in a manger, and the wise men bringin' gifts.

"That part of it's all right," says Mrs. Todd, "but that don't help Tombstone none. He's done recited all his mul-pi-cation tables, and that damn' Dog Rib Davidson done stole over half of his tickets. Ain't there no law in this place? I've been a lady all through these proceeding, but I'm shore goin' to forget m' bringin' up. Git up, honey, and poke him in the nose."

"Little mul-pi-cation won't hurt him none," says Dog Rib. "He don't know eighteen from eighty-one. He may be honey to you, but he's shore horseradish to me, ma'am."

"There ain't no law against hittin' a man with a boot, is there, Judge?" asks Hair Oil.

"Not specific, Hair Oil. It may be a breach of etikette."

"When he wakes up, he'll kill somebody," says Mrs. Todd.

"Not with his own gun," chuckles Dog Rib, " 'cause I've got it."

"He'll run you out of Yaller Horse, you sneakin' thief."

"Tootms two is eight," says Tombstone. "Tootms three is—is—"

"Eighteen," says Dog Rib. "Let's go ahead with the show."

"I came out here to explain the scene to you," says Testament. "Unless you understand what it all means, you won't know what it's about. In this scene, we aim to depict and duplicate a scene—"

"What happened to me?" chirps Tombstone, holdin' his head in both hands. "Where'd all this blood come from? I crave to know who hit me, that's what I'd crave?"

"Dog Rib hit you, honey," says Mrs. Todd. "He stole your tickets and your gun."

"I'll git your ears for this, Dog Rib!"

"You'll need 'em to replace the ones I got from you. While you're at it, you might as well stock up on other parts of m' anatomy, 'cause when I'm through with you, you'll need plenty fixin', Tombstone."

"Did he git number eighty-one?" asks Tombstone of his wife.

"If I didn't, I'm shore cockeyed," laughs Dog Rib. "Folks, I've shore pulled the fangs out of this old sidewinder. He's bossed Yaller Horse jist as long as he's goin' to. From now on, Dog Rib Davidson is—"

Dog Rib is standin' up to make his proclamation, when Telescope Tolliver, barytone of the Cross J quartette, flung a chair halfway across the room at Tombstone, and hit Dog Rib right on the head. Dog Rib shudders, folds up like a hat rack and disappears behind Tombstone Todd's chair.

"Si-eye-lent ni-i-i-i-ight," sings Telescope, startin' in where he left off when Tombstone knocked him out.

"Set down!" snorts Muley Bowles. "We're three murders and a homicide past that song, Telescope. Set down, before somebody kills you. This here peace on earth stuff means to keep down and protect your own head."

"And Tombstone Todd still bosses Yaller Horse," grunts Tombstone, as he helps himself to Dog Rib's gun and his own, while Mrs. Todd recovers most of the tickets.

I can see and hear all this from my perch on top of the chimbley, where I'm swayin' like a jaybird on a limb.

"Git ready to yank the curtain," says Magpie. "Put all them lanterns inside the manger. Makes it look better. Somebody blow out the lights out in front."

"Somebody calm this here bo-veen, will you?" I asks. "I'm gittin' seasick."

———————————⊰⊱———————————

I see the lights go out over the audience, and then I hears the curtain go rattlin' back. Every bit of light from all them lanterns is reflected upward, and there I set on that swayin' chimbley top, like an illuminated buffalo coat, decorated with brass sleigh bells, which are jinglin' every time that restless steer weaves back and forth.

I'm gittin' so dizzy I can't look down, and the rest of the world is all black to me.

"It's Ike Harper," says a voice out in the crowd. "The catspaw of Piperock!"

"Don't shoot, Tombstone! You might be mistaken!"

"I'd know him among a million. Don't jiggle m' arm."

"Stand still, you bald-faced *oreano*!" yelps Dugout Dulin, and then I hears the splat of that two-by-four across the rear end of the old steer. *Wham!*

That bullet picked off one of my numerous sleigh bells and sent her jinglin' up among the rafters, and I let loose with both hands. It wasn't quite the longest fall I ever had, and I lit sittin' down, for the simple reason that the chimbley kept me from turnin' over.

But I didn't reach the floor. That old steer's withers was between me and *terry firmy*, as you might say, and I lit a-straddle of 'em. I reckon I lit jist ahead of Dugout's next attempt to pacify the steer from behind, and we was both goin' ahead at the impact.

My nose and chin knocked the front out of that fireplace, and we came right out into that manger. I seen one horn of that steer hook into Dirty Shirt's curtain, and he seemed to kinda open up, like a newspaper in the wind. It must have scared Araby, 'cause in what short time I had, I seen that old camel's shoulders and hump comin' out through the wall, and the camel's mouth was wide open in a perfect "O", like somebody tryin' to blow smoke rings.

"Hook'm, cow!" screams somebody out in that dark audience, and that steer starts sunfishin' right across that platform, headin' for the audience, head down, tail up, and foghorn blowin', while behind us comes Araby, kickin' at everythin' in sight, but follerin' me and the bald-faced steer.

It's about eight feet drop to the floor off that platform, and I've got both knees locked right behind that steer's horns, when the fall started. I gets a flash of Paradise and Yaller Horse and Piperock, goin' backwards over their seats in the dark, and then we landed.

It shore was one awful jolt, but you can't discount the Harper fambly, when it comes to bulldoggin' a steer. I took that animile to the floor in one blaze of glory, as you might say. There's only a few shots fired. There was two fired close to the ceilin', and I think it's Judge Steele up there with his shotgun, judgin' from the sound of it. He was right in the path of Araby the last I seen of him.

I'm pretty much shook to pieces, but I still retain my fightin' instinct, and I got that steer by the horns, holdin' his head close to the floor. We knocked over all the chairs in reach, both of us growin' weaker and weaker as the battle progressed.

Finally the steer said—

"Well, damn you, hold my arms, but git your hair out of my mouth!"

There's a light comin' from somewhere, and I lifts my head to look down at the face of Dog Rib Davidson. One end of his mustache points up and the other points down, one eye swellin' shut and there's hair between his teeth.

The light stops beside us, and I look up at Dirty Shirt Jones, packin' a lantern. Behind him trails that colored curtain, and that's about all the raiment he's got. He looks us over by the light of the lantern.

"Who're you?" asks Dog Rib.

Dirty opens his mouth several times before he says:

"I'm one of the Wise Men who follered a star—but I lost the damn' thing."

"Huntin' for it with a lantern?" I asks.

"I 'member you," says he, his left eye doin' a few loops. "You're the feller who had ticket number eighteen, but I don't 'member your name, feller."

"I'm Sandy Claus."

"Oh, yea-a-a-ah!" snorts a voice, and I set up to see Tombstone and his wife. He's got both arms braced against her to keep her upright. She's got the seat of a chair balanced on her head, and her mouth is all puckered up in a silly smile.

"Look out for that steer!" yelps somebody, and here comes the danged animal, wild eyed, with a chair hangin' to one horn. I reckon he got hung up on somethin' around behind the platform, and jist got loose.

But that steer ain't mad; he's scared stiff. He throws up his head like a deer, bawls like a slide trombone, and comes right straight for me, kickin' busted chairs every direction. Tombstone Todd let loose of his wife and jumped out of the way, and the steer hurdled her. I fell sidewise, as the steer surged past, and grabbed holt of its long tail.

Never do that. I went up in the air, sheddin' busted chairs, got a flash of that shiny autymobile in the lantern light, and then my head hit somethin' so hard that all the big and little stars clustered around me. It shore was worth seein', but it got monotonous after awhile.

Suddenly I hears voices, and all them stars went zippin' away.

"Put her feet in, dang you! No, I want her all in. I tell you I'm goin' to take away what I own. Now, you show me how to start her, Dirty Shirt."

I raised up and looked around. I'm in the back seat of that danged machine, along with Mrs. Tombstone Todd, and in the front seat is Tombstone, with a six-gun in his right hand. I can't see Dirty Shirt Jones, but I can see the light of his lantern. Mrs. Todd is sprawled out, snoring lustily.

"Y—you—tut—turn that dud-dingus on that dashboard," sayd Dirty weak-like.

Zee-e-e-e! Somethin' kinda hummed a little.

Mrs. Todd jerked upright, surged ahead and grabbed the back of the front seat.

"My Gawd, I've had a nightmare!" says she.

Well, that sudden surge shoved that machine ahead, and it headed right down them two planks. It hit the floor and headed right for the openin' at the head of the stairs, with Tombstone Todd kickin' at every pedal with his feet and yankin' at every lever with both hands.

"Whoa, you locoed son of a tin-can!" he yelped.

Wham! Bam! Rer-r-r-r-r-r-ro-o-o-o-o-o-w!

I felt that machine jerk ahead like a buckin' horse, and that dark room was filled with lightnin' flashes, a cloud of smoke and the noise of a machine gun. I tried to jump out at the head of the stairs, but I hit against the side of the opening, and got knocked back on top of Mrs. Todd, who is yellin' for Tombstone to let her out.

We shot off the top of them stairs in the dark and I don't reckon we ever touched again until we shot out through that doorway, over the board sidewalk, bounced a couple times in that icy street, made a slight right hand turn jist in time to take every post out from under Buck Masterson's porch. The street is full of screamin' people, horses runnin' away, porch posts goin' up and comin' down.

That's when I lost Tombstone and his wife. The machine whirled around, kinda actin' bowlegged, righted itself, and about that time it must have hit somebody, 'cause I'm enveloped in a suit of clothes that's got somebody inside 'em, and all them little stars came back to play with little Ikie Harper.

I'm conscious of a dull crash, and then perfect peace. I open my eyes, but all is darkness. I can hear somebody movin' around, but I'm not much interested. Then a lamp is lit and I look around. I'm settin' in what's left of that prize machine, and behind me is a wrecked doorway. I look around, and there's Testament Tilton, standin' beside his pulpit, without hardly enough clothes on to flag a handcar. One eye is swelled shut and his nose looks like a pickled beet.

"We'll open services with a prayer," says he solemn-like. "After that I shall endeavor to explain the different scenes of our entertainment. This is Christmas Eve—the evening when peace on earth, good will to men predominates; the evenin' when all men are meek and mild, and a little child shall lead them."

———•◇•———

I dunno how I got out of there. That busted doorway wasn't quite big enough, 'cause both of my legs had different ideas of direction. I'm still wearin' part of that buffalo coat, and a long string of sleigh bells trail along behind me.

I didn't go uptown. There wasn't anythin' up there to interest me; so I cut across to my own shack. I found Dirty Shirt, Scenery Sims and Magpie there, and they're a fine lookin' lot of undertaker bait.

I just comes jinglin' in and rubs my hands over the fire. Magpie look sad-like at me, but don't say anythin'.

"The steer broke its neck," says Dirty Shirt. "Jumped through a winder and landed on its head."

"Araby died in convulsions," says Scenery.

"And the autymobile went to church," says I.

"Anyway, we're all alive," remarks Magpie.

"Nobody but a damn' optimist would say a thing like that," says I. "I hope you're satisfied, Magpie."

"Oh, shore. It accomplished what we set out to do. We'll have a new church and a bell in the steeple."

I helped myself to their jug, bent myself in the shape of a chair and sat down by the fire.

"Dirty Shirt," says I, "jist why did you and Scenery start this movement for a new church? It's a cinch neither of you got religion."

"Self-p'tection," says Dirty. "That church looked like a saloon. Me and Scenery got drunk and got in there by mistake."

"Ter'ble," says Scenery. "Ter'ble mishtake. Won't happen 'gain, y'betcha. Goin' to have a steeple and a bell; so she'll look and shound like that she is. Well, here's Merry Christmas to all and peace on earth."

I didn't have no gun, and my fists don't seem to be mates; so I took another drink and went huntin' for the horse liniment, as usual.

INJUNEERED

OLD RUNNIN' WOLF CLAIMS that he's the son of a chief. Most Injuns do, as far as that's concerned; but Runnin' Wolf covers too many tribes in his claim to greatness. On one bottle of kidney cure he can become a son of Sittin' Bull. Give him a couple shots extra of hair tonic, and he claims Chief Joseph, of the Nez Perce tribe, as his father. A pint of corn liquor drives him plumb back to Pontiac; and I've knowed him to mourn a heap over the death of his sister, Pocahontas.

Runnin' Wolf is six feet six inches tall, and if it wasn't for the size of his nose he could dive out of sight in a shotgun barrel. Nobody knows how old he is, and nobody cares. He's jist a mean lookin' old war whoop, who lives in a teepee outside the town of Piperock, schemin' all the time to get money enough to buy alcohol, and a little left over for a poker game. Can he play that pastime? Give him two deuces, and he'll win more jackpots than any livin' aborigine.

At one time in his distant past, Runnin' Wolf traveled with a medicine show. The owner was one of them sleight-of-hand fellers, crooked as a snake in a cactus patch, and he taught Runnin' Wolf how to play winnin' poker. And that war whoop, comin' straight from a long line of horsethieves, et cettery, shore absorbed knowledge. I wouldn't play him for a two-bit piece, if he'd let me do the dealin'. Yaller Rock County knows him so well that he's in the sere and yaller leaf, as far as winnin' anythin' goes.

Me and Dirty Shirt Jones are settin' on the hitch rack in front of Buck Masterson's saloon one mornin', like a couple old buzzards, lookin' for something to happen. Dirty Shirt ain't very big, but he's got a man sized capacity for anythin' you might mention. His left eye is his predominatin' feature, bein' as it ain't noways fixed like a regular eye, but kinda darts hither and yon, finally comin' to rest in the northwest section of his eye socket, peerin' up at the angle between his crooked nose and his eyebrow. All of which gives Dirty a cockeyed expression.

We're settin' there, tryin' to elect a Democrat President, when here comes old Burnin' Wolf, headin' across from the post office, trailin' his blanket.

"I ain't goin' t' lend that old marrowgut a cent more," declares Dirty.

But Burnin' Wolf merely scratches his shoulders against the rack post, picks up the butt of the cigaret I've jist dropped and asks me for a match.

"Gittum letta," he says.

"Who got a letter?" asks Dirty.

"Me gittum letta."

"Who from?"

The old boy fishes out a dirty envelope from inside his shirt and hands it to me. In one corner of the envelope it says, "Barker Brothers Great Consolidated Shows".

"Dirty Dora prob'ly died and they're askin' Wolf to take his place," says Dirty Shirt. "Open it up—the war whoop can't read."

Inside was a single sheet of paper; on it was written, kinda sprawly—

I em cum to veesit yu sunn.

                                                    CHEEF AXILGRISS

"What say?" asked the chief.

I reads it to him. He scratched his left knee with the toe of his right moccasin, and then he laughs kinda foolish.

"Who's Chief Axlegrease?" I asks.

"Long time ago I be with him in medicine show. Him Osage or Cherokee or somethin'."

"He's a hell of a lot like you, eh?" grunted Dirty.

"I'm a Sioux."

"Yeah—when you're sober."

"Pretty damn dry now."

"Yeah," says Dirty, "and if you don't quit drinkin' hair tonic, you'll have to eat moths to keep down the fur. So this here Axlegrease Injun is comin' to visit you, eh?"

"Um-m-m-m. Play damn bad poker."

"I suppose you'll skin him out of his moccasins, eh?"

"Um-m-m-m. Me no got money. Mus' have money for play poker."

"Yeah, we all found that out a long time ago, Mister Vanishin' Race."

It might be well to tell you somethin' about our town of Piperock and of the rest of Yaller Rock County. Piperock, Yaller Horse and Paradise are set in a sort of triangle. Yaller Horse grew up from a one shack horsethieves' hangout. I mean she growed up in size, but her morals remained dormant. The town is kinda mismanaged by Tombstone Todd, Yuma Yates, Hardpan Hawkins and

Smoky Potts, knowed by us Piperockers as Murderer's Row. Whenever folks enumerate the poisonous reptiles, they mention them four in connection with rattlers and copperheads.

Paradise is only of more consequence, because of a larger population. A horsethief got run out of Piperock, hid in a hole down the country, and out of spite he started a town, which they called Paradise. Bein' of the same minds and dispositions, Yaller Horse and Paradise buried the ax against each other, in order to concentrate against Piperock.

Piperock is a lovable old place, full of memories, tryin' to get along in a peaceable way and amount to something. If it wasn't for the folks in Piperock it would be a great old town. But even with our failin's, we're united. We don't need no outside help. We stand for a certain principle, and we back our own—right or wrong—and there ain't been an innocent bystander killed in years. We shoot straight. We go on the idea that if the law leaves us alone, we'll leave the law alone. Reciprocity, Magpie Simpkins calls it.

Magpie is built a whole lot like Runnin' Wolf, has sad, droopin' eyes, like a disappointed bloodhound, and a long mustache. And nature didn't cheat him, when it comes to noses. He's full of quaint ideas, all of which suffer a heap from missin' parts, and his main idea in life is to keep Piperock on the map.

Well, me and Dirty Shirt proceeds to forget all about Chief Axlegrease, and he ain't brought to our attention until the next day when a runaway bronc, bearin' Mighty Jones in the saddle, comes down through our main street like Paul Revere spreadin' his anti-English propaganda. Mighty ain't very big, but his hair is long and his voice is plenty resonant, as you might say.

When he's about in the middle of the town, wingin' along on that locoed animal, which is jist touchin' here and there, we hears him yelp—

"Ho-o-o-o-old your ho-o-o-orses!"

Jist one more *clickety-clack*, and he's faded out complete.

"That," says Dirty Shirt, "is damn' queer advice, under the circumstances. But mebbe he's like Old Testament Tilton, allus preachin' advice that he won't foller hisself."

"I'm pure in heart," replied Old Testament, who is also built awful high above his corns.

"Lotta bum watches have plenty good main springs."

"I'm meek and lowly," says Testament, pious-like.

"Yea-a-ah—right now."

"Well, f'r Gawd's sake!" snorts Magpie. "Will you tell me what this caval-cade is? Will you tell me—crip-puled crawlers!"

I didn't blame Magpie for his remarks. This here cavalcade turns into the main street from the south, and if it ain't a circus, I'm a hairy tarantaler. In front is one of them big decorated wagons, with four horses, and on the driver's seat is a big fat Injun, all dressed up in a shiny plug hat, cutaway coat and a high white collar.

Tied behind that wagon is a scrawny lookin' elephant, behind which comes another big wagon—one of them Queen of Sheba float wagons—hauled by two pinto horses and driven by a fat squaw; and in that float is at least sixteen Injun kids, from one year to sixteen. Towin' behind that comes one of them steam pipe pianos, and a tow headed jigger in a red uniform is playin' "Sweet Adeline" as loud as he can.

The big Injun drives up along the old sidewalk and stops his team, while we stands there and gawps at him, until "Sweet Adeline" fades away to a hoarse whistle. The fat Injun takes off his hat, polishes it on his arm, puts it on his head and looks us over kinda dignified-like.

"I like see Runnin' Wolf," says he.

Dirty Shirt's eye circles and circles, finally stoppin' abruptly.

"That," says he, "must be Chief Axlegrease."

"Big Chief," says the fat aborigine.

"Ex-cuse me," grunts Dirty Shirt.

Them Injun kids sees some candy in Wick Smith's store window, and they all puts up a yelp for it. The old boy picked up a rock from the seat beside him, and the yelpin' stops. That buck shore knows family control, 'cause even the fat squaw ducked quick.

About that time Runnin' Wolf comes lopin' up the street. He heard that music, I reckon. He stopped and looked at the steam organ, stopped and looked over the family wagon, and finally arrived among us. Him and the fat buck looks each other over. The fat one cocks his plug hat over one eye and looked down at Runnin' Wolf.

"Hyah?" he snorts, kinda like an explosion.

"Purty damn' good!" explodes Runnin' Wolf.

"You git letter?"

"Got."

"I come visit."

"Hm-m-m-m-m-m-m!"

The big chief waved a fat arm to encompass his equipage.

"Purty good, eh? Belong me. Oil well gusher. Too damn' much money. Where you live?"

It kinda dawned on us that the old chief had made a pile in oil, and this was his idea of travelin' in state. I moved down and takes a look at the greasy faced jigger at the piano. He ain't very big and he looks tired.

"What kind of an outfit is this?" I asks him. He shakes his head, spits out in the dust and blinks considerable.

"Ay am de calli-yupe player," says he. "My name is Yergens. Das out feet belongs to de Inchun. Ay am jus' de calli-yupe player."

"Rich Injun?" I asks.

"Ay am get pay for dis yob—you bet. Dis damn' road make me mees notes."

"Where are you from?" I asks.

"Ay am from Copenhagen."

"Play!" yells Axlegrease, and the Swede almost blew the tops off them pipes, and scared every bronc in the county.

Away they went, with Runnin' Wolf walkin' in the lead, and the parade follerin' him down to his little teepee, while the rest of us sets down on the sidewalk and laughs ourselves so dry that Buck Masterson does a rushin' business in a few minutes.

Some of the boys follered down to the teepee, and they comes back to tell us that inside the chief's wagon is a lion and a tiger.

"One of them big Affreecan lions," says Slim Hawkins. "Cross m' heart, if he ain't. And in the other end is one of them penitentiary pumas—with the stripes. Take a whole horse to feed them two f'r one day, not to mention that elephant. I've seen a lot of elephants in m' time, but I never seen one with a worse fittin' skin. He shore needs ironin' out. They got him staked to a tree and he's eatin' all the branches off; while them two buck Injuns are settin' there in Runnin' Wolf's wickiup, smokin' a pipe. The squaw and all the kids are cuttin' wood for the whoopee organ, and the Swede is actin' as horse wrangler and bull-cook. If that ain't a outfit, I'm a cow's nephew!"

About an hour later Yuma Yates, Tombstone Todd, Hardpan Hawkins and Smoky Potts rides in from Yaller Horse. They stands out there in the street for a while, lookin' around, before they invades Buck's place. It wouldn't take no Saint Peter to tell where them four will go when they die. Them four gents is hard for to get along with. Tombstone is the ringleader; him and his big buffalo horn mustache. In fact, they all kinda runs strong to hair, as far as that's concerned. They has a drink together, and we can see that they've been drinkin' on the way to town.

"Did it stop here?" asks Tombstone.

"What?" asks Buck.

"That red skinned war whoop and his circus."

"Oh, yea-a-ah—they're here. That's Chief Axlegrease, a wealthy Nin-copoop Injun, who struck oil. Him and Runnin' Wolf was in a medicine show together, and he's come to show off. He's the first Injun to ever git fancier than a hearse, when it comes to puttin' on the dog. He's got a whistle wagon, elephant, lions and taggers too numerous to mention—and a Swede."

"We seen it all," says Yuma, yawnin' wide and lettin' a full glass of red liquor drop down his throat. "Every hitch rack in Paradise is in ruins. Two horses went plumb into Hank Padden's saloon, and only one came out. They think the other one is under the bar, but they won't know until they git things cleared out. Half-Mile Smith wanted to telegraph for the militia, but Zeke Whittaker's wagon team ran straddle of a telegraph pole and the wires are all down. The last we seen of Hank he was loadin' a riot gun, swearin' that Custer would be avenged at last."

"You fellers ain't up here to mop up on the war whoop, are you?" asks Dirty.

"Not if he'll listen to reason," says Tombstone.

"Reason or no reason," says Magpie, "that Injun is bein' p'tected by Piper-ock, if anybody stops to ask you, Tombstone. He's a guest of our fair city, and as such, we stands behind him. If Paradise animiles are so danged ignorant that they stampedes regardless at sight of a few chariots and a misfit ele-phant, they ought to stand their loss."

"Oh, we don't mean no bodily harm to the Injun, Magpie. That ain't in our thoughts a-tall. But you don't need to get runty about it, as fer as that goes. We comes in peace, you understand—but p'pared for war."

"We shore do love peace," sighs Dirty, who is achin' for a crack at one of them Yaller Horsers, "but if there's any choosin' to be done, I've done made my selection."

"I'll shake dice with you t' see which one of us takes two," suggests Slim Hawkins to Dirty. "There's times when I kinda throw back to m' aboriginal ancestors, and at such times I hankers for hair."

"Peace," says Testament Tilton. "Peace, brothers. There's a time and a place for all things."

"Yeah, and I jist mopped this floor," said Buck kinda sad-like. "C'mon and everybody have a little drink on the house. No use goin' to war, unless we know what the shootin' is all about."

That buried the hatchet for the time bein', and them three thieves from Yaller Horse starts a poker game with Magpie, Testament and Slim Hawkins. Me and Dirty Shirt drifts down to Runnin' Wolf's teepee, kinda wishful to see what the layout looks like, and we meets Runnin' Wolf. The old buck looks kinda down in the mouth, but he stops and looks back.

"How're you and the circus comin'?" asks Dirty.

"Big mouth!" snorts Wolf. "Much money. Huh! Like play poker."

Dirty cocks his hat over one eye and looks at the old buck. Dirty knows how good the old boy is at poker, and he wonders how much Chief Axlegrease knows about the great American pastime.

"Likes poker, eh? Good player?"

"Hm-m-m-m-m! Talk too damn' much. Say I'm poor Injun. Huh! Needum fifty dolla."

"Will ten dollars set you up in business?" asks Dirty.

"Plenty. I go buy cards."

"What do I get out of it?" asks Dirty.

"Runnin' Wolf honest Injun."

"You git the ten, old-timer—and may your fingers never cramp. Soak this fat war whoop plenty."

"Plenty," agrees Runnin' Wolf, almost grinnin'.

Me and Dirty went on down to the teepee, and Chief Axlegrease looks us over as though we're poor relations. Them sixteen assorted kids sets on the edge of that float, like a lot of little mahogany faced mummies, while the fat old squaw fusses around the stew pot on a fire.

The Swede is busy with a rag, polishin' his steam piano, and every once in a while that lean-lookin' lion almost choked to death over his own noises. The big striped cat has got his nose against the bars, sleepin' out loud. The elephant is roped to a tree near the Swede's musical wagon, and he seems a lot interested in what the Swede is doin'.

Dirty looks the fat Injun over, and says—

"Pretty swell outfit you got, Chief."

"Belong me. I got too damn' much money. Strike oil."

"Paid a lot for her, eh?"

"Sixty-fi' hundred dolla."

"Sixty-five hundred!"

"Um-m-m-m-m. Two wagon, one thousand. Six horse, twelve hundred; elephant, ten hundred; smoke organ, two thousand; lion, five hundred; tiger, five hundred. Plenty damn' good outfit, you bet."

"Buy out a circus?"

"Um-m-m-m-m. Plenty money. What's matter your eye?"

"That," said Dirty, "is none of your damn' business."

The fat Injun looks sad, and don't say anythin'. Dirty rubs the palm of his right hand on the leg of his chaps, and I know he's wonderin' just where to shoot that Injun to hit a vital spot under all that fat. The Swede in the red uniform ain't payin' no attention to us. He steps back and squints at all them metal pipes on his instrument, his cap cocked on one side of his bushy head.

The elephant leans forward on his ropes, and the slack jist gives him room to reach the Swede, who lets out a yelp you could hear in the next county, and begins waving his arms and legs; but the elephant took up the slack in that uniform so quick that it cut off the yelps. He kinda dangles the Swede in his trunk, like a baseball pitcher gettin' ready to throw, and all to once he heaves him up sideways, lets out a mighty *woosh!* and here comes the Swede, floatin' horizontal through the air, preceded by the soles of two of the biggest feet I ever seen.

That Swede never lost an inch of elevation nor did he change his horizontal position until them two big feet landed square on the chest of Chief Axlegrease and knocked him backwards through Runnin' Wolf's teepee. The Swede landed on the back of his neck, rolled over and sat up, blinkin' his eyes.

"My name is Yergens," says he. "Ay am de calli-yupe player, da's all."

"You ought to stick to it," says Dirty. "Didja have a nice trip?"

The Swede didn't say; he jist sets there blinkin', one eye on the elephant. The fat squaw comes over and looks inside the teepee, while the kids all set there, grinnin'. The show was jist built for them. It kinda strikes me that the old buck must run his family with an iron hand, 'cause the fat squaw turns around and waddles over to the line up of kids, and says—

"Make no noise—papa sleep."

She's either dumb as hell or she's got a sense of humor. The Swede gets to his feet and twists his clothes around to kinda fit his body.

"Some day," says he, "Ay am going to keek hal from that brute."

"Yeah," says Dirty, "that's great. But if you're wise, you'll stick to your calli-yupe, Jergens."

"Ay am mad, by yinks! Das har yob no goot. Work for Inchun! Ay am free man, pas' twenty-two, and dis Inchun business mak' me seek. Ay don' like Inchun."

Clank! A can of beans hits the Swede in the back of the head and knocks his cap over his nose. The squaw threw it, and she's got another can, in case this one didn't register. But it did. Jergens straightens up, puts his cap on backwards and strikes a dignified pose and points his nose to the sky.

"O-o-o-o-o-oo lee-e-e-e oh layee-e-e-e-e-e-e-e-e," he yodels. "O-o-o-oh lee-e-e-e oh layee-e-e-e, oh lay-hee-e-e-e, hoo-o-o-o-o-o-o."

"Sing good," grins the squaw.

The Swede stops, rubs his head kinda hard and goes back to his steam organ, where he leans and looks at the elephant. I don't reckon the Swede remembers jist what happened, but he's got a suspicion. One of the Injun kids hops off the wagon, picks up the can of beans and gives it back to the squaw.

"Do it ag'in, mamma," says he.

"Mamma busy."

Me and Dirty wanders back to town. Chief Axlegrease was still asleep, I reckon. We finds Runnin' Wolf at the end of the street, talkin' with Tombstone Todd, and we wonders what they're holdin' a council over. Ordinarily Tombstone wouldn't speak to the old war whoop.

But we found out, after them Yaller Horsers had gone home. Magpie got it from Smoky Potts, who can't stand much liquor. It seems that them four crippled crawlers have been figurin' on startin' a Wild West Show. Smoky was a horse wrangler with the outfit from the 101 Ranch for a while, and when they saw Chief Axlegrease go through Paradise they decides to annex his outfit and start their show.

"They ain't got money enough to even hire the Swede," says Dirty. "That old Injun paid sixty-five hundred for the outfit, and he wouldn't sell for a million. Them Yaller Horsers make me laugh. Start a show!"

"Goin' to call it 'The Yaller Horse Wild West'," says Magpie. "Huh! Why, Piperock could start one a lot bigger n' better. I'd be willin' to head the aggregation."

"You would," says Dirty.

"I would—and guarantee a success. Piperock is jist as well able to buy that Injun out as Yaller Horse is."

"Yaller Horse ain't bought it out yet. I seen Tombstone Todd talkin' to old Runnin' Wolf, and I'll betcha they're framin' up somethin' on Axlegrease."

"Runnin' Wolf must be," grins Buck Masterson. "He bought two new decks of red backed playin' cards."

Me and Dirty and Magpie left Buck's place about midnight, and decided to go down to Runnin' Wolf's wickiup and see what's goin' on. There's a lantern in the teepee, and we hears voices. Goin' kinda careful like, we gets close to the teepee. That float wagon is covered with dark humps, where the squaw and their sixteen offsprings are wrapped in blankets and plenty slumber.

Them two buck Injuns don't hear nothin', 'cause they're playin' poker in the teepee. The Swede is propped up against a roll of blankets, snorin' plenty, while Chief Axlegrease and Chief Runnin' Wolf play poker on a blanket, with the lantern danglin' from a pole. The flap of the tent is wide open.

"Money all gone," states Axlegrease. "Plenty money in bank—no money here."

"Bet horse," suggested Runnin' Wolf. "How much you pay?"

"Two hundred dolla."

"Too damn' much; I bet hundred dolla."

"Deal."

Runnin' Wolf took plenty time dealin'. He got up, grunted a few times and sat down again—with the deck in his hands. Then he dealt slow.

"Bet one horse."

"Good! Raise hundred dolla."

"Bet two mo' horse."

"Raise two hundred. No more money. I got fo' aces."

Chief Axlegrease grunted and threw down his cards.

"You lose six horse," said Runnin' Wolf.

"My deal."

Both men passed. On the next deal Chief Axlegrease lost his elephant on a six horse bet. This time Runnin' Wolf had four kings. They passed on Axlegrease's deal—as usual—and on the next hand Runnin' Wolf won the lion, tiger and four sets of harness. He had four queens. On his own deal Chief Axlegrease wanted to bet, but Runnin' Wolf passed.

This time old Runnin' Wolf got up again, turned around once for luck and sat down again—holdin' the cards. We watched the deal, and I distinctly saw Chief Axlegrease look at his cards and slide them under the blanket. But he still had cards in his hand.

"How many?" asked Runnin' Wolf.

"No cards."

"No draw, dealer," grunted Runnin' Wolf.

"Pass," said Axlegrease.

"Bet one five hundred dolla wagon?" queried Runnin' Wolf. "I ante one lion."

"Good! I bet two five hundred dolla wagon."

"I raise one lion."

Chief Axlegrease thought it over.

"I got smoke organ, two thousand dolla. I call one lion and raise smoke organ."

"Fifteen hundred dolla, eh?" said Runnin' Wolf. "I call with one elephant and three hundred dolla cash, and raise one hundred dolla cash."

"Good! I call two set harness. What you got?"

"Plenty," grunted Runnin' Wolf, and spreads his hand.

Chief Axlegrease didn't say a word. He leaned forward, grabbed Runnin' Wolf by his thin neck and lifted him off the blanket. Old Wolf pasted him one in the belly and they went down together, landin' on top of the Swede, who let out a yell, like one pipe of his calli-yupe—the high pitched one. Somebody kicked the lantern out.

There's plenty moonlight outside, but it's shore dark in that teepee. Out comes the Swede, turns over twice and lands under the float wagon. Then out comes Runnin' Wolf and Chief Axlegrease. They fall in a heap, and Runnin' Wolf breaks loose, gits to his feet and lopes away in the night, makin' plenty good on his nickname. Chief Axlegrease lets out a weak war whoop, crawls to his feet and takes out after Runnin' Wolf.

The Swede must have hit the runnin' gears of that wagon, 'cause he's under there, singin' at the top of his voice:

Ay vas born in Minnie-sota,

Den Ay came to Nort' Da-a-akota;

Ride on Yim Hill's beeg red vagon,

Yeeminy, I feel for fight!

"What's the matter, mamma?" pipes up one of the papooses. "I hear papa yell."

"Sh-h-h-h-h," grunts the fat squaw. "Papa restless."

We sneaked inside the teepee and lit a match. There's both hands on the blanket, right where they laid 'em down. Runnin' Wolf had four aces and the joker, and Chief Axlegrease had four aces. The deck is still there, and with one of them hands, it's a full deck. There's cards scattered all over the place, and we follered Runnin' Wolf's trail half way to town and he's still sheddin' red backed cards.

"Well," says Dirty Shirt, "I reckon Runnin' Wolf wins the circus. I seen Chief Axlegrease hide the hand Wolf dealt him, and ring in a cold one from under his leg."

"All I seen was Runnin' Wolf sneak a cold deck from inside his shirt," laughed Magpie. "They had one regular deck. Runnin' Wolf had sets of four aces, four kings, four queens planted where he could get 'em for each bet, and he had one whole deck frozen for the grand climax; but Axlegrease stole them four aces and played 'em against the four aces and a joker Runnin' Wolf dealt himself from the cold deck."

"Well," said Dirty Shirt, "you got to give Runnin' Wolf a lot of credit for runnin' less 'n ten dollars up to a sixty-five hundred dollar circus and all the loose money the oil well Injun had with him. That war whoop knows a lot about poker—and he can outrun Axlegrease, that's a cinch."

The next mornin' we finds the Swede in front of Buck's saloon, settin' on the sidewalk. His uniform is split down the back and he's shy one cap. One eye is all purple, and he's lost a couple front teeth.

"Ay am t'rough," says he, sad-like. "Dat Inchun got no money now. Never since Ay come from Copenhagen do Ay get so many hurts. Ay am queet dis yob. De beeg Inchun seet on de vagon, with two barrel gon in hees hand, and hees say, 'Ay shoot hal from somebody pretty queek. Ay have been rob.' De lion and tiger not been feed for two day. Ay tal heem so, and hees say she feed pretty queek, when other Inchun comes back. Ay no git pay for de yob, an A'm bruck. Das is no place for calli-yupe player, by yimminy."

"How about a little drink?" I asks.

"Val, Ay take drink alcohol, please."

That calliope player's insides must have been made of rubber. He took a big scoop of raw alcohol and never grunted. Buck bought him another, jist to see him drink, and then Magpie bought one.

"My name is Yergens," says he. "Olaf Yergens, from Copenhagen."

"Write it down, Buck," says Magpie. "We'll have to put somethin' on his tombstone. This here Swedish jigger is embalmed right now."

While we're talkin', Smoky Potts, of Valier Horse, comes in. He offers to buy a drink, and we're so astonished that we accepts. Jergens takes another scoop of raw alcohol, and Smoky looks him over curious-like.

"Ain't that the jigger who plays the hot water accordion?" asks Smoky.

"Ay am de calli-yupe player," says Olaf, kinda bat eyed. "Ay queet de yob. You see, de Inchun played poker and loses de calli-yupe and everyt'ing. He can't pay my vages, so Ay queet de yob. Ay am Olaf Yergens, from Copenhagen."

"In alcohol," adds Magpie, "a few yards of bandages, and you're a first class mummy, Olaf."

"Who won all them there things?" asks Smoky.

"Runnin' Wolf," grins Dirty Shirt. "He cold decked the fat war whoop, and the last we seen, Runnin' Wolf was leadin' by a shirt tail."

"You mean Runnin' Wolf owns the whole danged circus?"

"From the neck yoke to the elephant."

"I'll be danged! Well, I've got t' be joggin' along."

After Smoky pulled out we put Olaf in a chair and folded his hands. Four big glasses of raw alcohol is enough to pickle a rattlesnake. We started a game of seven-up and are goin' along nicely, when Dirty Shirt gits a sudden idea.

"By golly, I've got it!" he snorts. "Runnin' Wolf is down at Yaller Horse, tryin' to sell that outfit. Smoky Potts comes up to find out if Runnin' Wolf did win that outfit, and now he's beatin' back there to make the deal."

"That's a cinch!" snorts Magpie.

"What's to be done?"

"Morally," says Dirty Shirt, "I own half of it, 'cause I staked Runnin' Wolf to ten dollars, and he'd have to split the profit with me."

Magpie almost dragged Dirty Shirt out of his chair.

"C'mon!" he yelps. "We'll spike their pants to the floor."

We didn't know what it was all about, but we seen 'em headin' for Judge Steele's little office. Scenery Sims, the sheriff, comes in and sets down with us.

Scenery is about as big as a quart bottle, and he talks with a queer, squeaky voice. He knows the world ain't none too good, and it worries him a heap to think he can't find out how to make it better.

Scenery wasn't in town yesterday, so he don't know a thing about the Injun circus. Magpie and Dirty comes back, and Dirty hands Scenery a legal paper. It's an attachment on one-half the circus, demanding one-half of the outfit, or the sum of three thousand two hundred and fifty dollars, bein' as the valuation is claimed to be sixty-five hundred dollars.

"What damn' circus is this?" squeaks Scenery.

"It's down at Runnin' Wolf's teepee," explains Magpie. "You can't miss it. We'll go down with you, Scenery."

"S'pose I've got t' serve it. Well, c'mon. Looks funny t' me. How did Dirty Shirt ever git to ownin' half a circus?"

"Lotta things you don't know," says Dirty Shirt.

We leads Scenery down there, and his eyes kinda bug out when he sees all that aggregation. On top of the animal wagon sets Chief Axlegrease, with a double barrel shotgun across his lap. The squaw and the kids are all under the other wagon, sleepin' in the shade. The elephant is backed against the tree and he's tore off every branch in reach. I reckon that's all the food he's had since they arrived. The lion acts as sore as a boil, and I'll bet he's hungry enough to eat hay.

"What you want?" asks the chief.

Scenery climbs up on a wheel and hands him the attachment. Axlegrease opens it up, upside down and looks it over.

"What say?" he asks, and Dirty takes it back and reads it out loud.

"Um-m-m-m-m! Man own half, eh? How he get half?"

"I'm sheriff," states Dirty Shirt, pointin' at himself. "That paper says a man owns half this damn' circus, *sabe*? I take half this circus for him."

"You take?" Axlegrease opens his mouth wide and stares at Scenery. "You take?"

"I take."

"You git!" Axlegrease shoves both barrels of that shotgun down in Scenery's face. "You git fast!"

Scenery is kinda hypnotized by them twin tunnels, and he backs plumb into that elephant, which kinda takes him to his bosom, as you might say. Scenery don't say a word, but his lips move in prayer. The elephant kinda makes a little squealin' noise, as though he was tickled stiff, and then he spins Scenery around, like one of the band leaders whirls his stick, and tossed him plumb up into that tree.

Scenery turned over, caught the open seat of his chaps on a snag limb, and hung there upside down, ten feet above the elephant's reach.

"Kill the dirty brute!" yells Scenery. "Kill him before he kills me!"

"They don't climb trees," says Magpie. "Stay where you are, Scenery."

The limb kinda cracks a little, and Scenery says:

"Now I lay me down to sleep; I—I pray—I—I pray—"

"I dunno who you're prayin' to," says Dirty Shirt, "but you don't need to lie about your position."

"This limb is gittin' weak!" wails Scenery. "Can'tcha help a feller? The blood is all rushin' to m' head."

"It can't leak out," says Dirty, "so don't let that worry you. Anyway, you seen your duty and you done it, Scenery. You're high and dry in the matter."

"If this limb ever breaks, I'm a goner—and if it don't break, I'll die, anyway."

"Either way we lose a sheriff," says Magpie. "Well, them is things we have to face in this life. I always said you was born to be hung, but I didn't never suppose it would be upside down. If you quit jigglin', you might die natural."

"I ain't jigglin'; it's that dang Injy rubber ox doin' it. Somebody cut him loose, won't you, before he uproots the tree?"

Magpie walks a little closer to Axlegrease, who seems to be enjoyin' it.

"Who takes care of the elephant?" asks Magpie.

Axlegrease shrugs his fat shoulders and sighs real deep.

"Damn' Swede!" he says. "He go way."

"Can he handle the elephant?"

"Um-m-m-m-m."

Pop! That limb busted up close to the tree, and poor Scenery turns over once, lands all spraddled out on the elephant's back, like a flyin' squirrel. I reckon the shock was too much for the elephant, 'cause he jist made a noise like one of them slip horns, swayed his whole weight on that big rope around his hind leg, and the rope busted like a twine string.

Mebbe the elephant wasn't expectin' to break loose, and when he did it was too late to miss the big animal wagon. He hit jist above the right front wheel, and the shock sent Chief Axlegrease up in the air, from whence he descended on top of Scenery Sims, and away went that runaway elephant, headin' for the open country, blastin' away like a trumpet at every stride, while Scenery and Chief Axlegrease, arms wrapped around each other's necks, suspendin' out from each side like a pair of pack sacks, went along with the elephant.

I took a look around, and there goes mamma and her sixteen copper colored offsprings, headin' for Piperock like a flock of scared quail.

"Dirty," says I, "I reckon your attachment took."

"Looks thataway, Ike."

"We'll do the proper thing, under the circumstances," says Magpie. "Git the harness on them horses and we'll move this outfit up to the livery stable, where they'll be safe from all harm."

"Meanin' Yaller Horse, eh?" grins Dirty.

"Well, yea-a-ah. C'mon."

***

We had quite a parade among us. I drove the animal wagon, Magpie drove the big float, while Dirty Shirt rode on the musical boiler, towin' behind Magpie's outfit. Pete Gonyer, who runs the stable, yelped like a peevish wolf. He didn't want no danged circus in his stable. Wasn't nobody goin' to stable lions and tigers in his stable—not if he was alive to see it.

"Where's the elephant?" he asks, after we've stabled the outfit.

"Scenery Sims went out for a ride," says Dirty Shirt.

"On the elephant?"

"Right on to him, Pete."

"Took nerve, didn't it?"

"All he had. You better feed them lions and tigers."

"Feed 'em—what with?"

"Listenin' to 'em right now, I don't reckon they'd be particular. Mostly they eat dead horses."

"I ain't got no dead horses."

"Well," says Magpie, "if them two cats git loose, you will have. Them things are attached by the law, and it's up to you to guard 'em with your life."

"Thasso? Huh! This place gits locked up right now. I'll move out every danged bronc in the place—and let nature take her course. Guard 'em with *my* life? Who the hell is takin' liberties like that with my life? If Scenery Sims wants these here animiles guarded, let him quit lopin' around on a elephant and take care of 'em hisself. Them is my sentiments."

"He'll prob'ly be mad at you, Pete," says Dirty Shirt. "You better be here and let him stable the elephant."

"I'll put them broncs out in the corral, and I'll wait a reasonable length of time. If he ain't here by that time—well, I'm runnin' a livery stable—not a damn' jungle, I'll tell you that."

Them two cats smell horse, and they're clawin' at the bars and makin' all kinds of noises. The horses ain't noways meek and mild themselves, and Pete has a man sized job in gettin' 'em out past that cage.

We went back to Buck's place and had a drink. We shore needed one, after what had happened. Somebody suggests that we go huntin' for the remains of Scenery and Chief Axlegrease, but we don't go. Scenery wouldn't be the first sheriff of Yaller Rock County to pass out with his boots on. Mrs. Axlegrease and her sixteen offsprings are perched on the sidewalk across the street, waitin' for papa to come back. I reckon they've got plenty faith in his ability to take punishment, 'cause they're eatin' candy while they wait.

The Swede is still a little woozy, but willin' to imbibe, if we'll buy. We gave him a slug of alcohol, and he grows reminiscent in Swedish. We gave him another shot, and he tried to start a war with all of us.

"Ay am strong man," he declares. "Ay feel for fight."

And then he turns Swedish agin.

"The elephant busted loose," Magpie tells him. It took Olaf a long time to get this idea.

"You say das bull bruck de rup?"

"Shore—broke the rope. He's gone away."

"Yeeminy! Das bull is bad. He teep ofer house. Where he goes?"

"Nobody knows. Do you reckon he'd hurt anybody?"

"Das bull like to play. Ay tal you something—" and then he makes us a long speech in Swedish, his eyes jist poppin' when he finishes.

"That's different," says Magpie, solemn-like. "You get all our votes. What'll you have to drink?"

"Ay tak' scoop from alcohol, t'anks. You good faller."

About fifteen minutes later Scenery Sims comes staggering in through the back door. If Scenery ain't a first class wreck, he'll do, until we do get one.

He staggers up to the bar and looks us over, kinda pop-eyed.

"Fall off?" asks Dirty.

Scenery nods and fingers his throat.

"Fuf-fuf-five tut-tut-times. And every tut-time that dud-damn' elephant pup-put me back. The la-last tut-time, he pup-put me too fuf-far."

Scenery's voice went up so high it broke off, and his chin quivers from the tension.

"Where's the elephant?" I asks.

"Huh-huntin' for me, I s'pose. Can I have a drink?"

"Where's Chief Axlegrease?"

"He fell off in a cactus patch. Gimme liquor, can'tcha?"

We got Scenery quieted down after six or eight drinks, and he starts braggin' about what a rider he is. About that time Tombstone Todd, Yuma Yates, Hardpan Hawkins and Smoky Potts ride in, tie their broncs and come in. They look Scenery over.

"What happened to him?" asked Tombstone.

"I rode the Injy rubber ox to a fare-thee-well and never pulled leather," brags Scenery. "Match that, can you?"

Tombstone cuffs his hat over one eye and considers Scenery.

"You rode what?"

"That danged elephant."

"Our elephant?"

"Your—say, have *you* got one, too?"

"We've got the only one there is in Yaller Rock County."

"No you ain't—you ain't got the one I rode. Nobody ain't got him. He's what you might call a independent elephant."

"Uh-huh. You're speakin' of the one the Injun brought here?"

"Yeah, and the one what took the Injun away from here, too, if you want to be particular."

Tombstone looks us over kinda meanlike.

"We're holdin' Piperock responsible f'r any harm done to that elephant," says he. "You see, we own that aggregation of jungle beasts."

"Thasso?" says Magpie. "How come you own it, Tombstone?"

"Bought out Runnin' Wolf."

"We're up here to take the outfit back to Yaller Horse," says Smoky.

"Barrin' my legal claim, you might," says Dirty Shirt.

"Your what?" roars Yuma. "Say that agin, feller."

"It's thisaway," grins Dirty. "I staked Runnin' Wolf with poker money to play with Axlegrease, and Runnin' Wolf promises me half what he wins. The fat Injun says the outfit is worth sixty-five hundred dollar, so I levies my attachment on half of the circus, or asks thirty-two hundred and fifty dollar in cash."

"You got any legal papers to prove he promised you half?" roars Tombstone.

"I've got Ike Harper for a witness, ain't I, Ike?"

"You shore have," says I. "I heard every word of it."

"Anyway," says Dirty, "my paper has been served, and we've got the whole works, except the elephant, locked up in the livery stable, until this here modest claim of mine has been satisfied at one hundred cents on every dolla."

"But we bought the whole works from Runnin' Wolf!" yowls Yuma. "We've got his mark on a bill-of-sale."

"Arrest him f'r obtainin' money under false pretense," suggests Buck.

"Now, listen t' me," says Yuma. "We expected Piperock to do us dirt. It ain't no surprise. But we're here to git them animiles—and git 'em we will. All the legal papers in the world won't stop us. Ain't that right, boys?"

"Right," says Tombstone.

"What the hell's this comin' in?" grunts Magpie.

We all runs to the doorway. Here comes Eph Whittaker, standin' up on a big load of hay, drivin' like a Roman chariot driver, and his pinto team on the dead run. They go through town so danged fast that you can hear Eph's whiskers poppin' in the wind; and as far as you can see 'em, they're still goin' high and handsome, and about two hundred yards behind 'em is that danged elephant, trunk stretched out, tail stretched out, chasin' that load of hay. He don't pay no attention to the town, but when them three broncs from Yaller Horse see that apparition goin' past, they take the hitch rack with 'em, and starts off across country, buckin' and bawlin'.

Tombstone, Yuma, Hardpan and Smoky take out after their horses, runnin' and swearin', while the rest of us sets down on the sidewalk and has a good laugh. Even Olaf Jergens from Copenhagen got a laugh out of it.

"Ho-ho-ho-ho-ho!" he whoops. "Das elephant hungry, by yimminy. I buy drink, if I have money."

It was worth a lot to see them four sinners from Yaller Horse chasin' their runaway broncs; so we treated the Swede liberally. About fifteen minutes later Chief Axlegrease limps in from the lower end of town, stoppin' now and then to pick out some cactus. He sets down on the sidewalk with his family, but they don't pay any attention to him. After while me and Dirty go over to see him.

"You take circus?" he asks.

"Shore did," grins Dirty. "Runnin' Wolf won it from you, and he's supposed to give me half, because I staked him to play poker with you; but he went down to Yaller Horse and sold it to four men down there. I locked her up 'cause I own half of it, *sabe*?"

"Mm-m-m-m-m-m. Where's Runnin' Wolf?"

"He's down at Yaller Horse or Paradise, prob'ly spendin' the money he got."

"Um-m-m-m-m."

He gits up, picks out a few more cactus spines, speaks to his family, and away they go, travelin' in single file, headin' down the road toward Paradise.

"Well, there's one objector out of it," grins Dirty. "If we can send Yaller Horse down the road, talkin' to themselves, we've got a circus."

***

Yaller Horse didn't show up that afternoon, but we wasn't fooled by that. We *sabe* that bunch pretty good. Eph Whittaker was intendin' to unload that hay at the livery stable, but he ain't never come back yet. Magpie wanted to take a posse and go after that elephant, but none of us had any desire to hunt elephants.

"That's Runnin' Wolf's share he sold to Yaller Horse," said Dirty. "Let 'em worry about that hay burnin' quadruped—we'll keep the lion and tiger."

Well, we had a few more drinks, and Dirty Shirt made me a present of the lion. I took him. It was the first lion I ever owned. It was almost dark when we went down to look at our animals. The stable was locked, but we busted open the back door and went in, takin' Olaf Jergens with us. Olaf is sufferin' from acute alcoholism and a desire for music. The calli-yupe is in the stable, but there ain't no steam in her.

"Ay am de calli-yupe player," declares Olaf. "Ay vant moosic."

"That's fine," says Dirty, who is so cockeyed that he can't even see Olaf. "We've got to have a musician, Ike; so we better take the Swede in partnership. Olaf, you are now an owner in a circus. What do you think of that?"

"Ay am de calli-yupe player. My name is Yergens and Ay am from Copen-hagen." Dirty tried to bow to him, and hit his head on the lion cage.

"What do you think you are, a woodpecker?" I asks, holdin' the lantern up. "Instead of knockin' your head against wood, you better figure out some way to save this outfit. If Yaller Horse comes back, we've got a fight on our hands."

We went into executive session right there.

"You can't hide an outfit like thish," declares Dirty, owlish-like. "There's sixsh horshes in the corral, b'longin' to us, but they ain't worth mush. Our visible assets are the lion and tagger. They're worth money. Wonner what their names are? Olaf, what's the names of lion and tagger?"

"De lion," says Olaf, "iss Chudas, unt der tiger iss Chessie Chames."

"That's a swell name for that pet of mine," says I.

"He kill seex men," says Olaf.

"And," says Dirty, "everybody says seven is a lucky number. If we could only hide them animals somewhere."

Dirty produced a bottle, and we all had a drink.

"I've got a swell idea," says Dirty. "We'll hide them animals in the grain room, and if Yaller Horse overpowers us, they'll take away an empty cage."

"Ay tank das been goot yoke," says Olaf.

"You know how to get 'em out of the cage?"

"Sure, Ay know how."

I dunno yet how we done it, but the three of us managed to wheel that wagon around and against the door of the grain room, which is a place about fifteen feet square, built inside the stable. There's a end door to the cage, and a way of liftin' the bars in between the two cages. The door of the grain room opens in; so Dirty tied a rope to the handle. Olaf let the lion into the tiger's cage, before he opened the end door, and they shore told each other a few things in jungle talk. There's fur flyin' out through the bars of the cage when Olaf opened the end door, and both of them animals went crashin' into that grain room. Dirty yanked the door shut behind 'em, and we wheeled the wagon away from the room.

I reckon them two cats stopped fightin' to examine their new quarters, 'cause everythin' is quiet again. We had another drink, and then we heard somebody fussin' with the lock on the front door. Dirty sneaked down there, but comes back in a minute, and tells us that Yaller Horse is back.

"Das goot yoke," chuckles Olaf.

"Let's git up in the loft," suggests Dirty, which was a good idea.

Yaller Horse would never look up there, and none of us were capable of stoppin' 'em from taking the rest of the outfit. It was quite a job to get Olaf into the loft, 'cause he wasn't in no climbin' mood, but we got him there.

At the street end of the loft is a hay hole, about five feet square, where the moonlight shines through. We're above the level of the hills, and all we can see is a lot of stars. We crawls toward that hay hole, and we're only about fifteen feet from it when Dirty grabs me by the arm and I came down on my chin.

"My Gawd!" wails Dirty. "There's a stairway up from the grain room, and we never locked it!"

Right in the middle of that hay hole stands Judas, the man eatin' lion, with the moonlight makin' a light streak all around him.

"Where de hal iss dat hole we come oop?" wails Olaf, tryin' to back up.

"You—you know lions, Olaf," whispers Dirty. "Say somethin' to him, can'tcha?"

"Ay don't unnerstand," complains Olaf. "Ay vant to git out from dis place." Judas turns his head and looks at us.

Wham! The report of Dirty's six-shooter almost blew my hat off. I dunno where that bullet hit Judas, but he let out a squawl you could hear for a mile, and he went back past so fast that he missed the stairway door to the grain room, and hit the wall.

I got to my feet and headed for the hay hole as fast as I could run, and Dirty Shirt was right behind me. We never stopped to see what was below, but sailed out of there like a couple of birds. It's fifteen feet to the ground, as the crow flies, but I reckon Ike Harper made a runnin' broad jump record, 'cause I came down flat on my back in a waterin' trough full of cold water.

It knocked all the wind out of me, and the vacancy was immediate and soon filled with water. I reckon I was goin' down for the third time, when somebody pulled me out.

Everythin' was kinda confused for a while. Instead of rollin' me over a barrel, they seemed to be rollin' me up in a rope. I coughed out about a gallon of water and hayseed mixed, and then begins to find out that things ain't so cozy after all. I've been all roped up by Yaller Horse, it seems. Dirty Shirt lit so hard that he's recitin' the Lord's Prayer in Chinook. They only had one rope, as far as I can understand, and I'm tied up with one end, while Dirty is tied up with the other. There's about fifteen feet of slack between us.

"Well, we've got the ones we needed," says Yuma. "It's a cinch now."

"We can git in the back door," says Tombstone. "C'mon."

"What'll we do with these two snake hunters?" asks Smoky Potts.

"Better gag 'em," suggests Hardpan; and that's what they done.

"Lock 'em in the grain room," says Tombstone. "Somebody'll find 'em in the mornin'."

I tried to yell, but it wasn't any use. I wanted to tell 'em that the grain room was full of wild animals, but all I could do was glub a little. I knowed dam' well nobody would find us in the mornin', unless they performed an attopsy on a lion and a tiger. My gun was gone, my hands tied and my voice cut off just behind my tonsils.

Dirty was makin' a lot of funny noises, but 'nobody paid any attention to him. They shoved us around to the back door, which they had opened. The lantern was still lighted. Smoky comes in, leadin' several of them circus horses.

"Better unhook that front door," says Tombstone. "It locks from this side. We want to be all set to git out of here. P'session is nine points in the law, and we p'sesses right now. Git them harnesses on and let's git goin'."

We hears one of 'em slidin' that front door open kinda easy-like.

"Unfasten that grain room door," says Yuma, "and let's git these two jiggers off our hands. No use of me holdin' 'em, when there's more important work to be done."

I look at Dirty in the lantern light. His hair is standin' up on end, and his one loose eye is doin' a war dance. He's tryin' to tell 'em why we don't want to go in that grain room, and it sounds like a hawg diggin' for roots.

"Oof gloogl oof oof glug mff glug oogle," says he.

"Shut up, you damn' Eskimo!" snorts Tombstone. "Open the door, Yuma, and I'll see how far inside I can kick these two Piperockers."

And he kicked me so far inside that my vertebrae knocked a chunk off my solar plexus. Me and Dirty landed on our hands and knees jist inside the door, when a cross between a yaller streak and a locomotive went between us. That is, he went between us as far as the rope would let him, and then he took up the slack. I went upward and backward and my spinal column rattled like a handful of poker chips when my back hit the wall beside the door.

It's my opinion that the rope broke, but I won't swear to anythin', except that I bounced off that wall and landed with my nose against the side of the big grain bin. I see a lot of stars that ain't never been seen by any telescope, but I didn't lose my presence of mind. Somethin' seemed to be sayin', "Ike Harper, esquire, don't forget that even with the lion out there somewhere, eatin' up

Yaller Horse and Piperock, you are still among the tiger; and while the lion is the king of beasts, the tiger is the minister of war."

And that still, small voice made me forget my sore nose and unjointed vertebrae. But the Harper fambly are fighters from the belt both ways. The door is shut, but I can hear sounds of conflict outside. The rope comes loose from m' hands, and I gathers m' muscles—what's left to gather—and gits ready for anythin'.

It's awful dark in there, and I've lost all track of direction, but m' ears are tuned plenty. Then I hears that tiger—Jessie James. He's goin' soft, kinda sniffin', sniffin' along. I've fought all kinds of things in one way or another, but I don't *sabe* the proper attack on tigers; so this is kinda new to me, and jist about the time I'm tryin' to figure out a plan of battle, as they say, Jessie James rubs agin me.

As I said before, I'm plumb lackin' in feelin's, but the fightin' instinct is strong within me, and I took to that tiger like he was m' long lost brother. Did we have conflict? Ask the man who has took to a tiger. There wasn't no furniture in that grain room to hamper us—jist four walls and some big grain bins—plenty room to show the superiority of the white race agin' the striped.

We went around and around that place in the dark, kickin', bitin', scratchin', bumpin' into the walls. Sometimes the tiger is on top, and agin Ike Harper rises above all obstacles and whangs that man eater from above. We're both active, as you might say, but I hit m' head on the wall a few times, and I've got inside information that unless the tiger has had about enough, the fight is goin' agin the white race. And about that time I gits my hand on what feels like a loaded quirt, and the next time I gits on top, I socks Mr. Tiger over the head with all my remainin' strength. It was plenty. The tiger sighs kinda deep, relaxes, and Ike Harper rolls off on his back, weak but triumphant. Barrin' that one wallop with the quirt, I've whipped a man eater with m' bare hands. I'm takin' a lot of deep breaths and wonderin' how much of this is goin' to be believed, when I hears a weak voice sayin'—

"Ay don't like dis haar t'ing."

"Olaf, is that you?" I asks

"Ay am de calli-yupe player," says he. "My name is Yergens, from Copenhagen."

"C'mon down, Olaf. Everythin' is all right—I've whipped the tiger."

"Ay am down."

With a hand that feels like it belonged to somebody else, I finds a match and managed to scratch it on the floor. Beside me lays Olaf Jergens, minus most of his clothes, both eyes blacked and a long scratch across his nose. We stare at each other until the match goes out.

"Where's the tiger?" I asks.

"Ay don't know," says Olaf painful-like, "Ay have whip heem, Ay t'ink. Yeeminy gosh, we have fight!"

"And you let him git away from you?"

"Ay t'ink de ruff fall in on me."

I tried the door, but it was locked. Olaf wasn't very steady, but he followed me up the stairs to the loft. I've lost all fear of that tiger, but my legs don't track good; so I gets down on my hands and knees and starts crawlin' toward that hay hole agin, with Olaf crawlin' behind me. He don't know what it's all about, but he's too dumb to ask questions.

We reached the hay hole, when I happens to turn my head, and there's the two shiny eyes of that tiger behind us. He must have been hidin' in the loft. I sat up with my back toward the hay hole. I wanted to save my life as much as ever, but I didn't want to take that fifteen foot jump agin. Mebbe the tiger had an idea that we had him cornered.

Jist then the floor seems to kinda raise under me, and the stable begins to shake.

"Yo-o-o-o-o-owr-r-r-r-rr!" yowls Jessie James, and he came between me and Olaf Jergens like an arrer from a bow.

I made one grab with both hands, got me a flyin' tackle on some part of that tiger, and went out through that hay hole with such a jerk that I yanked my backbone into place agin. I let loose in midair and landed with a splat right on the broad back of that elephant, which is half-way through the door of the livery stable and don't seem to be able to go either way. That was what was givin' us an earthquake feelin' up there.

There's horses and people runnin' everyway, yellin', givin' advice.

"Shoot him!" yells Pete Gonyer.

"Shoot him."

I reckon they meant me, 'cause the first bullet nicked a chunk off the bridge of my nose. The elephant is surgin' and gruntin', and the old stable is loosenin' in all her joints. And then there comes another sound. The only thing I ever heard make a noise like that was the old automobile Tombstone Todd won at the Piperock raffle. It had a horn on it that sounded like the wail of a lost soul. Yaller Rock County forbid Tombstone from runnin' it, and he stored it in a blacksmith shop in Paradise.

Nearer and nearer she comes, wailin' plenty. Even the elephant stops his house wreckin' and tries to pull loose. And then we see it in the moonlight, and it's an automobile, runnin' like a comet, with fire shootin' out the rear end. It hit a little culvert at the end of the street, about a hundred feet from the stable, whirled around on one wheel, and in less time than it takes to tell it, the danged thing hit the elephant square in the rear end.

The front end was jist high enough to knock the elephant loose from his hind legs, and he came backwards with the whole front of the livery stable, and we all crashed down in a shudderin' heap. My light went out then. It had been flickerin' badly, anyway.

When I woke up, I'm settin' in a chair in Buck's saloon. There's Yuma Yates, Hardpan Hawkins and Smoky Potts. All three of 'em look like the climax of a nightmare. It seems as though all of Piperock is there. Propped up in a chair is a stranger. He's wearin' what's left of a checked suit, a white collar sticks straight up the back of his neck, and around his neck is the brim of a derby hat. Both of his eyes are black and his nose looks like a peeled beet.

"Here's another one," says Magpie.

Runnin' Wolf comes in through the doorway, and he's shore a downtrodden lookin' aborigine. He's been hit so hard that he's more bow-legged than ever, and all he's wearin' is about half of a boiled shirt and a twisted eagle feather.

"Set down," orders Magpie. Runnin' Wolf tries to, but he can't bend.

"What happened?" asks the stranger, plenty hoarse. "I don't remember much. I was in that town they call Paradise and I wanted to come up here. That Indian had an automobile and offered to take me up here with him. We missed the road and knocked down a lot of little trees, I think, and some of them must have hit me in the head."

"The Injun was drivin' it, eh?"

"I drive," nodded Runnin' Wolf. "Go like hell."

"Where did you git that horseless carriage?" asks Magpie.

"Tombstone traded it to him for the circus," groans Yuma.

"Traded for what circus?" asks the stranger.

"Oh, the one an Injun brought in here."

"Traded? Say, that outfit belongs to me! I rented it to that Injun. He wanted to put on style, and I needed the money. Where are my animals?"

I've been listenin' to all this, but my eyes have been on the back door, where Dirty Shirt is standin' with his back toward us, pullin' on a rope which extends around the corner. He turns his head and says:

"I dunno where the rest of your damn' mee-nagerie is, mister—but I've got the lion. Gimme a hand, will you?"

"You—you got the lion on that rope?" yelps Magpie.

"Yea-a-a-ah—and he's balkin' on me. Gimme a hand, will you?"

In less than three seconds there's only me and Dirty Shirt left in the place. I managed to git to my feet and go wobblin' down to Dirty, who is bracin' his feet, pullin' awful hard. I slips out my knife and cut the rope, and Dirty went over backwards against the wall.

I helped Dirty to his feet and we went wobblin' down to the front door. He thought the rope broke. We went outside, hangin' on to each other, and almost run into Tombstone Todd. He's got a rope tangled around his neck and one arm, and he ain't got enough clothes on to build a handkerchief.

"Wh-where's the lul-lion go?" he asks.

We didn't know.

"It dragged me all over the damn' town," he wails. "Tried to drag me into the saloon, but the rope busted. I'm through. I traded Runnin' Wolf my horse-less carriage for his damn' circus, but I take my loss cheerfully."

An apparition limps in out of the dark. It is Olaf.

"Ay am de calli-yupe player," says he. "My name is Yergens, from Copen-hagen."

"Did you know Chief Axlegrease only rented that circus outfit?" I asks.

"He tal me, 'You say Ay buy dis outfit, and Ay pay you ten doolar.' Ay don't get no pay. Ay am what you call socker."

"And," sighs Dirty Shirt, "when Barnum said that he didn't jist mean that they had to be born thataway. Lotsa grown folks git that way. I lose ten dollars, too."

"I'll make that damn' Injun give me back my gas buggy," groans Tombstone.

"If I'm any judge," says I, "you'll have to take it out of the elephant's hide."

Next mornin' they found the lion and tiger sleepin' together in their cage, and the elephant eatin' up all of Pete Gonyer's haystack; so the owner paid Pete for his loss and took 'em away. I was glad to see 'em leavin'. I've always been a great lover of animals—but I owned a lion onct. His name was Judas.

HENRY GOES PREHISTORIC

"Judge" Van Treece was mad; so mad that he deliberately threw his beloved, and badly dog-eared copy of Shakespeare, across the office, where it fluttered to the floor, like a wounded duck. He didn't even look at the poor thing, as he sat, tilted back in an old chair, his high heels hooked around a rung of his chair, which brought his bony, overall-clad knees, almost up to his chin. Judge had the features of a tragedian, and just now he glared his hate at nobody in particular.

Henry Harrison Conroy, the sheriff of Tonto City, got up from his creaking desk chair, retrieved the dog-eared copy and placed it on his desk. While Judge was inches over six feet in height, and as skinny as a sand-hill crane, Henry Harrison Conroy was barely five feet, seven inches in his high-heel boots. However, Henry was fashioned after the specifications of the well-known Humpty Dumpty. Henry had very little hair, a face like a full moon, small eyes and the biggest nose that ever gleamed above the footlights in vaudeville. That nose had been known from one end of most vaudeville chains to the other, featured, in fact.

He looked quizzically at Judge, as he sat down.

"After all, Judge," he said, "you can not blame William Shakespeare."

"I have," declared Judge hollowly, looking straight ahead, "a notion of resigning. I still have my pride, sir. My body may belong to Wild Horse Valley, but my soul is still my own."

"Ah, yes—pride and soul; resignation—no!" mumbled Henry. "No, that is not the solution, Judge. There must be some other way to handle the situation. We'll fight this out to the bitter end."

"So you think there will be a bitter end, Henry?"

"Let us look calmly upon the matter at hand," suggested Henry. "I must admit that those Commissioners are irksome. They did decry our lack of ability in coping with the crime wave, which seems to be washing upon our shores. It is very unfortunate that recent gold strikes have filled Tonto City to overflowing with some damnable riff-raff, which always drifts in with new gold strikes, like buzzards after a dead animal. Our once-peaceful pueblo of

Tonto is filled with covetous folk, who work not, neither do they spin. And we, you and I, Judge, are the Keepers of the Peace—such as it is."

"Keepers of the Peace," repeated Judge. "I like that, sir. But that is not what the *Clarion* called us. Isn't bad enough to read such damnable, scurrilous, infamous—er—"

"Enlightening," suggested Henry calmly.

"Well," sighed Judge, "I was about to indicate that I did not relish the reading of the editorial by the Commissioners. Damme, they didn't have to read it aloud to us! We had read it. It is deplorable that a chuckleheaded nincompoop like James Wadsworth Longfellow Pelly can influence public opinion. He suggests that we resign at once. And damme, that Board of Commissioners agreed with him. In fact, they—well, were you going to say something?"

"No," replied Henry calmly, "I merely opened my mouth for air."

"Well, do you not resent the attitude of the three Commissioners, Henry? Are you a man or a mouse, sir?"

"Biology," sighed Henry, "is in my favor; I have but two legs."

"Will you please hand me that book?" asked Judge. "I hate to ask it, but my damn legs are so cramped that I would never be able to regain this position again. Thank you, sir—you are kind."

<hr />

Judging from appearances there was little wonder that the Scorpion Bend *Clarion* called these two men, plus Oscar Johnson, their jailer, the Shame of Arizona. Oscar was a giant Swede of tremendous strength, but low IQ.

When vaudeville waned and faded from American stages, Henry Harrison Conroy, like thousands of other vaudevillians, was out of work. An uncle, whom he had never heard about before, died in Wild Horse Valley, leaving Henry as sole owner of the JHC cattle ranch. Henry knew nothing about the cattle country, but he accepted his inheritance, came to Tonto City, wearing tailored clothes, spats, pearl-colored derby hat, and twirling a gold-headed cane.

Arizona loved Henry at once. His courtly manner, sense of ridiculous humor, and enormous thirst intrigued them. He took over the JHC, much to their delight, and really went Arizona himself. Shortly after he became acclimated an election came along, and, as a good joke, the cowboys got together and wrote Henry's name on their ballots. The next morning he found that he was sheriff of Wild Horse County. A cowboy summed it up in his statement that, "We've shore played a joke on this county."

Henry saw the humor of the situation clearly. In Tonto City lived Judge Van Treece, who had never been a judge, but a really fine attorney, until an insatiable thirst made him a derelict. Henry, as a humorous gesture, and also because he liked Judge, appointed Judge as his deputy. And as an extra gesture, he appointed Oscar Johnson, a horse-wrangler, as jailer. It completed as queer a trio of peace officers as any county ever had. Men laughed and made fun of them, but, as a matter of fact, they had managed to keep crime at a rather low ebb in Wild Horse Valley, until now, when things were getting out of hand, due to an influx of rather unsavory characters, lured by new gold strikes.

Judge had barely settled in his chair, thumbing the pages of his old book, when John Campbell, the big, prosecuting attorney came in. Campbell had been present with the Commissioners, when Henry and his staff had been severely taken to task.

"One gloat out of you, John, and I shall cram this copy of the Bard of Avon down your gullet," declared Judge soberly.

John Campbell laughed shortly. "I don't blame you, Judge. No, I came not to gloat, gentlemen."

"To bury Caesar?" queried Henry quietly.

"No, Henry. I talked with those men after we left here. They are merely barking, not biting—as yet. As a matter of fact, Henry, this Mr. Thomas Akers, the gentleman from Scorpion Bend, has an axe to grind. He is stumping for his cousin, Pete Gonyer. If you can be induced to resign, or if he can talk the others into forcing you out of office for cause, he hopes to have Pete Gonyer appointed as sheriff of Wild Horse Valley."

"That broken-nosed high-pockets!" snorted Judge. "Why, that—"

"So Pete Gonyer, owner of the Circle G, is a cousin of our esteemed Commissioner from Scorpion Bend, eh?" remarked Henry. "Now I see the light. And Mr. Thomas Akers is a friend of James Wadsworth Longfellow Pelly, ye editor of ye *Clarion*."

"In fact," added Campbell, "Mr. Akers rents the *Clarion* building to Mr. Pelly."

"Astoundingly simple," snorted Judge. "Back-scratching!"

John Campbell laughed. "All you have to do now, Henry," he said, "is to put a halt to all this high-grading and gold stealing in Wild Horse Valley. Personally, I don't envy you the job."

John Campbell went back up the street, leaving Henry and Judge, looking at each other. A team and vehicle drew up in front of the office, and two men got out. One of them was of featherweight size, with a murderous-looking mustache, bow-legs—and a gallon jug. The other was tall and thin, tired-eyed, buck-teeth and inquiring eyebrows. The smaller one was Frijole Bill Cullison, the cook at Henry's JHC ranch, and the other was Slim Pickins, Henry's lone cowpoke.

They went slowly into the office, with Frijole in the lead, carrying the jug in front of him in both hands, like a man bearing a valuable gift—or something dangerous. Both Henry and Judge turned quickly, looking at the procession, which came to a halt in front of the desk, where Frijole carefully set the jug. Then they both backed away and stood at attention.

"Damnable mumbo-jumbo!" snorted Judge.

Frijole winced. "Don't say that, Judge," he pleaded. "You are now in the presence of the finest batch ever made. Twelve hours of age, and as prime as anythin' that ever come out of a pot. That, gentlemen, is m' masterpiece. Put yore ear agin that jug, and yuh can hear her hum, like a wire in the wind."

Slim just stood there, grinning foolishly, eyebrows arched.

"Well done, thou good and faithful servant. What is in it this time?" Henry asked quietly.

"The soul of a great distiller," replied Frijole gravely. "M' life's work is done. If the world knew what I know—"

"We would all be half-witted," added Judge soberly.

The jug looked innocent enough. Henry touched it with his finger. Frijole said, "Slim, you tell 'em what happened to Bill Shakespeare."

"Have done!" exclaimed Judge. "Not that, Frijole. I can swallow your prune whiskey, but not the fantastic tales of that damnable rooster. I do not believe a word of it—even from Slim."

"I cain't tell it," whispered Slim. "You go ahead, Frijole."

"The two biggest liars in Arizona," sighed Judge.

"I believe," stated Henry soberly. "Go ahead, Frijole."

"Well, this ain't no lie," declared Frijole. "I seen it with m' own eyes. Yuh see, Henry, I've been 'sperimentin' on a new mash. I fermented some maguey, like they make tequila, mixed it with some spuds, and a batch of Indian corn."

"Don't leave out the horse liniment," suggested Judge.

"No, I didn't, Judge. When that batch of mash got to the whistlin' point, I put in the liniment and then I—"

"No one is interested in a recipe," interrupted Judge. "Get down to the distorted facts."

Frijole grinned slowly. "Well, yeah—I shouldn't expose my formula. I won't tell yuh how me and Slim had that mash in a keg, with a anvil on top of it, and it blowed the anvil plumb through the kitchen roof, and when it hit—" Frijole whispered huskily, "that anvil was shrunk to the size of a tack-hammer. I won't tell that part of it, 'cause it's hard to believe. Anyway, you know how fond Bill Shakespeare, the rooster, is of mash. I was so scared of him a-gettin' this mash and killin' himself that I put it in a sack and hung it in a tree, aimin' to dry it out and burn it. But do you know what happened? It leaked—and there was Bill, settin' on his hind-end under the tree, bill open, drinkin' in the drippin's.

"By the time I seen him, Bill was swelled up like a balloon. His crop was plumb filled with mash-drippin's, and he was as loaded as a lumber-jack on pay-day. He staggered away from the sack, with joy in his soul and rubber in his legs. The hens all kept away from Bill—them a-settin' on the corral fence in executive session, while Bill goes lookin' for what he may devour.

"Well, sir, there's a old diamond-back, which lives in the day-wash, and I suspect he's livin' partly off baby chickens. He's a old sockdolager, with about twenty rattles. Bill finds him out in the weeds behind the little chicken house, and the first thing I know, here's that big rattler, all cocked and primed, buzzin' his tail, a-warnin' Bill Shakespeare to stay back.

"I know that Bill don't like that rattler, but he ain't never been able to figure out jist how to whip the crippled crawler. I just says to m'self, 'Bill, yo're a goner this time, if yuh don't back-track real pronto.' But Bill don't back-track. He staggers in close, and that dog-gone rattler hits him square in the crop. Then he rears back and socks poor old Bill another. I kinda shut m' eyes and turns away. I—I love that old featherless son-of-a-gun." Frijole choked a little.

Henry was leaning across the desk. "So Bill died, eh?" he said.

"Nossir," replied Frijole, "he didn't. Bill walked away, kinda proud-like and went down to the corral—and yuh don't have to believe me, Henry, but a few moments later that big rattler went into convulsions, and died on the spot."

"Slim!" exclaimed Judge sharply. Slim jerked convulsively.

"Slim, did you see all this?" asked Judge.

"No, I didn't exactly see it, Judge," replied Slim soberly. "Yuh see, I was out in the blacksmith shop, tryin' to make a couple new iron lids for the cook-stove. When we was makin' this mash, it kinda boiled over on the stove and et up two lids, jist like a Piute eats hotcakes. Why, I jist got in the steam of that batch, and it et all the rivets out of m' overalls."

Henry put one hand on the jug and shut his eyes. "I can see it all," he said soberly. "A wonderful tale—and well told, Frijole. Thanks to you, Slim, for the additions. Judge, if you will be kind enough to procure the cups—"

The testing of a new batch of Frijole's distillation was a ceremony. They drank from tin cups which held almost a half-pint. Sometimes Henry or Judge offered a toast, but usually they merely nodded to each other, held the cups high, and drank swiftly. This was no liquor to be sipped.

For several moments after the drink no one spoke. In fact, it was a physical impossibility. Slim's whisper came first—"Don't anybody light a match!"

Gradually as they recovered speech and action, Henry said, "That is proof positive, gentlemen."

"What does it prove?" husked Judge.

"It proves the story of Bill Shakespeare and the snake, sir."

"And I," said Judge soberly, "feel sorry for the snake."

"And why, may I ask, sir?"

"For wasting its efforts. One strike would have been enough."

<hr />

Rumors of new, rich strikes were common in Tonto City, most of them were false, but a man brought a story of a rich strike to the sheriff's office. Old Ben Todd, a veteran prospector of Wild Horse Valley, had struck a bonanza. He was spending raw gold in the saloons; not the washed nuggets of a placer mine, but chunks of gold from a quartz vein. Henry tried to find Old Ben. He liked the eccentric old-timer, and had done favors for him. Not that Henry wanted any part of Old Ben's find, but did consider that the old man might need protection.

However, he was unable to locate Ben. He talked with a bartender in the King's Castle Saloon, who had seen Ben's gold, and the bartender said it was true. Old Ben had his pockets full of the stuff, and was drinking heavily.

The Yellow Warrior mine had been the hardest hit by thieves. It was the oldest mine in the valley, and had been once virtually abandoned as through, but a small syndicate of eastern men had purchased it and struck a new vein, which was so rich that high-graders had managed to steal the bulk of the output. Not only had they swiped the jewelry-ore piecemeal, but had broken in and got away with twelve sacks of selected stuff, ready to ship.

An organized bandit gang had made it difficult to send gold or payrolls over the regular channels, and the sheriff's office had not been able to cope with all the various crimes against the law. Bob Stickler, manager of the Yellow Warrior, was one of the leading agitators against the present regime of Henry Harrison Conroy. Stickler wanted protection—not a comedy trio.

The Three Partners and the Smoke Tree mine were not complaining vocif-erously. They had little high-grade stuff to steal, but they were concerned over the robbery of the Yellow Warrior payroll.

The Yellow Warrior syndicate had also purchased the King's Castle Saloon, which was being operated by Mack Greer, a newcomer to Tonto City. Henry sighed over the changes in Tonto. He told Judge, "When a man complains about changes in his community, he must be getting old."

"You are," nodded Judge soberly.

"I am not!" Henry was emphatic, and added quietly, "I love peace and quiet. This damnable town clatters like a tin-pan shivaree for twenty-four hours, on end. Let us go out to the ranch and put our feet on the porch-railing, Judge. I would enjoy the song of a little bird."

They were an incongruous couple on horseback. Judge rode a short-cou-pled roan, and his long feet almost reached the ground, while Henry perched high on a leggy sorrel, his legs reaching only to the middle of the lanky animal. Judge hated a saddle. In fact, he rarely used the stirrups, preferring to let his legs dangle loosely, and instead of the high-heel boots he wore what was known as Congress-gaiters, well-worn and the elastic sides gaping.

Oscar Johnson was left in charge. The giant Swede, who dwarfed that little office, nodded solemnly when Henry said they were going to the ranch.

"Ay vill run it, Hanry," he said, "and Ay hope Tames Vadsworth Longfeller Telly comes ha'ar. Ay have bone to pick vit him."

"What bone is that, Oscar?" asked Henry.

"His," replied Oscar blandly.

There was nothing ornate about the JHC ranchhouse. The old frame house tilted west, while the front porch tilted east, and the railing around the porch sagged to the north. Frijole had a mulligan stew on the stove, and more of his devil's brew in a jug.

Thunder and Lightning Mendoza, two of Henry's general helpers, sprawled on the shady side of the house. "Henry don't need those two any more than he needs shoe-laces for a boot," Judge had said.

"I love every bit of ivory in their unused heads," declared Henry. "They amuse me."

Henry looked them over soberly. He loved to question them as to just what they had done for the past week. Lightning seemed to be the more intelligent of the two.

"Oh, we feex the corral," he said expansively. "Put out ol' fence-pos', leave een a new ones. Cut leetle wood. Ver' busy pippil."

"Sure," agreed Thunder. "Ver' nice jobs—I theenk. You know Profeezil?"

Henry scratched his chin thoughtfully. "Profeezil?" he asked.

"Sure," grinned Lightning. "Profeezil. Got the long leg, glass on hees eye."

"Aw, he means Professor Fossil," informed Slim Pickins.

"Sure," grinned Thunder. "We see heem."

"He came past here a while ago," said Slim, "packin' a short pick and a sack of rocks."

"Oh, yes," murmured Henry. "Professor Fossil."

His right name was Charles Winston Norbert, Archaeologist. He was tall, thin and slightly stooped, possibly from carrying rock specimens. He had been in Wild Horse Valley for weeks, and had taken up his temporary abode at the Circle G ranch, from where he sampled the country. Even Pete Gonyer considered the man slightly touched in the head. Nearly every day he brought in a sack of samples, which he studied carefully, making voluminous notes in his book.

"Except for eddication," declared Frijole, "he'd make a first-class shepherd. He's got the legs for it."

"*Mucho loco*," declared Lightning. "Rock too damn h'avy."

"Ver' seely pippil," added Thunder. "He theenk feesh leeve on rock."

"Fossil fish," explained Henry.

"Sure—weeth a peek—not weeth a hooks," said Lightning.

"I think it is about time to surrender," sighed Judge.

They were in bed that night, when Oscar Johnson came out there, knocking so hard on the front door that the whole house shook. Frijole opened the door, and said Oscar, "Val, hallo dere, Freeholey. Ay yust come out."

"That's what I thought, when I heard yuh knock. What's wrong? Have the Norwegians taken Tonto City?"

"Norvegians! Ay can lick any Norvegian Ay ever—oh, hallo, Hanry!"

Henry had stepped from his room, clad only in his full-length underwear, which had been made full-length for a full-length man. Henry was one succession of wrinkles.

"What is wrong, Oscar?" he asked.

"Oh, Ay forgot," said Oscar, "Ol' Ben Todd is dead."

Henry paddled out a little closer. "Ben Todd?" he asked. "You mean to say that Ben Todd is dead?"

"Ay have de opinion of Doctor Bogart"

"What killed him?"

"Buckshot—t'rough a vindow."

"My goodness! Judge! Oh, Judge! Frijole, saddle our horses! Judge! Wake up! We have a murder!"

Judge mumbled something about not being a Recording Angel, as he struggled into his clothes. Frijole had gone to saddle their two horses.

"Ben Todd vars in his little shack," said Oscar, "and somebody shoots bockshot t'rough de vindow at him. Ay t'ink he vars dronk, but yust de same, he died."

"That's queer!" declared Henry, struggling with his boots.

"Nothing queer about murder," said Judge. "Sordid, I'd say."

"Possibly, Judge. But why kill Old Ben? He was—oh, I forgot about the new strike they say he made!"

"He vars spending gold," said Oscar.

"Ay saw it."

"Chunks of raw gold," remarked Judge. "I saw some of it. Crushed out of gray quartz. And now he's dead."

"You have your shoes on the wrong feet, Judge," said Henry.

"It might change our luck," said Judge. "Let 'em stay."

<hr />

The body of the old prospector had not been moved. Doctor Bogart, the coroner, was waiting for them. Ben Todd had a little, old shack a short distance off the main street, where he batched, when in town. A load of buckshot had blown out one of the windows, and Ben Todd was sprawled on his bed. Evidently he had been killed, just as he was about to retire.

His pockets still held several chunks of gold, possibly worth twenty dollars, but he had no money. On a shelf was an old, tin tobacco box, in which were some odds and ends, and in it was a folded paper. Henry unfolded it on the table. It was Ben Todd's will, written in an inky sprawl, and said:

I hereby give every thing I own to Violet La Verne because she grub-staked me. I ain't got no relatives.

—Ben Todd.

"Violet La Verne?" queried Doctor Bogart.

"One of the King's Castle damsels," said Henry grimly. "You know her, Judge."

"Why me?" asked Judge testily. "Everybody knows her."

"So she staked Ben Todd," muttered Henry.

"The will isn't dated," remarked the doctor.

"No, that is true, Doc—but, still, it is a will."

"And Ben Todd was murdered," pointed out Judge. "Just one more incentive for a *Clarion* editorial."

"I read that last one," said the doctor. "Something should be done to muzzle Mr. Pelly. We better get some help to move the body. You take charge of that will, Henry."

"Probably worthless," said Judge. "He had nothing to leave."

"You forget his rich strike," said Henry. "He may have plenty."

"Yes, I forgot," admitted Judge. "At least he had enough to get himself blasted off this mortal coil—or presumed to have."

There was no use going back to the ranch, so they went up to their room at the Tonto Hotel. It was miserably hot up there. Judge kicked off his gaiters, flung his hat in a corner and sat down, a miserable specimen of the genus *homo*.

Henry said nothing, sitting there on the edge of the bed, deep in thought. Judge got up slowly and went over to a small closet, where he picked up a jug and shook it carefully. Henry said slowly:

"'And lately, by the tavern door agape,
Came shining through the dusk an Angel
Shape bearing a vessel on his shoulder;
And he bid me taste of it; and 'twas the Grape.'"

"Omar," said Judge, "had the right idea, but in our case it was prune-juice and horse liniment. Have a small portion, sir."

"About three inches in a bath-tub," nodded Henry soberly.

Tonto City was not greatly perturbed over the murder of Old Ben Todd. Henry gave the will to John Campbell, the prosecutor, who said that if Ben left anything of value it must be given to Violet La Verne. Henry went to the county recorder's office and looked over the records, but Ben Todd had not recorded a mining claim for over a year.

Later in the day he found the girl in the honkatonk at the King's Castle, and sat down with her. Violet had little resemblance to her namesake. She was of undeterminate age, blonde, by choice, with dark roots showing.

"Did you call me over to buy me a drink?" she asked curiously.

"I have no objections, my dear," said Henry soberly, "but alcohol was not my main reason. You knew Old Ben Todd, I believe."

"Yes. I grub-staked him. Gave him fifty dollars. He said he'd cut me in on any strike he made."

"You knew he was killed last night, did you not?"

Her eyes narrowed a little. "I heard he was," she nodded.

"It is true, my dear—he was murdered. But evidently Ben Todd was as good as his word—he—that is, you are his sole heir. He wrote a will, in which you get everything he had."

"He did, eh?" Violet leaned across the table. "What?"

"Who knows? I understand that he made a rich strike."

"He was throwing money around. That is, he was throwing gold. It must have been a rich strike—don't you think?"

"Didn't he tell you where it was?" asked Henry.

Violet shook her head. "He didn't tell me anything. But if he made a strike, he must have—I don't know what you call it—"

"Recorded it?" asked Henry, and she nodded quickly.

"That's what I meant," she said. "He must have done that."

"Unfortunately—no," said Henry quietly. "I examined the record book, and Ben Todd did not record his location notice—if he ever made one out. My dear lady, I'm afraid that it will go down in history as the Lost Todd mine, along with many more."

Violet La Verne looked bleakly at Henry.

"Then I don't get anything for my fifty bucks, eh?"

"The clothes he had on, a pocket-knife, a six-shooter, very old and very battered, a mule—I believe. I'm not sure of the mule—but who is? Oh, yes, about twenty .45 caliber cartridges, somewhat corroded. I believe that covers his assets."

Violet La Verne got up from the table. "What about that drink?" said Henry.

But Violet La Verne walked away, not even looking back. Mack Greer, the new manager of the place, came over and sat on the edge of the table. Greer was rather handsome, tall, slender.

"What about Ben Todd? I heard he was murdered," he remarked.

Henry nodded thoughtfully. "That is true, Mr. Greer. You see, he left his entire estate to Violet La Verne."

"Yea-a-a-ah?" whispered the gambler. "That's fine. I heard that she grub-staked him."

"It mentioned that in the will."

"It did, eh? Well, he had plenty of raw gold, and he said there was plenty more where that came from."

"It must have been rich," said Henry, "if all the tales are true. He had only a few nuggets left, and no money."

"That grub-stake was a lucky hunch for Violet," said Greer.

"That's what she thought," said Henry.

"What do you mean, Sheriff—thought?"

"Yuh see, Mr. Greer," explained Henry carefully, "Ben Todd forgot to record his claim. There isn't even a location notice to prove that he ever located a gold claim."

The gambler looked keenly at Henry. "You mean—he never put his claim on record at all; that nobody knows where it is located?"

"That seems to be a fact, sir. Unless Ben Todd imparted the knowledge verbally to someone—the secret died with him. That man with the shotgun was premature."

"It would seem so," agreed Greer.

Henry was crossing the street to his office, when he saw two men just entering the place. Henry groaned quietly. One of the men was Thomas Akers, merchant of Scorpion Bend, and a member of the Board of Commissioners, while the other was James Wadsworth Longfellow Pelly, editor of the Scorpion Bend *Clarion*, and the pet obsession of the sheriff's office. Judge and Oscar were both in the office.

Henry came up to the doorway as quietly as possible, and heard Judge say:

"We are not allowed to announce the name of the murderer of Ben Todd, until Sheriff Conroy gives his permission, sir."

"You mean—you—er—know?" asked Pelly in a whisper.

"Ay know von t'ing—" rumbled Oscar's voice, and the creak of a chair indicated that the giant Swede was getting up.

Henry had started to enter the office, when a flying Pelly hit him squarely in the middle. Pelly was more or less of a lightweight, but with a distinct muzzle-velocity.

Henry was knocked speechless for the moment. Thomas Akers came out swiftly, skidded a heel on the threshold, and came down to a sitting position with rather a dull thud. It knocked his hat down over his eyes, and he just sat there, wheezing audibly. It was all rather embarrassing. Judge and Oscar came to the doorway. Judge had tears in his eyes, but they were not from sympathy.

"All Ay done vars get up," declared Oscar stolidly.

James Wadsworth Longfellow Pelly sat up in the dust, looking dazedly around, until his eyes centered on Thomas Akers. Then he said accusingly, "I told you it wouldn't do any good."

Akers got up, too. He braced one hand against a side of the doorway and felt behind him, his hat still over his eyes. Then he took off his hat, fanned himself a little and stared at J. W. L. Pelly, who was trying to brush off the dust.

"Gentlemen," said Henry huskily, "I believe I am entitled to an explanation."

"A what?" husked Pelly. "Explanation of what?"

"Of your attack on me, sir. Do not deny it! I start to enter my own office, and you fly at me—actually fly, sir! You are not satisfied with slanderous attacks on me in your filthy newspaper—you attack me physically. And you, Mr. Akers! Why did you jump up and down in the doorway of my office, blocking me from entering? Damnable discourteous, to say the least."

Thomas Akers opened and shut his mouth several times, but no explanation came forth. He seemed in pain.

"As I told you before, it didn't do any good, Mr. Akers," Pelly said.

After Pelly delivered his "I told you so," he started back up the street, flexing his knees, like a place-kicker getting ready to boot a football. After a moment of indecision, Mr. Akers followed him.

Henry stepped into the office, leaned against his desk and gave way to his emotions. Judge sat down, bent over as though in prayer, and groaned painfully, "I—I can't stand it! As long as I live, I shall never forget what I just witnessed."

Henry managed to fall into his deskchair, his moon-like face glistening with tears.

"Ay vill be dorned! Did somet'ng go wrong, Hanry," said Oscar Johnson soberly.

"Something," choked Henry, "went just right, Oscar."

"Das is gude," said Oscar. "Ay vill get de yug."

They had finished their drink, when John Campbell came in. The big, good-natured prosecutor, looked at the tin-cups and smiled but shook his head. He had experienced a drink of Frijole's brew, and wanted none of it.

"I just came up from Doctor Bogart's place, where Mr. Akers and Mr. Pelly were consulting medical science," he said.

"O-o-o-oh!" said the surprised Henry. "And what ails them?"

"That seems problematical, Henry," laughed the lawyer. "Their testimony is contradictory. Mr. Akers is of the opinion that he must have slipped, while Mr. Pelly favors an attack theory. However, Mr. Akers does not remember any attack."

"And what was Doctor Bogart's diagnosis, John?"

"He advised a pillow for Mr. Akers and a sense of humor for Mr. Telly."

"Oil Ay did vars get oop," declared Oscar soberly.

"Well," laughed Campbell, "I guess the incident is closed. By the way, Telly hinted that you know the name of the murderer of Ben Todd."

"That," said Judge, "is as far-fetched as his attack theory. I merely told them I was not allowed to name the killer, until the sheriff gave his permission."

"And I," smiled Henry, "am very close-mouthed, John."

It was late that afternoon, and Henry and Judge were standing in front of the general store, when Pete Gonyer and Professor Fossil came to town in a buckboard. Pete Gonyer was of medium size, swarthy, possibly forty years of age. Professor Charles Winston Norbert, jokingly called Professor Fossil, was well over six feet in height, bony and angular, with a deeply-lined face, and wearing thick-lense glasses.

Pete Gonyer went over to the King's Castle Saloon, while the Professor came to the store. Henry had never met the man, but Judge had, and he introduced Henry.

"And how are the fossils coming, Professor?" asked Henry.

"I beg pardon, sir—but fossils do not come—they have been here for aeons."

"Sorry—my mistake," said Henry.

"I presume that you meant to ask if I had been successful. Yes, I believe I have, thank you."

"The fossil fish of this valley—are they of the upper Palaeozoic or of the Mesozoic rocks, Professor?"

Professor Fossil looked keenly at Henry Harrison Conroy.

"That I shall have to determine," he replied. "I have them classified as to location and depth, and I can assure you that I have some wonderful specimens."

"Perhaps I am foolish to ask you, sir," said Henry, "but have you found a specimen of the *Ichtus Fillari*?"

"No, I haven't, sir—much to my regret. I doubt if any exists in this local formation. However, I am still searching."

"I wish you luck, sir," said Henry soberly.

"Yes—thank you, gentlemen. Well, I must do a little shopping."

Henry and Judge went on over to the hotel porch, where they sat down to wait for the supper bell to ring.

"Henry, what in the name of all that is holy, is an *Ichtus Fillari*?" asked Judge.

"I am not exactly sure myself," replied Henry soberly. "It must have been a fish."

"Have you ever seen one, Henry?"

"Judge, I give you my word, I never even heard of one before."

"You—you made that name up, sir?"

"I believe I did, Judge. I feel that it is possible to create a fossil fish that even an archaeologist hasn't found yet."

"Hm-m-m-m," hummed Judge thoughtfully. "I had no idea you had ever studied such things. Palaeozoic and Mesozoic rocks. Your knowledge amazes me, Henry. I wonder what Professor Fossil thinks of your—shall we say, knowledge of archaeology?"

"It might be rather interesting to know," said Henry quietly. "Somewhere, sometime I read an article on prehistoric rocks. The names of the Palaeozoic and the Mesozoic came to mind, and I used them in the right spot, it seems. Hm-m-m-m-m. I seem to remember something—"

"It is my opinion," remarked Judge, "that if you have any urge of concentration, you might well try thinking of something that will clear up the local crime situation. What happened a million years ago will have little bearing on high-grading and murder."

"Perhaps you are right, Judge. Ah, there is the dinner-bell. I jump from the Palaeozoic to—well, to hash."

The inquest over the body of Ben Todd attracted few people. Violet La Verne was called as a witness, because of the fact that she had been the sole heir to Ben Todd's estate. She was defiant, tight-lipped, but stated that she had grub-staked Ben Todd about a month ago.

"Did Ben Todd tell you he had made a rich strike?" Doctor Bogart asked her.

"He never talked to me," she replied.

"How much money did you give Ben Todd, Miss La Verne?"

"I don't know—hundred dollars, I guess."

"You told the sheriff that you gave him fifty dollars."

"Did I? Maybe I did. What's the difference?"

"Mathematically—fifty dollars," said the doctor dryly.

"All right," she said angrily, "it don't make any difference. I lose—and the amount is my business."

"Did you know that Ben Todd had made you his sole heir?"

"No!" emphatically. "He said he'd split with me—if he found a mine. Why should I be a witness in this—I don't know who shot the old coot."

They excused Violet La Verne, and she swept out of the courtroom. The six-man jury grinned and brought in the usual verdict, killed by a person, or persons, unknown.

"That woman knows something," declared Judge quietly.

"At her age—and occupation—she should," agreed Henry.

As they walked back to the office Judge said:

"If that La Verne woman knew that Ben Todd had willed everything he owned to her—"

"But she says she didn't, Judge."

"My dear, Henry, you are a trusting soul. What is her word worth? She lied about the amount she gave Ben Todd."

"Only a matter of fifty dollars, Judge. It is possible that the woman is poor in mathematics."

"We are all entitled to our theories, sir," said Judge, "and mine is that somebody was greatly surprised and pained when they discovered that Ben Todd did not locate and record that gold mine."

"It would, I believe," said Henry soberly, "have added to his estate."

"As Shakespeare said," smiled Judge, "there is something rotten in Denmark."

"At least, it is worth a sniff or two," said Henry.

In the afternoon mail came a notice from the express company that a new buckboard, consigned to the JHC ranch, had arrived in Scorpion Bend, and was ready for delivery.

"Something more for those half-wits to destroy, Henry," remarked Judge.

"I hope they will be careful, Judge. This one has yellow wheels, red body, and is appropriately decorated."

"I shudder to think what it will have after Frijole, Slim or Oscar have a try at it. We should keep it here in the livery-stable, and only use it on state occasions."

"Such as?" queried Henry.

"Well—going between here and the ranch, for instance. You know how I hate to ride a horse. Possibly we could use it for a trip to Scorpion Bend."

"It might give Mr. Pelly an idea for a new editorial," laughed Henry. "The Shame of Arizona on Yellow Wheels."

"Anyway," sighed Judge, "it is money wasted. Those prune-juicers at the JHC have no regard for property. I shudder to think what that buckboard will look like in a week."

"Well," said Henry soberly, "when I told Frijole what I had ordered, he said that he would protect it with his life. Frijole, I believe, likes nice things. Slim also has a feeling for art. Why, I've seen him stand for long periods of time in front of that picture in the King's Castle, studying it intently."

"What picture?" asked Judge curiously.

"The one at the end of the bar-room, Judge. A beer advertisement, I believe. It depicts a member of the female sex, leaning over a rock, peering into a spring. Rather nicely done, too."

"Oh, that!" snorted Judge. "I happened to note Slim Pickins studying the print at close range, and I asked him if he was interested in the technique of the artist, and he said, 'Hell, no! I'm tryin' to see what she's a-lookin' at.'"

Henry grinned slowly. "Maybe Slim is a realist, Judge."

John Campbell dropped in and they discussed the inquest for a while, but finally Campbell said:

"You probably don't know it yet, Henry, but the Commissioners are holding a special meeting tomorrow afternoon at Scorpion Bend. I have not been asked to attend."

Henry looked at the big lawyer thoughtfully, but did not comment. The implication was plain. They were going to decide to ask for his resignation.

After a long pause, the lawyer went on. "I hear that James Wadsworth Longfellow Pelly is spending a few days at the Circle G, where Mr. Thomas Akers has also been the guest of Peter Gonyer. I heard that they bought a case of bourbon from the King's Castle."

"Mr. Akers," remarked Henry, "is the chairman. But will the others vote with him, John?"

"I don't know, Henry—but I'm afraid they will."

Frijole, Slim and Oscar came in from the ranch, driving a young team to a battered old buckboard. Judge said, "You can look at that equipage and know what that new buckboard will look like in a few days."

They met the three men on the sidewalk and Henry said to Frijole, "You take the team over to the livery-stable and hitch them to a spring-wagon. We are going to Scorpion Bend to bring back our new buckboard."

"Vit yellow veels?" asked Oscar. "Yudas, Ay von't to see it."

"Who is going?" asked Judge quickly.

"Don't you want to go, Judge?" asked Frijole.

"Ride over Lobo Canyon grades with any of you three doing the driving—at night?"

"I shall do the driving, Judge," assured Henry soberly. "We shall be back before morning."

"In that event," said Judge firmly. "I shall stay right here in Tonto City. You drive! And how on earth will you bring that pristine vehicle back, if I may be so bold as to ask?"

"Tie her on behind and trail her home," said Slim.

Judge shrugged. "I still shall stay here," he decided.

They secured the two-seated spring-wagon, and with Henry at the lines, seated with Frijole, they rode away, with Oscar and Slim Pickins on the back seat, holding a gallon jug between them.

"Ay am crazy to see a bockboard vit yellow veels," declared Oscar.

"Yo're crazy," agreed Slim soberly. "The rest is superfluous."

"This is not a pleasure trip," informed Henry. "For your information, Oscar, the Commissioners are meeting tomorrow in Scorpion Bend to decide to ask me to resign as sheriff of Tonto. It will mean that you are out of a job, along with Judge and me."

"Ay vill now open de yug," stated Oscar.

"No," said Henry, "we will not do any drinking—yet."

"Ay vant to be yoyous, ven Ay get to Scorpion Bend, Henry. Ay am going to have a vord vit Mr. Pelly."

"Unfortunately, Mr. Pelly is at the Circle G ranch, Oscar."

"Ya-a-a-ah! Das son-of-a-gon! Vaal, Ay am so downhorted that Ay must have drink."

"Oh, go ahead," said Henry. "You'd do it sooner or later."

They were able to travel the Lobo Grades in daylight, on their way to Scorpion Bend, a picturesque but dangerous road, which wound around the cliffs above Loco Canyon, only wide enough for one vehicle, except at rare intervals, where there was barely room for two wheeled vehicles to pass each other. Jack-knife turns, where the road ahead was blocked from view, until completely around the turn, increased the hazard, even in daylight. Sheer cliffs blocked the inside, but there was no guardrail on the other side.

It was after dark, when they arrived at Scorpion Bend. Frijole, Slim and Oscar were rather mellow, but Henry did not take a drink. He declared, "I am going to make this trip in safety, if it is the last thing I ever do."

"Tha's a good idea," agreed Slim. "I admire any man who is wishful to get back alive."

They ate supper, and Henry tried to get the boys to go up to the depot, but they didn't want to go back too early.

"Man, when we go back," said Frijole, "we don't want nothin' else on the grade."

So Henry waited. There was a dance in Scorpion Bend, and it was after ten o'clock when Henry managed to gather his brood and go to the depot after the new buckboard. A peevish depot agent accepted the money from Henry, and unlocked the storeroom. The whole buckboard was crated, wheels separate, and Henry's helpers were in no condition to do mechanical labor.

They managed to move everything outside, borrowed the agent's lantern and hammer. There was a monkey-wrench in the spring-wagon, and, after an infinite lot of argumentative labor, they got the wheels and tongue on the buckboard. It glistened like a circus wagon in the lamplight. With a section of chain they fastened the tongue to the rear axle of the wagon, and were all ready for the trip to Tonto City.

Slim and Oscar declared that they were going to ride in the buckboard, and Henry was too weary to argue.

"It's all right, Henry. If the blamed thing busts loose, they can take care of it—until found," said Frijole.

"I believe you are right, Frijole."

--- ◦ ---

They drove slowly, until satisfied that the coupling was sufficient, and then headed for Tonto City at their usual pace, which was a cross between a harness race and a runaway. They heard Slim yelling to Henry to stay on the road, but paid no attention. At the foot of the grade they stopped for inspection. Slim said wearily, "I'm shore glad yuh stopped. Every time we tried to take a drink out of the jug—we can't. Man, I never rode in anything as rough as this buckboard. Oscar's very sick."

"Ay am sea-sick," gasped Oscar. "Some-t'ing is wrong vit us."

The buckboard seemed intact, unmarked. Henry and Frijole lighted matches and looked things over. Slim asked, "What's wrong with it, Frijole?"

"Not a blamed thing. Cork up that jug—we're travelin'."

"I dunno," said Slim. "I've rode a lot of things in m' life, but this'n has got em all beat. How are yuh, Oscar?"

"Viggly," whispered Oscar.

They drove on. Frijole was chuckling, and Henry said, "What is so funny?"

"That buckboard," choked the little cook. "We got a hind wheel and a front wheel on each end. No wonder Oscar feels viggly!"

"My goodness!" exclaimed Henry. "Hadn't we better remedy that?"

"No. It can't hurt anythin'—except their feelin's. Keep goin'."

There was no moon, and a slight overcast ruined the starlight for illumination. Henry had to trust to the team entirely. On the first sharp turn they felt a decided jerk, and heard a crash. The team stopped short, when Henry applied the brake.

"W'ere de ha'al do you t'ink you are going?" wailed Oscar.

"I see!" grunted Henry. "Sharp turn, and the buckboard did not make it in time. Hm-m-m-m!"

Oscar and Slim were scratching matches at the buckboard, and Slim came up to report, "You almost knocked the hubs off both wheels, scratched the body and some of the spokes pretty bad."

"I shall try and do better on the next one," promised Henry.

"Yeah," said Slim, "you do that. Yuh can roll when ready."

As they started on Henry said, "I shall swing wider on the next curve, Frijole."

"Could yuh see where yuh swung?" asked Frijole.

"No, I could not, but I'll swing wider next time."

"Not with me on this side—yuh won't. Even in the dark I could look straight down into that canyon, and I seen a eagle's nest with six aigs in it."

"Well, I don't want to knock *all* the paint off that vehicle."

Frijole had taken the jug from the buckboard, and now he drew out the cork. They were on an upgrade, and at the top was the worst jack-knife curve on the whole road. Frijole said,

"Have a snort, Henry—it might cushion yore fall."

Henry shoved on the brake very tight and stopped the team.

"Cushion my fall!" he snorted. "The idea!"

"The idea is good," said Frijole. "That curve ain't twenty feet ahead, and I don't believe we'll make it—not in this dark. That buckboard won't swing far enough. Mebbe we better untie it and take it around by hand."

"I believe I can make it, Frijole," said Henry, but there was doubt in his voice. Frijole said, "Anyway, I'll get out—until yuh do. After all, there should be one survivor of the tragedy."

"What'sa delay?" yelled Slim. "This ain't no place to stop."

"We're figgerin'!" yelled Frijole.

"Git out, Oscar, and hug the rock—they're a-figgerin'!" exclaimed Slim.

"Ay vill help dem," declared Oscar. "Ay am gude from figures."

"He-e-ey!" howled Slim. "Where-at is the jug, Oscar? We've done lost it!"

"Hang onto yore seat!" yelled Frijole. "We're goin'."

Henry kicked off the brake and they started ahead, but just at that moment something loomed out of the darkness just ahead of them. They heard the rattle of a wagon, the rasp of shod tires, skidding on rock, and the yell of warning. Henry swung heavy on his left line, throwing his team in against the cliffs. It was a violation of driving rules, trying to pass on the left, but Henry had no liking for that outside edge. A moment later came the crash, a babel of excited yelps.

Henry jumped ahead of the crash, tripped over a front wheel and dived headfirst into a bushy manzanita against the foot of the cliff, breaking his fall, but taking great toll of his clothes. He had a dim idea of horses rearing over him, but he was helpless to do anything about it. He heard a man yelling:

"Help! Help! Help!" and suddenly realized that it was himself. He heard Frijole's voice calling, "Whoa, you buzzard-heads! Whoa, whoa! Where are yuh, Henry?"

Slim said, "Stop yellin' and help me git this horse back on his feet, Frijole!"

"That ain't no horse—that's Oscar."

"It is, huh? How can yuh tell, in the dark?"

"He's got on high-heel boots. What happened? Didn't I tell yuh that buck-board wouldn't make the turn? Didn't I—huh?"

Henry managed to extricate himself from the manzanita and staggered around the end of the wagon, where he almost fell over somebody. He grabbed the end-gate of the wagon and felt for some matches.

"Henry must have got killed, Slim," came Frijole's voice.

"Yeah," said Slim vacantly. "We lost the jug, too."

"Well, what happened?" asked Frijole. "I seen somethin'—Slim! It was a wagon and team! I 'member now. But where did they go?"

Henry managed to light the match and look down. He was standing astride of James Wadsworth Longfellow Pelly, and the vitrolic editor of the *Clarion* was staring up at him, blinking slowly. Frijole and Slim came over and lighted more matches. Pelly was fast recovering. Slim said, "We have to take the bitter with the sweet—he ain't dead."

"Henry ain't dead, too," said Frijole in amazement. "Henry, what happened to you?"

"Never mind me," replied Henry. "What happened to that other team and wagon?"

"You saw it, too, huh?" asked Slim. "I didn't. I was huntin' for that jug in the back of the buckboard."

"Did you find it?" asked Oscar's voice, very weakly. "Ay could use it."

"I had it before the crash," said Frijole.

"Vait a minute!" snorted Oscar. "Ve must check up. Slim, are you and Hanry and Freeholey oil right?"

"No," replied Henry, "but we'll do, I suppose. Why?"

"Ay have found somebody else."

Oscar scratched a match, and yelled, "Yudas Priest! Das is Professor Fossil!"

They all stumbled over and made a match-light examination of Professor Charles Winston Norbert. He was all dressed up in a black suit, white shirt and very high, starched collar. Slim said, "From the way he's dressed, he must have knowed—"

James Wadsworth Longfellow Pelly managed to get up and stagger over toward them.

"I—I can't get this straight," he said huskily.

"You never got anythin' straight—so don't worry," said Frijole. "Stop tee-terin' —that aidge is too close."

"Let him weave," said Slim quickly. Henry took hold of the editor's arm and steadied him. "How did you get here Pelly?" he asked.

"In a wagon," whispered Pelly. "I—I was at the Circle G—visiting. The professor was going home; so I decided to ride back with them. Cooler at night, you know."

"How many of you on that wagon?" asked Henry anxiously.

"Th-three," stammered Pelly. "The professor, Jud Bailey and myself. But what happened—anyway? Don't you know?"

"I hate to say this, gentlemen," remarked Henry slowly, "but I'm very much afraid that Jud Bailey and his equipage went into Lobo Canyon."

No one said anything for a while, and then Slim remarked, "Well, they ain't here now, they didn't go past that buckboard, and I'm fairly sure that they never backed up, Henry."

"I remember a little," said Pelly shakily. "I—I thought we were going a little too fast for that curve. Then it happened."

"Well," said Slim dryly, "all I can say is that you and Professor Fossil was lucky to get off on the right side. It was shorter that way. Shucks, you could be a-fallin' yet."

But the professor was not dead. He sat up, took a few wheezing breaths, but was unable to talk. An examination showed that their two horses were still intact, but the right front wheel of the wagon was gone and the body badly ditched on that side. They took the team, hitched it to the buckboard, piled everybody aboard, and headed for Tonto City, with Frijole and Slim taking care of the speechless professor.

"Don't talk with yore hands," said Slim, "'cause we can't read no hand-talk in the dark."

"Das is the lousiest deal Ay ever had," declared Oscar sadly.

"What was that?" asked Henry.

"Losin' de yug," replied Oscar.

They finally arrived at Tonto City and routed Doctor Bogart out of bed. Professor Fossil was able, with some help, to walk into the doctor's office. He had only spoken a few words on the way home, but he was able to tell the doctor that he was all right. He had a cut scalp, numerous bruises, and the doctor decided that he was suffering from shock. Pelly shrugged off any medical attention, although he had an egg-sized lump on the side of his head. Henry had numerous cuts and bruises, most of them from the sharp limbs of that manzanita, and also declined any assistance from the doctor. Slim had brought Judge down there to hear what happened. The doctor put the professor to bed and came back to the office.

"The professor required a sedative," said the doctor. "He has suffered considerable shock, and is very nervous."

"You can't blame him," said Pelly. "After all his work in this valley, all his samples and trophies have gone into Lobo Canyon."

"Oh, that's too bad!" exclaimed Henry. "I didn't realize—"

"Mr. Gonyer wanted him to ship them out on the stage," said Pelly, "but he decided to handle them himself."

"Quite a collection, I suppose," said Henry.

"Two large boxes," said Pelly. "At least five hundred pounds of fossil-bearing rocks. And his trunk and valises, too."

"They might be recovered," suggested Henry. "Lobo Canyon is a difficult place to get in and out, but perhaps we can—"

"I must get to Scorpion Bend," interrupted Pelly. "My paper must be published. I almost forgot about it."

"Not a bad idea," said Judge soberly. "I'm sure that the public would thoroughly admire your negligence."

Although Pelly was not in physical shape to flare-up—he made an attempt. He turned on Henry and declared, "I am announcing your resignation, Conroy."

"My goodness! But what if I do not resign, sir?"

"You will—or get fired. By resigning you escape the stigma of being ousted bodily. I have it on such good authority that I have the story all written. And after what happened tonight—"

"You are blaming me for that?" queried Henry soberly.

"You deliberately turned the wrong way, Conroy. You forced the wagon over into the canyon."

"Instead of going down there ourselves," said Henry. "Yes, I did that, Mr. Pelly. You have admitted that your driver was traveling too fast for that dangerous road, and you must admit that he was crowding the outer edge, making it impossible for me to have stayed on that side. I have the evidence of your own words, spoken before witnesses. One word of accusation against me in your paper, and I shall sue you for criminal libel, my boy."

James Wadsworth Longfellow Pelly looked around the room. Oscar Johnson, Slim Pickins, Frijole Cullison, Henry Conroy, Judge Van Treece, all looking at him.

"You can't scare me," he said weakly.

"Not any worse than you are now, Pelly," assured Henry.

"It's a wonder Professor Norbert and I were not killed, too," said Pelly huskily.

"We can't have everything our way," sighed Judge.

------◆------

Slim, Frijole and Oscar took the buckboard and headed for the JHC, while Henry and Judge went up to their room. It was almost morning. Henry's face was scratched, his clothes badly torn. He took off his boots and sank down in a chair.

"Well, my friend, it looks as though *finis* has been written for the Shame of Arizona," remarked Judge.

Henry drew a deep breath, flexed his tired hands, and said, "Judge, a Conroy always goes down fighting."

"Against whom—if I may ask, sir?"

"My opponent has not been selected yet."

"And today—they hold that meeting. The time is short, sir."

"Aye, my friend—but not too short. We must sleep on it."

Someone knocked timidly on their door, and Henry said, "Come in."

It was Slim Pickins, who announced, "We've decided to stay here t'night, Henry."

"You have? And why, if I may ask, Slim?"

"Yuh see," explained Slim, "Oscar was drivin', and he knocked the left front wheel off the buckboard against the sidewalk."

They were barely asleep, when another knock sounded.

"Don't bother lighting a lamp, Henry. The professor is gone," came Doctor Bogart's voice.

"You mean—he died already, Doc?" asked Henry huskily.

"No, I mean he pulled out. Opened a window in the bedroom and left it open. Took all his clothes."

"My goodness, Doc! Why, the man must be out of his head!"

"I wouldn't swear to that, Henry—but he is out of my house."

"Should we make a search for him—do you think—I hope you do not?"

"No, I don't believe that would do any good, Henry. I just thought you'd like to know about it. Good-night."

"Good-night, Doc."

Doctor Bogart closed the door and Henry sank back.

"The professor must be wandering in his mind," commented Judge.

"With brains enough left to dress himself and crawl through a window? He may be wandering, Judge—but not in his mind."

Henry slid out of bed and lighted the lamp. Judge sat up in amazement and saw the sheriff starting to dress. Judge ran his bony fingers through his mop of tousled hair, shut his eyes tightly and then looked at Henry again. The fat man was struggling with a rather tight pair of overalls.

"You must have been hit rather hard, too, Henry," said Judge.

"I suspect that some of my sense of balance has been disrupted," agreed Henry, "but I am normal again—thank you. Get into your clothes, Judge; and I would advise boots, instead of those disreputable slippers you have been wearing. And chaps, too, if you do not mind."

"Have you gone mad?" gasped Judge. "We haven't been to sleep yet."

"Oh, get dressed and do not quibble. You must realize that a man died in the depths of Lobo Canyon tonight, and, in spite of Mr. Pelly's diagnosis, we are still the peace officers of Wild Horse Valley, and it is our duty to remove that body."

"Heavens above!" snorted Judge. "You mean—no, you can't mean that, Henry— at this time of the night!"

"Explain, Judge."

"Well, I—Henry, you do not intend going into Lobo Canyon at this ungodly hour —or do you?"

"I do, my dear deputy—and you will be at my side—except where we are obliged to ride single-file. Stop moaning, and dress."

"I wish I could contact Doctor Bogart about this," whispered Judge. "He would know what to do about it."

"I suppose we should take rifles along," muttered Henry, yanking at his boot.

"Rifles?" Judge sat on the edge of the bed and stared at Henry. "Why—uh—the man is dead, isn't he, Henry?"

"Get dressed," said Henry. "It is almost daylight."

"What you need is a sedative, sir," declared Judge.

"What I need is a deputy, I'm afraid."

Judge grabbed a boot and glared at Henry. "Indeed? Until you fall on your head—I am satisfactory. Do not blame *me*, Henry—you do not realize your condition." Henry selected an old, leather coat and drew it on, saying, "I'd advise that you wear a leather jacket, Judge—that brush tears cloth badly. I'll meet you at the office—with the horses. Do not keep me waiting, my boy."

"You have your boots on the wrong feet, Henry."

"I have not, sir; I am toeing-out—to keep my balance. It has been a hard night."

Henry walked out and shut the door. Judge stared at the boot in his hand for several moments, before putting it on. He said aloud, "The man is as mad as a hatter—and I must humor him." Then he donned the rest of his clothes and left the hotel.

It was about nine o'clock when Oscar, Slim and Frijole came down to breakfast. They were all limping, more or less. They found James Wadsworth Longfellow in the restaurant. He flinched, but did not speak. The three were subdued, having little to say. Doctor Bogart came in and asked them if they had seen Henry or Judge. He had been up to their room, but they were not in, nor were they at the sheriff's office.

"Henry hit on his head," said Slim soberly, "and Judge ain't too intelligent to wander off with him."

"You boys don't look too good this morning," remarked the doctor.

"Pers'nally, Doc," said Frijole flexing a sore shoulder, "I think I'm in the sere and yaller leaf, as yuh might say. I ain't as flexible as I was last night, I know that much. Slim slept on the floor. He said that the bed was too soft, after what he'd been through. Sa-a-ay!" Frijole's eyebrows lifted suddenly. "Yuh don't suppose them two old galoots have gone into Lobo Canyon, do yuh, Doc?"

"That's possible, Frijole. Better see if their horses are gone."

They finished their breakfast first. The horses and saddles were not in the stable.

"Looks at it thisaway, fellers," said Slim soberly. "Them two galoots ain't got no more right in Lobo Canyon than David had in the lion's den. That's one awful tough spot. I've been there and I know. What's to be done about 'em?"

"Our best bet," said Frijole, "is for one of us to get a horse at the livery-stable, go out to the ranch and bring back enough rollin'-stock for all three of us. And make it quick. We'll match coins—odd man goes."

"You ve got a head on yuh," said Slim soberly. "All right, get out yore money."

Slim and Frijole's coin showed heads—so Oscar went to get the horses at the ranch. It always worked—and Oscar never got wise to their scheme.

<hr>

Slim and Frijole met James Wadsworth Longfellow Pelly on the street. Pelly had talked with Doctor Bogart, and found that the professor was missing. Pelly wasn't in perfect physical condition, and he had lost his glasses.

"Somebody should go out and tell Mr. Gonyer," said Pelly. "He don't know what happened last night."

"As a matter of fact," said Slim Pickins gravely, "it's too late for Pete Gonyer to do anythin' about it, Pelly. He's shy one team and wagon—and a squint-eyed cowpoke."

"Yes, I'm afraid that Jud Bailey is dead."

"If he ain't, he's the most durable cowpoke that ever lived. It's three, four hundred feet to the bottom at that place, and he shore got a divin' start."

"You knew that the professor is missing, didn't you?"

"Missin'?" gasped Frijole. "Missin' what—his valise?"

"No—he's gone," said Pelly. "Doctor Bogart went in to look at him, after we had left there last night—or this morning—and the professor had dressed and went out the window."

"Lovely dove!" snorted Slim. "Let's go to the office and find the jug—I need medical assistance."

"Thank you," said Pelly, "I do not need that stuff. I feel bad enough, as it is."

Slim had a key to the office, and they located the supply. They were enjoying their third cupful, when Bob Stickler, manager of the Yellow Warrior, came into the office, looking for Henry.

"What was this about the accident on the grade last night?" he asked. "I've heard two or three versions."

"What did yuh hear?" asked Frijole soberly. "We don't want ours to be the same. Yuh see, we was there, and maybe we saw it all wrong."

"Oh, I see—trying to make it sound funny, eh?"

"It wasn't funny," said Slim. "The Circle G team and wagon went into the canyon, along with Jud Bailey, who was drivin'. He came around a jack-knife bend too blamed fast, shoved us in against the wall, and went off the edge."

"I see. Yes, I heard all that. How badly was the professor hurt?"

"*Quien sabe?* Doc put him to bed, but he dressed and sneaked out a winder."

"Probably didn't know what he was doing."

"Yuh mean—before or after he fell?"

"So you don't know where the sheriff went, eh?"

"Just between me and you—and I want this held in strictest confidence, Mr. Stickler—I don't. All we know is that he's gone, Judge is gone and so are their two horses."

"I might add to the confusion," said Frijole owlishly, "by sayin' that they've prob'ly gone to find the body."

"Jud Bailey's body?" asked Stickler.

"Well, yeah—that seems to be the only one we have on hand at the present time. Have a drink?"

"No, thank you."

Stickler left the office, and they filled the cups again.

"Lizzen," said Slim, "if we drink two more cups of this stuff we won't even be able to find Lobo Canyon."

"Don'tcha think we ort to drink this'n, Schlimmie?"

"Well, I wouldn't shay that—but I will shay that we ort to drink it a little slower, par'ner."

Henry and Judge, shivering in the false dawn, rode off the main highway and followed an old trail, which led to the lower end of Lobo Canyon. The trail was little used, because only on rare occasions did anybody go into the canyon. Cattle kept away from it. There were a few pools of water down there, where quail, bobcats and an occasional lion slaked their thirsts, but the bottom of the gulch was a tangle of brush and rocks, making it very difficult to travel. The main canyon was about nine miles in length, and in most of it the sun never shone.

Judge had spent most of the trip complaining. His boots hurt, he hated leather chaps, and his rheumatism was acting up again.

"Here we are," he stated dismally, "poking into an ungodly spot, risking our lives, while those damnable Commissioners are meeting to throw us out of our jobs. We may come out alive, but without visible means of support. Henry, what on earth shall we do for a living?"

"Let us get out of Lobo Canyon with our lives, before we do too much worrying about the future, Judge."

"You admit that it is hazardous?"

"Yes, I believe it has its dangers. Rocks do let loose and come down here, they say. Slim swears that he saw a rattler as long as a lariat and as big as a stove-pipe. Well, here is the trail into it, Judge. Just let the horse pick its own way, and we'll be down there in a jiffy."

The entrance to Lobo Canyon was not too difficult nor dangerous, but the trail ended at the bottom. From there on it was a case of work out your own salvation.

"At least seven miles to where the wagon went over—and if we make a mile an hour we shall be going mighty fast," groaned Judge.

"One thing," said Henry soberly, "there is no danger of us getting separated."

They started up the canyon, seeking places where their horses could travel, but after about a mile Henry said:

"It gets worse every foot of the way, Judge. New slides have blocked us ahead, I believe."

"In a way, I am glad," said Judge. "We can go back now."

"Go back?" asked Henry in amazement "And admit defeat? I'll have you know that a Conroy is never conquered, sir."

"You admitted defeat."

"I admitted defeat—on horseback, sir. We will leave our noble steeds here and proceed on foot."

"Well," said Judge resignedly, "I suppose that is what I get for playing Sancho Panza to an addle-pated Don Quixote. But I may assure you that these high-heel boots were never made for this sort of usage. We will never get out alive—unless somebody carries us out, Henry."

"I hope we are alive—when carried," remarked Henry soberly.

———◇———

They started ahead, crawling through brush, over rocks, keeping alert for rattlers, which abounded in Lobo Canyon. Henry was so stiff and sore that it was difficult for him to keep going. They rested often, but were making fair progress. They struck about a mile of fairly open traveling, but ran into another slide, which halted them for a while.

"Isn't there another way to get into this canyon, Henry?" Judge panted.

Henry sprawled on top of a rock to get his breath, nodded and rubbed a sore elbow.

"I've heard there is, Judge. Somewhere near the upper end, but I don't know just where."

Judge took off a boot and examined his sore toes. It was very quiet down there. Finally Judge said:

"Henry, we're two old fools! We ruin ourselves, trying to get in here to find the body of a dead man. Suppose we do find him—we can't carry him out. Why, we will be lucky to get out ourselves."

Henry sprawled on the rock, looking up at a circling buzzard, far up in the blue sky.

"Two old fools," he said slowly. "That's right, Judge. Fighting to keep a job, getting all busted up physically. This is a young man's job, Judge. Maybe Pete Gonyer—who knows?"

"Pete must be forty."

"A mere child, Judge. Well, we must be going on. It is noon. At this rate, we will fight our way out in the dark."

"But about taking the body out, Henry."

"The first thing to do is to find the body, Judge. Come on."

They went on, circling, crawling, tearing their way through the brush. Circling a pot-hole in the bottom of the canyon, they reached a steep slope, reaching up into more rocks and more brush. Judge was ahead, hunched over, clawing his way up, when Henry saw the head and shoulders of a man ahead of his deputy. Henry reached for his bolstered gun, when his feet slipped and he dropped to his knees on the slope. The gun slipped out of his hand, and before he could recover it, he heard a voice snap:

"All right—come on up—and keep yore hands in sight!"

Henry managed to straighten up. Judge was above him, hands up above his shoulders. There were two men now, and one of them had a gun pointed at Henry. Taking a deep breath, Henry managed to negotiate the slope. Judge sank down on a rock, panting heavily. One of the men yanked the gun from Judge's holster, and came to Henry to disarm him.

"Where's yore gun?" he asked sharply.

"I—I lost it," panted Henry. "Let me sit down—please."

There were two men, both masked, watching Henry and Judge.

"What are you two doin' here in the canyon?" asked one of them.

"We are on an errand of mercy," replied Henry painfully.

"Yeah? What do yuh mean?"

"A man fell into the canyon last night, and we are searching for his body."

"Well, ain't you nice and kind. Who are you?"

"I am the sheriff, sir," replied Henry. He was getting his wind back now. The man laughed.

"Sheriff, eh?" he snarled. "A fine sheriff, you are! Well, Fatty, yo're all through."

"So you knew about it, too, eh?" remarked Henry.

"Knew about what?" asked the masked man.

"About the Commissioners going to force me to resign."

"They are, huh? Well, we'll save paper and ink for 'em, feller."

He turned and called, "One of you fellers fetch a rope."

And as he turned to speak Henry slid off the rock, hit that slope, and went sliding. The man yelled for him to stop. Perhaps he thought it was an accident. At any rate it only required a second or two, before Henry slid onto his gun, grabbed it with both hands, crashed feet-first into the brush and turned over. He had dust in his eyes and misery in his body, but he lifted the gun and shot point-blank at the man at the top of the slope. At that moment Judge fell backwards on the rock, both feet in the air. The man jerked back and yelled:

"Damn him, he hit me! Look out—he's got a gun!"

Henry scrambled to his feet and went into the brush, away from that slope, coming up among some huge boulders. He reloaded his gun, ears alert for sounds. A man was cursing viciously.

"I'll get him—don'tcha worry about that!" he said.

"He outsmarted yuh once," said another voice. "Where'd he get that gun? Where's the other one?"

"Get away from that openin', you fool! He's down at the foot of that slope."

"Where'd he hit yuh?"

"My right arm. Damn him, I've got to shoot left-handed."

For a while there was no noise, no conversation. Then somebody began throwing rocks into the brush—rocks about the size of a baseball. One of them crashed off a rock and filled Henry's eyes with rock-dust. Then a man's voice said harshly:

"Aw, that won't do no good. We've got to git above 'em and shoot down. Yuh can't see a damn thing in this brush."

"You do it—I can't. That arm hurts—yeow! Look out! They're throwin' rocks, too! That'n hit me in the back. Get down!"

For several minutes there was not a sound. Henry hugged the rocks and listened. He knew that any movement must make a noise. Then he heard a man crashing brush, stumbling, panting. He stopped at the foot of the slope, but went on up, his breathing plainly audible. Henry tried to see who he was, but the brush was too thick. Then he heard a thud, a muffled cry, and a crash.

"Who was that?" one of the masked men called.

"I presume it was one of your friends," replied Judge's voice. "He stopped a rock. Now, if you will kindly show yourselves—"

"You blasted old fool!" snarled one of the men, and fired three shots in Judge's general direction, but all it brought was a derisive laugh from the deputy.

Henry, peering through the brush, saw a movement, caught a flash of color. He steadied the gun over the rock, holding it in both hands, and squeezed the trigger. The rattling report brought a yell of pain, and a general scurrying around in the brush. A man was cursing, and Henry heard him say:

"We've got to git out of here, I tell yuh! I've got some busted ribs. If the boys ain't finished—we can't help it."

"Lettin' two old fossils like that whip us," complained the other man. "Pull yore shirt tight over them ribs, can'tcha?"

From far up the canyon came the rattling report of a gun.

"He-e-ey! What's goin' on up there?" came from one of the men.

"C'mon! That don't sound good!"

Henry could hear the two men going up through the brush. He backed out and called to Judge. After a few moments he heard Judge say, "I just wanted to be sure they had really gone, sir. Are you all right, Henry?"

"The latest reports from outlying precincts," replied Henry, "would indicate that I am not running too well. Who did you hit?"

"He is there at the top of the slope, where we were captured."

Henry managed to climb up there, where Judge was looking down at his victim. Judge and Henry looked at each other, and Judge said blankly:

"Where does Bob Stickler fit into the pattern of things?"

"I don't know," replied Henry. "Why did he come here, I wonder. Look at that knot on his head! Judge, if he came here to help us, I'm sorry, but if he came to help the other team, I'm mighty glad for your pitching ability. Listen!"

The canyon echoed with more shots. Henry scratched his head and squinted thoughtfully at Judge. By mutual consent they moved into the brush, where Judge picked and hefted another rock.

"Or Slingshot Van Treece," he said grimly.

"I hit two of them," said Henry.

"Knowing how well you shoot," said Judge, "I believe in miracles."

"I suppose the meeting is on now," remarked Henry. "Mr. Akers is on his feet, extolling the virtues of Peter Gonyer. By the way, I wonder what became of James Wadsworth Longfellow Pelly?"

"And Professor Fossil," added Judge.

Henry was staring into space, and now he gasped, "I have it!"

"You—uh—have what?" whispered Judge.

"Palaeozoic and Mesozoic," whispered Henry. "There are no fossils in the Mesozoic."

Judge shook his head. "Probably just a slight recurrence of shock," he said quietly. "You should have stayed in bed."

"He said he would have to determine, Judge. Ridiculous!"

"You take the rock and let me have the gun, Henry."

"No, I—"

Another splattering of shots, but closer now. A man was running wildly down through the brush, and they saw him now. Hatless, his clothes torn, tall, thin, running clumsily, trying to look back. He wasn't looking for anyone ahead of him, and he was heading for Henry and Judge. He jerked to a stop, gun raised, when Henry hit him in a clumsy football tackle. In fact, Henry missed him with both hands, but his ample girth struck the man just behind the knees with terrific force, and he went down backwards, flinging his gun far into the brush.

Both of them were knocked out. Judge went over carefully and looked them both over. Henry sat up, his face purple, as he tried to wheeze air back into his tortured lungs, but the other man lay quiet, arms outstretched, breathing heavily. Henry's gun was on the ground, and Judge picked it up.

Another man was running down through the brush toward them. Judge cocked the gun, his face grim, as the man came ahead, really smashing his way. He crashed into the opening, stumbled to a stop, and stood there staring at Judge. It was Oscar Johnson, torn, disheveled, but very much in earnest.

He came on and squatted on his heels beside Judge. Henry was beginning to recover. Oscar looked at the other man, and a slow grin spread across his big face.

"Ay vill be yiggered, Yudge!" he exclaimed.

Henry drew a deep breath, and whispered, "Professor Fossil."

"Yah," grinned Oscar. "Ay vass chasing him, Hanry. By golly, das faller can run!"

"You—were—chasing—him?" panted Henry.

"Yah, sure. How are you, Hanry?"

"I do not know, Oscar. I doubt if I shall ever know again. How on earth did you get down here?"

"Oh, that vass easy. Freeholey know the odder trail. Ve caught all free of dem, Hanry."

"All three of them?" queried Henry weakly. "Three, you said?"

"Yah—su-re. Couple of dem vere vounded, but Pete Gonyer, he vars all right, until he vent crazy and tried to shoot us. Who is that yigger over dere, Yudge?"

"That," replied Judge, "is Bob Stickler."

"Yudas Priest! How did he get here, Yudge?"

Judge shook his head. "He just came, Oscar."

"Three?" queried Henry. "Pete Gonyer and who else?"

"Lou Greer and Yud Bailey."

"Jud Bailey? Oscar, Bailey is dead!"

"No-o-o," drawled Oscar. "All he got is bullet in his arm."

"But—why—didn't he go into the canyon last night?"

"He yumped," said Oscar. "Ve missed him, and he valked to de ranch."

<hr />

Bob Stickler stirred and managed to sit up. He rubbed his head and stared around, looking at each of them separately, as though trying to reason out what this was all about. Then he tilted his head and looked up at the canyon walls. The professor was moving his arms and legs, as he recovered. The three men watched them. Consciousness came quickly to the professor, and with it came realization. Then he sat up, flexing his legs.

Stickler started to get up, but Oscar went over to him, and the manager of the Yellow Warrior sat down again.

"Yust stay like you vere," said Oscar.

Another man was coming down the canyon. It was Frijole. He broke into the open, gun in hand, and stood there, staring at them.

"Velcome de party, Freeholey," grinned Oscar.

"Yeah," said Frijole, and came on slowly, staring at the professor and Bob Stickler.

"Slim's got the others," said Frijole. "They're roped. Where in hell did these two come from?"

"Mr. Stickler came up the canyon," said Judge, "and I hit him with a rock. Mr. Fossil came down the canyon, and Henry tackled him around the knees."

"Nice work!" grunted Frijole. "We found 'em, startin' up the trail, Henry. They've got four pack-horses, loaded with—do you want to tell 'em, Professor?"

Professor Fossil didn't. Henry said, "Loaded with jewelry ore from the Yellow Warrior, Frijole?"

"You knowed, Henry?"

"No—I merely guessed. What'd your version, Stickler?"

"I am not talkin'," said Stickler sullenly.

"Pete Gonyer was the leader of the gang," said Frijole. "That dad-blamed Jud Bailey confessed. He thinks he's goin' to die from a bullet in the arm. Where-at is yore horses, Henry?"

"About a mile from the other end of the canyon. You know where it makes a sharp right-hand turn? You do? Well, the horses are on the left-hand side, in a little thicket. But how—?"

"We'll get 'em from the other end—later. Let's drift."

Both Stickler and the professor were able to walk. Less than a quarter of a mile up the canyon they found the others. They unpacked the horses and tied Pete Gonyer to a saddle. He was in bad shape, as were the others, but they were able to get back to the grades.

They had the four pack-horses, and seven saddle-horses. The trail was bad, but they got up to the main road without mishap, just as the valley-bound stage came into view. The driver pulled up beside them and looked with amazement at the cavalcade.

Out from inside the stage came Tom Akers and two others of the Board of Commissioners, staring, mumbling. Akers said:

"What happened to Pete Gonyer? Conroy, what does this mean?"

"It means," replied Henry wearily, "that we have busted up the high-graders—and Mr. Gonyer, whom you were going to appoint as sheriff in my stead, was the leader. Professor Fossil was here, merely to be able to ship samples back to his home—samples of Yellow Warrior gold. Mr. Stickler handled things for them at the mine. You see—"

"My God!" gasped Akers. "It can't be true!"

"It looks true to me," said one of the Commissioners dryly. "Congratulations, Sheriff Conroy."

"I don't understand," complained Akers. "Pete Gonyer isn't that sort of man. Why, I'd bet my soul—"

"If you do not mind, gentlemen," interrupted Henry, "you will ride horseback the rest of the way, and we will use the stage as an ambulance. Later we will recover the Yellow Warrior gold."

The cavalcade came into Tonto City, the stage almost an hour late, and drew up at Doctor Bogart's house, where the wounded were unloaded. James Wadsworth Longfellow Pelly was there, trying to find out what on earth had happened.

"Did you," he asked Akers, "hold that meeting and decide to remove Henry Conroy?"

Tom Akers looked bleakly at Pelly, but said nothing. This was no time to talk of resignations. He followed them to the jail with Stickler and the professor.

Stickler said, "I'll sue the county for false arrest, Conroy. You can't prove anything against me."

"We shall try, sir," said Henry wearily. "What do you think, Professor?"

"After what has happened," replied the professor soberly, "I'm sure you will try."

------◇------

With their prisoners behind the bars, Henry led the way over to the King's Castle. There was quite a crowd in there, discussing what had happened. Mack Greer, the manager, saw Henry and came to him.

"Good work, sheriff," he said. "Mighty good work."

"All praise aside, sir," said Henry soberly, "I would like to see Violet La Verne."

Greer looked curiously at Henry and at the other men with him. Then he turned to one of the other girls, who had come in close, and asked, "Where is Violet?"

"She's up in her room, packing up, Mack—she's quit."

They trooped up the stairs and knocked on her door.

"All right—in a minute. Take that rig around to the back and I'll meet you out there," said a voice from inside.

"She hired a livery rig to take her to Scorpion Bend," whispered one of the curious girls. Henry nodded.

Then the door opened and Violet La Verne stood there, staring at the crowd. She was dressed for traveling, and had an old valise in her hand.

"Who shot Ben Todd?" asked Henry quietly.

The valise dropped from her hand and she closed her eyes for a moment. Henry went on kindly:

"You see, my dear, I happen to know that Ben Todd couldn't read nor write; so that will had to be a fake. All the rest of the gang are either in jail or being probed for lead, so you might as well talk and save what skin you have left."

"Stickler killed him," she whispered huskily. "I grub-staked Ben Todd—I—I honestly did. Stickler wrote that will. He thought Todd had struck it rich and that he'd record the location—but it—it wasn't recorded—because it wasn't a mine—he stole two sacks of high-grade ore from the Circle G. That's the truth—and—and nothing but the—"

And then Violet La Verne went flat in a faint.

Back in the office, thirty minutes later, Henry, Judge, Oscar, Slim and Frijole sat there a tin-cup in hand. They were a bedraggled crew. Stickler had confessed—and the troubles of the sheriff's office were over for the time being.

"You see," explained Henry, "about a year ago I helped Ben Todd make out a location notice. He could neither read nor write, and I felt very sure that he could not learn in a year. That was their first blunder. I suspected theft of that gold by Todd, because he did not record his claim. Todd was careful."

"But why did you suspect the professor?" asked Judge.

"His lack of knowledge of the rocks, Judge; and he was supposed to be an archaeologist. I am not versed in it, but somewhere I had read of them, and I'm sure that either the Palaeozoic or the Mesozoic rock contains no fossils, while the other is filled with them. I believe the Palaeozoic is the blank rock. But, Judge, the professor said he would have to classify them."

"And what other clues?" asked Judge.

"Well, when the professor escaped from Doctor Bogart's place last night, I realized that he was going to warn Pete Gonyer; so I—well, Judge, I decided to beat them to the fossils."

"Speaking of rocks," said Judge soberly, "I wonder just what I hit Stickler with."

"Well, here's luck," said Frijole. "Everythin' turned out fine."

"You forget somet'ing, Freeholey," said Oscar soberly.

"What was that, Oscar?"

"Das lef' front wheel of the bockboard.

DANCING DEVIL RANGE

A LONG, DUSTY FREIGHT train rattled and clanked through the desert hills, seemingly in no hurry to anywhere. Outside it was almost dark, and there were no lights inside the caboose, where Hashknife Hartley sprawled on an uncomfortable seat and gazed wearily through a dusty window. Across the aisle was Hashknife's partner, Sleepy Stevens, stretched out on the seat, his head pillowed on his war-sack.

Hashknife was inches over six feet tall, of slender, steel-muscled manhood, his sombrero pulled low over his gray eyes. Sleepy Stevens was less than six feet tall, broad of shoulder and beam, slightly bow-legged. Sleepy had a grin-wrinkled face, wide mouth and innocent-looking blue eyes, which seemed amazed at the world.

In garb they were merely a pair of drifting cowboys; well-worn Stetsons, colorless shirts, stringy vests, little more than a depository for tobacco and papers, faded overalls and high-heel boots. There was nothing fancy about these two cowpokes. Their gun-belts were home-made, form-fitted by wear, and even their Colt guns, tucked into short holsters, had plain wooden butts, blackened by wear.

A sleepy-eyed brakeman climbed down from the cupola and wiped a grimy forearm across his dusty eyes and lighted his lantern. He said, "We're pullin' into Northgate, boys."

Sleepy swung around on the seat, yawned widely and picked up his war-sack. The train was slowing down, as they came out on the platform. Each one of them picked up a heavy saddle and stepped down. There were few lights in Northgate, the railroad point for all of the Dancing Devil range.

There were huge loading corrals along the tracks, indicating that much livestock was shipped from Northgate. The train stopped, with the caboose close to the depot, and the two men swung down. The conductor crossed in front of them, going into the depot, where a kerosene lamp yellow-lighted the windows. A man came from the near corner of the depot, walking swiftly toward the rear platform of the caboose.

He had just reached the steps and was about to enter the caboose, when a shotgun blasted from down behind the loading platform. The man twisted around, tried to grasp the doorway, but missed, and went backwards off the platform, falling in the middle of the tracks behind the caboose.

Hashknife and Sleepy dropped their impedimenta and ran over to the caboose. There was no sign of the shooter. The conductor, depot-agent and a brakeman came running. They picked the man up and placed him on the platform while Hashknife told them where the shot came from. There was no one in sight. The victim had stopped a dozen buckshot, and was beyond any medical assistance.

There was no law officer in Northgate, the sheriffs office being at Tomahawk Flats, thirty miles south, center of the Dancing Devil range. Someone summoned a doctor, and other curious people arrived. A cowboy said, "I know who he is—he's Oren Blakely. I think he worked for the Circle H, down at Tomahawk Flats."

Hashknife and Sleepy secured a room at a little hotel, and, after considerable haggling, bought two horses from the man who owned the livery-stable and feed corral. They told him they were leaving for Tomahawk Flats in the morning. He said, "if yo're lookin' for work down there—"

"What about it?" asked Hashknife quickly.

"I just meant that they prob'ly ain't lookin' for cowpokes. Yuh see, the bank went busted and that busted most of the cowmen, makin' things kinda bad down there. If a feller was lookin' for work— But that's yore business."

"Much obliged," said Hashknife, but he didn't say whether it was for the advice or the information.

Over at the hotel they heard a man say that they had sent for the sheriff and the coroner. Another man said, "It ain't goin' to be a very merry Christmas down there this year."

In their little room, Hashknife sprawled on the bed, smoking a cigarette, while Sleepy looked moodily from a dusty window. Sleepy said, "I just hope we ain't playin' Sandy Claws for Bob Marsh."

Hashknife laughed shortly. "Where'd yuh get that idea?"

Sleepy sat down and began manufacturing a cigarette.

"Distrust of Bob Marsh," he replied. "Bob sets there at his desk, his big, brown eyes as full of honesty as a coyote pup is full of fleas, and explains that all on earth he wants us to do is come down here, get the best possible price on three, four cattle spreads, and let him know."

"Well?" suggested Hashknife curiously.

"That's all we've got to do," sighed Sleepy. "No rustlers, no horse-thieves—just a couple real estate men on horseback."

"Sounds all right to me," said Hashknife. "We get paid so much for the job, and if the deals go through we get more money. It's an honest job, Sleepy. Bob Marsh, as secretary of the Cattlemen's Association, can't afford to be mixed up in a crooked deal."

"Yeah, I know but—well, a man was murdered tonight."

"Men," remarked Hashknife quietly, "are murdered every day."

"Yeah, I know, but—you heard that man at the livery-stable, sayin' that everybody in the Dancin' Devil country are broke. The bank went busted—"

"Are you lookin' for boogers, Sleepy?"

"No, I'm tryin' to figure out why Bob Marsh got us down here. If he can't get us into trouble one way, he'll—well, all right."

"I've just thought of somethin' else," said Hashknife soberly. Sleepy looked sharply at him and said, "Yeah? What?"

"It ain't long until Christmas, pardner."

"I heard that mentioned tonight, High Pockets. Christmas! Heat and dust. Yuh know, I'd like to spend a Christmas in the snow agin, Hashknife. It ain't Christmas down here, except on the calendar. We had real Christmases in Idaho."

"We had 'em in Montana, too," said Hashknife. "My old man, bein' a range preacher, was strong for things like that. I 'member the church trees decorated with popcorn in strings, popcorn balls, and little, red sacks of mosquito-nettin', full of hard candy, with a tired-lookin' orange in the bottom. They'd read telegrams from Santa Claus, showin' that he was comin'—and then he'd come, all in a bear-skin coat, sleigh-bells, whiskers—"

"Bringin' a pair of skates for little Hashknife," suggested Sleepy.

"They called me Henry," smiled Hashknife, "but I never got any skates. A range preacher didn't make money enough—and we had a whopper of a family. We was poor folks, Sleepy."

"Poor folks in Tomahawk Flats, too, they say. Be a bad Christmas down there—and we're goin' down to try and buy 'em out as cheap as possible."

Hashknife nodded slowly. "That's life, Sleepy."

"It's a tough life for busted folks. Yuh know," Sleepy began rolling a cigarette, "I'll bet yuh a dollar agin a doughnut that we don't buy any spreads."

"Anythin' to base that bet on?"

"Bob Marsh. Listen, tall-feller; Bob Marsh used that as an excuse, or my original name ain't Stevens. He wanted us to come here and let Nature take her course. Yuh can't fool me, feller; I'm wise to Bob Marsh. No, I don't say that Bob's crooked, but he's allus been a connivin' critter."

"He told the idea as straight as a string, Sleepy."

"And here we are," added Sleepy. "We get off the train—and what happens? A man is blasted down with a load of buckshot, that's what happened. He poked cows for one of them poverty-stricken outfits at Tomahawk Flats."

Hashknife grinned. "A coincidence, Sleepy. Prob'ly a grudge between two men—nothin' to do with us."

"No? Nothin' t' do with us, sez he. Huh! And yore long nose has been wigglin' and sniffin', like the nose of a bloodhound, ever since that poor devil done a hooligan off the end of that caboose. Nothin' to do with us, eh? Let's go to bed, before yuh get me all riled up."

Hashknife laughed. It was like Sleepy to complain of things that might happen. They had been together a long time, these two drifting cowboys, always trying to find out what was going on over the next hill, only working long enough to suffice for their few wants, and then going on, always looking, helping some under-dog, asking nothing for themselves.

—◇—

Hashknife, with his ability to solve range mysteries, could have sold his services to the law, and made money. But neither law nor money meant anything to them. They had seen the law miscarry too often. They loved justice—which is not necessarily law. At rare times they worked for the Cattlemen's Association, asking only that they be given a free hand and not be hampered by rules. But neither of them enjoyed nor appreciated the work. Bob Marsh would have almost given his right hand to have them work for his organization. In fact, he used every sort of ruse to get them on certain jobs, knowing that Hashknife, confronted by a problem, would never give up, until it was solved. That was why Sleepy mistrusted Bob Marsh's casual suggestion that they make some money for themselves by asking prices on some cattle ranches.

They found the depot-agent in the little restaurant next morning, eating breakfast with Nick McGarvin, the sheriff, and his deputy, Frenchy Arnett. The agent recognized them, and told the sheriff that these were the two men who had just arrived on the freight train, and were present when Oren Blakely was shot. Hashknife introduced himself and Sleepy, and sat down at their table. He was unable to tell them any more than they already knew about the shooting.

Nick McGarvin was a big, two-fisted sort of person, and Hashknife mentally listed him as a much better man with his fists or gun than with his brains.

Frenchy Arnett was small, dark, hatchet-faced, with a sour disposition and need of sleep. The agent went back to the depot, and the sheriff remarked:

"You two came in on the freight, packin' saddles, bought two broncs from the feed-corral, and said you was headin' for Tomahawk Flats tomorrow morning—that bein' today."

"The corral man told yuh," said Hashknife. "Did he also tell yuh what else we said?"

"No, he didn't. What else did yuh say?"

"I don't remember," replied Hashknife. "It was prob'ly just as important as what he told yuh."

The sheriff nodded, but Frenchy grinned and looked sideways at the sheriff. Frenchy said, "It's allus best to write it out. Things like that require study."

"What are you talkin' about?" asked the sheriff.

"Nothin', Nick."

"Tells us some more about us," suggested Sleepy soberly. "It's shore interestin'."

"We don't know any more," replied the sheriff. "It's my duty to know things."

"Yuh mean—findin' out about everybody's deep, dark past?" asked Sleepy.

"Askin'," corrected Frenchy. "Nick's good at it."

"Any idea who shot the man, Sheriff?" asked Hashknife.

"No. He's worked for the Circle H for over a year, and I ain't never knowed him to have trouble with anybody. 'Course, I'll have to check up with Sam Hack—he owns the Circle H. Sam might know who Oren was feudin' with—I dunno."

They finished breakfast, and Hashknife and Sleepy decided to ride to Tomahawk Flats with the two officers, who had, so far, failed to find out why Hashknife and Sleepy were going there. As they were saddling at the livery-stable, a rider, on a very tired horse, swung off the street and into the stable:

The sheriff said, "Hello, Jim."

Jim Bailey swung off his saddle and came over close to the sheriff. He said, "Nick, I got here as quick as I could. Somebody shot and killed Chiquita Morales last night!"

The big sheriff stared at Jim Bailey, while Frenchy Arnett said, "Aw, Gawd, they didn't do that, Jim!"

Bailey nodded grimly. "She musta been in town, Frenchy—in a buggy. They tied the horse about a mile out of town and shot her."

Hashknife did not ask any questions as the sheriff said wearily, "We're headin' home right now, Jim. Doc Miles left about three o'clock with the body of Oren Blakely."

"It's shore gettin' to be a awful tough country," sighed Jim Bailey. "She was settin' there in the buggy—"

"Shut up!" snapped Frenchy sharply. He dropped his reins and walked over to the big, sliding doors, where he stood, staring out at the street. Jim Bailey shook his head.

"Chiquita was Frenchy's sweetheart," whispered the sheriff.

"That's what *he* thought—mebbe," said Bailey.

Bailey and Frenchy rode ahead, leaving the sheriff to ride with Hashknife and Sleepy.

"We heard that the bank went busted in Tomahawk Flats," remarked Hashknife.

"Robbed," corrected the sheriff. "Three men."

"Cleaned it out, eh?"

"Nothin' left—and it busted a lot of folks. Yuh see, Thomas Colton owned the bank—the Cattleman's Independent Bank. Old Ed Weed was the cashier. It was a good bank, too, with plenty cash. Tom Colton is a fine feller—everybody liked him. He played square with everybody—never hounded 'em on mortgages and all that.

"Well, a short time ago, three men got into Ed Weed's house, made him give 'em the combination of the safe, took his keys, tied Old Ed up so tight that he ain't rid of the kinks yet, and took their sweet time in bustin' the bank. They emptied the vault. As far as we can find out, there wasn't a thin dime left. It broke a lot of folks, I'll tell yuh that. I lost seven hundred dollars myself."

"Where," asked Hashknife, "does this Chiquita Morales figure in the deal, Sheriff?"

"She don't. Her father, Pete Morales, owns a little rancho. Chiquita is about eighteen. I reckon, and as pretty as a bug's ear. I'm past forty and I'm married, but every time she looked at me and grinned—I lost at least fifteen years of age. They're poor, them Morales are. Poor old Pete, this'll hit him hard."

"No idea who busted the bank, eh?" queried Sleepy.

The sheriff sat disgustedly. "We've got a prisoner," he said.

"Oh, yuh caught one of 'em, eh?" remarked Hashknife.

"Quien sabe? Yuh see, it's thisaway. Andy Davidson—we call him Uncle Andy, and his wife, Aunt Judy—the finest folks yuh ever knowed—have a son, Johnny. Johnny's fine. Hell, yuh can't have a pa and ma like them, and not be fine. Johnny's engaged to marry Nell Frawley on Christmas Eve. Well, Johnny's in jail."

"It don't seem to work out," said Hashknife.

"That's right—but there he is. Yuh see, Johnny wears a ring. That is, he did. Navajo, I reckon. Big ring, silver and with a turquoise cross. Anybody'd know that ring. Tom Weed says that one of the men who robbed the bank wore that ring. Johnny didn't have it on his finger when we arrested him, and he can't tell us where it is. He just sets there in his cell, staring at the bars. It's a tough situation, Hartley."

"Well, can't he prove where he was that night?" asked Sleepy.

"If he can—he won't. Yuh can't get a word out of him."

"What does his girl think of the deal?" asked Sleepy.

"Nell Frawley. Lord, I dunno what she thinks. Nell is one of the finest yuh ever seen, and yuh can't beat her folks. They got hit awful hard in that bank bust, but I don't reckon they got hit as hard as Uncle Andy Davidson. He's flat—but he ain't kickin'. If Johnny was out of jail—well, I don't think Uncle Andy is givin' a thought to losin' the money."

"I can imagine," said Hashknife thoughtfully. "A fine Christmas for folks like that."

"That's right, Hartley—I'd plumb forgot about Christmas. Peace on earth—don't fit so good in Dancin' Devil Valley this season."

After a full minute of silent riding the sheriff commented, "I plumb forgot to ask you fellers how come yo're headin' for Dancin' Devil Valley?"

Hashknife studied the bobbing ears of his horse for several moments, his eyes narrowed thoughtfully. Then he looked at the sheriff and said, "Sheriff you know what a wild goose is, don't yuh?"

"Of course, I do."

"We're chasin' one," said Hashknife.

The sheriff scratched his stubbled chin, looked sideways at Hashknife, but rode on, thinking it over. These two rather puzzled the law officer. They looked like a pair of drifting cowpokes, but why would a drifting cowpoke be looking for wild geese in the Dancing Devil country, he wondered. Funny thing, too—when that Hartley person looked at you and said something—you believed him. Even such a fantastic thing as chasing a wild goose.

It was afternoon, when they arrived in Tomahawk Flats, and the sheriff and coroner left immediately to get the body of the murdered Mexican girl. Men had guarded it since the discovery. Hashknife and Sleepy registered at the hotel, where folks talked about the crime wave.

The murder of Oren Blakely was secondary in importance. A man might get killed at any time, but for somebody to deliberately murder a girl—that needed attention.

"I seen Pete Morales and his old woman a while ago," one man said. "Gawd, you'd think the roof fell on both of 'em."

"It shore did," nodded a grizzled cowman. "I lost one—once—but she wasn't shot to death. That's worse—if it can be."

"Yeah, I knew. Mrs. Morales just sat there, countin' her beads, movin' her lips, never looked up at all. She wasn't cryin'—jist countin' 'em, I reckon."

"I kinda figured that her and Frenchy would get hitched," said another of the men. "They used to go down into Mexico to dances, and all that. Frenchy can talk Mexican pretty good."

Hashknife and Sleepy went up to their room to leave their war-bags. Sleepy flung his bag into a corner and stood there, his hands on his hips, looking at Hashknife, who sat down to roll a cigarette.

"Go ahead, pardner—say it," he remarked.

"Yeah! Just a couple real-estate men on horseback!" snorted Sleepy.

"Bob Marsh didn't know things like this would happen, Sleepy; he's no fortune teller. It just happened, that's all."

"Yea-a-ah? All right—be stubborn. We're here, ain't we? Pitch-forked into it by Bob Marsh. He knowed the bank was busted. Mebbe he knew Johnny Davidson was in jail. We came straight from his dog-gone office. Real-estate, yore eye!"

Hashknife lighted his cigarette and inhaled deeply.

"It's a terrible thing—murderin' a girl, Sleepy."

"That's right—terrible! Terrible thing to murder a man, too."

"Even if Bob Marsh knew—"

"Losin' faith in him, eh? That's fine. Now we can start even."

"And there's a job to be done, Sleepy," after a long pause, "we've got a good alibi for bein' down here—real-estate men on horseback."

They ate supper in a little Mexican restaurant, where they found Frenchy Arnett, more than half-drunk, imbibing tequila with his meal. He didn't speak to them—merely looked at them through bloodshot eyes, and went on drinking. Frenchy was gone, when they paid for their meal.

"Frenchy fill pretty bad—I theenk so," said the Mexican proprietor.

"Tequila won't help him much," remarked Sleepy.

"Notheeng help heem much, *amigo*. Too bad."

The murder of Chiquita Morales had sobered Tomahawk Flats. Even in the big Pasatiempo Saloon men talked in subdued tones, placed chips carefully into the jack-pots. The roulette-layout was not even uncovered. A man said, "I'd shore like to pull the rope on that dirty murderer."

Another man laughed shortly and said, "Fine chance. The best our sheriff can do is put Johnny Davidson in jail. Wouldn't have got him, if the blamed fool hadn't worn that ring."

"One cinch," said a gambler, "they can't put that onto Johnny; he was locked up tight. But I can't figure out why anybody'd shoot the girl. As far as that goes, why was Oren Blakely shot?"

"Oren was a good *hombre*," remarked another. "I talked with Sam Hack a while ago, and he said that all he knew was that Oren left the ranch, headin' for here. Why he went to Northgate, nobody seems to know."

"Somebody did," said the gambler, "and that somebody had a shotgun and a load of buckshot. Well, I dunno—it beats me."

"Beats the sheriff, too," said another. "You watch—he'll never get either of the killers."

Hashknife and Sleepy slept late next morning, ate breakfast in the hotel dining-room, and when they came back to the lobby they saw an elderly couple, talking with the hotel-keeper. The man was small, thin, bow-legged, smooth-shaved, almost bird-like in his movements. The woman was gray-haired, tall, slender, sad-looking. The hotel-keeper saw Hashknife and Sleepy come from the dining-room doorway, and motioned to the man, who got up very quickly from his chair and came over to Hashknife.

"Your name is Hartley?" he asked quietly.

"That's right," smiled Hashknife.

"I'm Andy Davidson—AD spread. Mind talkin' to me for a few minutes?"

"I'd like to, Mr. Davidson."

"Everybody calls me Uncle Andy."

"My friends call me Hashknife, Uncle Andy."

"Yeah, that's what—that's the name in the letter I got a few minutes ago. I'll show it to yuh."

Hashknife read the short letter from Bob Marsh, which said:

> I am in receipt of your telegram a few minutes ago, and in reply I can say that two men, Hashknife Hartley and Sleepy Stevens are either now in your town, or soon will be. I have perfect confidence in them and their ability. Please keep this confidential. For that reason I am writing you, rather than to use a telegram.

There was a postscript, which said, "Give my regards to Sleepy."

Hashknife smiled slowly, folded the letter and gave it back to Uncle Andy, who was looking closely at him. Hashknife motioned to Sleepy, who came over.

"Uncle Andy," said Hashknife, "I want you to meet Sleepy Stevens. Sleepy, this is Uncle Andy Davidson. He just got a letter from Bob Marsh."

"Bob's quite a hand to write letters," remarked Sleepy. "Did he send me his regards?"

"By doggies!" exclaimed Uncle Andy. "He did just that!"

"He always does," said Sleepy. "Anyway, I'm glad to meet yuh, Uncle Andy."

They shook hands, and Uncle Andy introduced them to Aunt Judy Davidson, who also shook hands with them soberly.

"We're in a peck of trouble, boys," said Uncle Andy.

"We heard about it," said Hashknife quietly. "Trouble seems plentiful around here. Yuh see, we just got off the train at Northgate when Oren Blakely was shot."

"Oren was a nice boy," offered Aunt Judy. "I'm sorry about him. Isn't it terrible about Chiquita Morales? I liked her."

"Is there anybody you dislike?" asked Hashknife smiling. Aunt Judy thought carefully, finally shaking her head. "I just can't remember any," she said seriously.

They sat down and Uncle Andy said, "How much of the story have you heard, Hashknife?"

"The sheriff told us most of it, ridin' down here."

"Nick has been awful nice to us," said Aunt Judy. "It isn't his fault—he had to do his duty."

"She excuses everybody," said Uncle Andy.

"You, too?" queried Sleepy.

"Not always, Sleepy. I'm about the only person she ever blames."

"Tell me about this ring—the evidence against yore son," said Hashknife.

"Well," replied Uncle Andy, "Johnny bought it from a feller in Northgate. It's a big, silver contraption, and the settin' is a turquoise, cut in the shape of a cross. Anybody'd remember it, if they seen it once. Awful gaudy, I thought."

"Beautiful," added Aunt Judy. "It was a little small for Johnny, and he had to wear it on his little finger. Very heavy."

"Ed Weed recognized it," said Uncle Andy sadly. "He'd seen it lots of times. But Johnny, darn his soul, won't tell what he done with it. Just sets there and shakes his head. Yuh see," Uncle Andy cleared his throat harshly, "yuh see, Johnny and Nell Frawley was due to get married Christmas Eve."

"Loveliest girl I ever knew," said Aunt Judy wearily.

"I'm wonderin' if Johnny would talk with me," said Hashknife.

Uncle Andy shook his head. "I don't believe he would. Won't talk to anybody, not even a lawyer. Stubborn's a bull calf."

"He might," said Aunt Judy hopefully, but added, "He ort to. Nobody can help him, if he won't talk."

"Let's try it," suggested Hashknife. "He can't no more than refuse."

"All right," replied Uncle Andy. "We'll try, but don't say I didn't warn yuh, Hashknife."

<hr>

They found Nick McGarvin in the office. He didn't think that Johnny would talk, especially to strangers, but was willing for them to try. Johnny Davidson was a good-looking young cowboy, but he had stubborn eyes and a stubborn chin. Uncle Andy introduced Hashknife and Sleepy to him, but he didn't seem interested.

"These here men want to help yuh, Johnny," explained Uncle Andy. "But before they can help yuh, they've got to hear yore story."

"I have no story," declared Johnny stonily. "Nothin' to tell."

Hashknife moved in close to the bars, and Johnny looked at him, rather defiantly, at first. Their eyes met for several moments, and Johnny turned away, looking at his mother.

"Johnny, you ought to talk to him," she said quietly.

Johnny looked at Hashknife again, and a weak smile twisted his lips for a moment. Then he said, "All right, what do I talk about?"

"That ring, Johnny," replied Hashknife. "We've got to know what yuh done with it."

Johnny shook his head. "It won't do a bit of good," he said. "It can't do any good now—it's too damned late, Hartley."

"Why is it too late?" asked Hashknife.

"Because Chiquita Morales is dead. Oren Blakely is dead, too."

Uncle Andy said, "What did Chiquita—"

"Wait!" interrupted Hashknife. "Johnny can tell us—in his own way. Go ahead, Johnny."

Johnny gnawed at his lower lip for several moments, his eyes bleak. Hashknife noticed that his hands were clenched behind him. Finally he said:

"I traded that ring, to Chiquita Morales for a pinto horse. She wanted the ring—I wanted that *pintado*. I—I was goin' to tell Nell about it. I dunno—mebbe Nell was a little jealous of Chiquita. She didn't mean anythin' to me, Chiquita didn't. There wasn't any bill-of-sale—nothin' to prove I traded. I was goin' to get the pinto—and that's all there was to it.

"She wanted the ring to wear to a dance—so I let her have it. I was down at Agua Verde that night, but I left there about seven o'clock. On the way back, at a little rancho, there was a lot of music, so I stopped to see what was goin' on. It was a dance—a pretty wild dance, too. Chiquita was there with Oren Blakely. Everybody was drunk, except Chiquita, and there had been several fist-fights. Oren was drunk, too. Chiquita wanted to go home—to get away from the place. Well, at least, I'm a gentleman—I hope. We got Oren on a horse, and all three of us came back across the line. Oren wasn't too drunk then; so we put him on the road to the Circle H, and I took Chiquita home."

"And you was afraid that Nell would find it out?" asked Uncle Andy.

"Yeah, I was," admitted Johnny. "Maybe I had no business doin' it—takin' her home, and all that—but I did."

"Was she wearin' the ring at the dance?" asked Hashknife.

"No, she wasn't," replied Johnny. "I asked her where it was, and she told me she left it at home, because it was too big, and she was afraid she'd lose it."

"I'll explain it to Nell," offered Aunt Judy.

"Thanks, Ma—but I'd rather tell her. I didn't take Chiquita to the dance—didn't even know she was there—and when she explained that she was scared to stay there—what could I do?"

"Couldn't anybody at that rancho testify that you were there, instead of robbin' a bank?" asked Uncle Andy.

"I doubt it, 'cause I didn't mix in the dance. And, anyway," said Johnny, "nobody knows what time of night the bank was robbed. Ed Weed didn't know. They woke him up, but he never seen a clock."

"I heard that Chiquita was to marry Frenchy Arnett," said Hashknife.

"*Quien sabe?*" Johnny smiled sourly. "Chiquita liked to have fun. She asked me to not tell Frenchy. I wouldn't, anyway. It wasn't my business."

"Johnny," said Hashknife, "do you know of anybody who hated Oren Barkley enough to shoot him? Maybe somebody who knew he took Chiquita to a dance."

Johnny shook his head. "No, I don't, Hartley. Frenchy was supposed to be keepin' steady company with Chiquita. Frenchy was either in Northgate, or on his way up there, when she was killed. Oren wasn't quarrelsome. In fact, that night was the first time I had ever seen him drunk. Oh, he took a drink now and then, I suppose, but not enough to affect him."

"Well, much obliged, Johnny," said Hashknife, shaking hands through the bars.

"Yo're welcome, Hartley. Glad to have met yuh—and you, too, Stevens."

He kissed his mother between the bars, and they went out. Aunt Judy took hold of Hashknife's shoulders and turned him around on the sidewalk, looking straight into his eyes.

"I just wanted to find out why Johnny talked to you," she said as he smiled slowly at her.

"Don't be silly, Ma," grinned Uncle Andy.

"I'm not silly," she said quietly, and turned away. Hashknife patted her on the shoulder.

"I dunno how it was done—but it was," Uncle Andy said. "Hashknife, we want you and Sleepy to make the ranch yore home. We've got room out there, and we'd sure admire havin' yuh stay there."

"Later—maybe," said Hashknife. "Thank yuh both a lot."

"Make it when yuh can; we'll be lookin' for yuh."

Nick McGarvin, the sheriff, was a little amazed over the willingness of Johnny Davidson to talk to a stranger. And he was also a bit curious as to just why Andy Davidson had brought these two strangers to the jail for the conference. He asked Johnny, who thought it over for several moments.

"I don't know, Nick," he said. "Mother and Dad brought 'em in here, and Hartley, the tall one asked me questions."

"Which you answered," said the sheriff dryly.

"That's right, I did—but don't ask me why, Nick. It is kinda funny. Somethin' about him—I dunno what."

Pete Morales and his wife came to town, and the sheriff asked Pete if he knew anything about Chiquita trading a pinto horse to Johnny Davidson for a turquoise ring.

Pete shook his head sadly. "*Mi amigo,*" he said wearily, "I know notheeng, excep's Chiquita ees died. I see no reeng."

"Did you know that Chiquita went to the dance in Mexico with Oren Blakely?"

Again the little Mexican shook his head. "No," he said huskily. "I tell her, 'Kip to hell from those dance at Miguel's rancho. Bad pippil down there.' But I theenk she go anyway."

Nick McGarvin went back to his office. Frenchy hadn't showed up yet. The death of Chiquita Morales was a terrible blow to the little deputy—and he was drinking too much.

Sam Hack and his only remaining cowboy, Gus Staley, came over to the sheriff's office. Hack was a tall, gaunt man, with deep-set eyes, long arms and huge, bony hands. Hack was really a newcomer to the Dancing Devil range, having bought the NK spread from the bank, which had it on a foreclosure, and registered his own brand. Oren Blakely had been one of his two men. Gus Staley was rather a nondescript cowpoke, who liked liquor and cards.

Hack wanted action. He said, "Nick, you've got to do somethin' about the murder of Oren. Yuh can't let things like that go—"

"Suggest somethin'," replied the harassed sheriff. "It's easy to talk about, Sam. Nobody knows why Oren headed for Northgate, nobody knows who wanted to shoot him. Everyone seemed to like him. If you know anythin' else, let me know."

"Well," replied Hack soberly, "I wish I could, Nick. Has Johnny Davidson talked yet?"

"Johnny talked this mornin', Sam. He wouldn't talk to me, and he wouldn't talk to his ma and pa—but he talked to a stranger."

"Meanin' what?" asked Hack flatly.

The sheriff shook his head. "I dunno, Sam—I can't figure it."

And then the sheriff told them what Johnny told Hashknife.

Sam Hack and Gus Staley listened closely while the sheriff related Johnny's story, and the sheriff finished with:

"I asked Johnny why he told all this to Hartley, when he wouldn't talk with anybody else, and he said he didn't know."

"Kinda funny," remarked Hack. He turned to Staley, "Gus, did you know that Oren took Chiquita to that dance?"

Staley shook his head. "Oren didn't talk much," he replied. "He was drunk when he got back to the ranch that night, but he didn't say where he'd been, I figured he got drunk here."

"Gus," said the sheriff, "you've been with Oren a long time. If I remember right, you came here with him. Do you know anybody who hated him enough to shoot him?"

"Hell, no!" snorted Gus Staley.

"Well, there yuh are," said the sheriff, shrugging helplessly. "Gus has been bunkin' the man all this time, and even *he* don't know who'd shoot him."

"Who is Hartley and Stevens?" asked Hack.

The sheriff smiled. "I rode all the way down here from Northgate with them two," he said, "and all I know is that they've each got two legs and two arms. Yuh might ask Andy Davidson—he seemed to know 'em."

"Just a couple driftin' cowpokes, eh?"

"You name 'em," replied the sheriff. "They came in on the freight-train, got off at Northgate, just before Oren climbed on and got shot. They had their saddles along with 'em, and I know they bought two horses at the feed corral."

"Well," yawned Hack, "we've got to be driftin', Nick. When is the inquest?"

"Tomorrow mornin', Doc Talbert told me. You'll be here?"

"Yeah. After all, Oren was one of my boys."

Hashknife and Sleepy sprawled on chairs under the porch of the hotel. Hashknife, as relaxed as a cat, smoked thoughtfully, paying little attention to activity on the street.

"How much of Johnny Davidson's story do yuh reckon a jury would believe?" inquired Sleepy.

"Very little, Sleepy."

"Do you believe him?"

"Certainly, I believe him. With all the lies possible, he told a story that can't possibly help him. The girl is dead—and he didn't have to tell the truth about the ring. The kid's honest."

"Yo're like Aunt Judy—everybody is all right."

Sam Hack and Gus Staley came past the porch and went on up the street. Both of them looked curiously at Hashknife and Sleepy. Frank Olds, the hotel-keeper, standing in the doorway of the hotel, waved a greeting to them, and he said to the two cowboys:

"That's the feller Oren Blakely worked for—Sam Hack. He's the tall one; the other is Gus Staley."

"Is Hack an old-timer down here?" asked Hashknife.

"No, he came here a little over a year ago and bought out the NK. Bought it from the bank, I reckon—they held a big mortgage, and Kinney, the owner, couldn't make the grade."

"You knew Blakely?" asked Sleepy.

"Yeah. Nice boy, too. I know most everybody. Growed up here."

"I hear," remarked Hashknife lazily, "that the bank bust hurt folks pretty hard around here."

"Busted some of 'em. Yuh take Andy Davidson and Ed Frawley, they got hit awful hard. Had most all their money in the bank, I've been told. Davidson just sold a train-load of cows, and they tell me he lost every cent in the bank. Frawley got hit about as hard. They ain't kickin'—'cause they ain't that kind."

"What do yuh think of Johnny Davidson's chances?" asked Sleepy.

"Well, I'll tell yuh; with that ring as evidence, and with a Dancin' Devil jury, he's got about as much chance as a celluloid cat has in hell. The jury will believe Ed Weed. I hate to see it happen to the Davidson family, but Johnny is stuck."

"What happened to the banker?" asked Sleepy.

"Oh, he's still livin' here. Tom Colton's his name. Got sort of a no-good son, named Harry. He tried to make a banker out of him, but it didn't work. Make a better banker for a faro game, I reckon. Drinks like a fish, Harry does."

After all this information Frank Olds went back to his hotel work, and Hashknife and Sleepy walked over to the livery-stable. The stableman was also a loquacious soul. He was standing in the rear doorway of the stable, staring out at a rather dilapidated top-buggy. He said, complainingly, "I wish they'd take that damn thing away from here."

"Why?" asked Sleepy.

"That's the buggy Chiquita Morales was killed in. They brung it here. Said that it was mebbe evidence. Huh! Blood all over it, too. I sleep in the tack-room—and I dream about that blasted, old buggy. Chiquita was awful pretty. I dunno, I reckon it'll stay there, until the sheriff takes it away."

Hashknife walked out and looked it over. Not much of a buggy, the worn cushion spattered with gore, dried black now, a broken buggy-whip in the old socket, ready to fall off the dash. Sleepy and the stableman had turned to talk with someone, when Hashknife pulled the seat-cushion loose from the back. Something rattled loosely, and Hashknife readied in and picked it up. One swift glance and he put the object in his pocket, shoved the cushion into place and walked back to the doorway.

A young man was talking with the stableman, paying him some money. He was wearing "store-clothes," except for his high-heel boots, and seemed just a trifle inebriated. A good-looking young man, too, except for the deep lines of dissipation in his face. After he went out, the stableman said:

"That's Harry Colton, the busted banker's son. He keeps his horse here in the stable, and pays his bills regular. I hate to see a young man drinkin' thataway. His old man tried to keep him straight, but I don't reckon it was any use. Too much money and nothin' else to do."

"Mebbe," suggested Sleepy, "he won't have too much money now."

"Did yuh hear what he said?" asked the stableman.

Sleepy shook his head.

"He said he'd prob'ly have to sell his horse. Can't afford to pay feed bills much longer."

"He might cut down on his whiskey bills," suggested Hashknife.

"You don't know Harry," grinned the stableman.

They walked back to the hotel and went up to their room, where Hashknife took the object from his pocket and placed it on the table. It was a huge, Mexican silver ring, with a turquoise cross. Sleepy stared at it, picked it up gingerly and examined it. He put it back on the table and sat down by the window.

"It was under that seat cushion," said Hashknife.

"Maybe," suggested Sleepy, "Chiquita thought she was bein' held up, and hid it under the cushion."

"It kinda figures out like this," said Hashknife. "Chiquita made the trade with Johnny. She wasn't in love with Johnny, but it kinda seems that she—well, she wasn't a one-man woman. Before the robbery, she let some-body have that ring. Maybe she got it back. Maybe she was scared to keep it. Maybe she hid it under the cushion. Maybe—"

"After all that," interrupted Sleepy, "what do yuh think actually hap-pened?"

"I don't know," grinned Hashknife, and pocketed the ring.

"This can't help Johnny none," said Sleepy.

"I don't reckon it can help anybody," smiled Hashknife, "but it's a mighty pretty ring."

They went back to the hotel lobby, where they were accosted by an elderly, well-dressed man. He said, "You are Mr. Hartley?"

"That's my name," nodded Hashknife.

"I am Thomas Colton, Mr. Hartley. Shall we sit down?"

Sleepy sprawled on a chair near a window, while Hashknife and Thomas Colton, former banker, sat down together.

The banker said, "I have a confidential letter from a land syndicate in Phoenix, saying that they are interested in buying cattle ranches in the Danc-ing Devil range, as an investment, and asking about prices. Today I received this telegram, which I will show you."

The telegram was sent to the banker, and signed James Morison. It read:

ADVISE YOU THAT A MR. HARTLEY IS AUTHORIZED TO CON-TACT RANCH OWNERS AND CONSULT THEM ON PRICES.

Hashknife read the telegram and handed it back to Colton, who said quietly, "The bank holds paper against nearly every ranch down here—rather big paper, I might say, and—"

"I understand that," interrupted Hashknife, "but mortgages have nothin' to do with my job. I merely ask prices."

"And I might say," continued the banker, "that few, if any, can meet their mortgages. Confidentially, Mr. Hartley, the ranches of this valley are in bad shape. I mean, financially, of course."

"Nothin' wrong with the ranches?" queried Hashknife. "This looks like a good range."

"Oh, it is, indeed! That is one reason that the bank was generous. Have you made any inquiries, Mr. Hartley?"

"I didn't want to rush 'em," said Hashknife. "Why?"

"Well, I—no reason at all, except that I—well, I might be able to get a better price than you could—knowing conditions."

Hashknife smiled as he looked at Colton. "Maybe yuh don't think I'm the right man to buy cattle ranches," he suggested.

"No, no, I didn't mean that! After all, the Cattlemen's Association wouldn't recommend a—well, a man who wasn't capable."

"Thank yuh," said Hashknife dryly. "You go ahead, Mr. Colton. Maybe you can do better than I could. Anyway, it's worth tryin'."

"Well, thank you, Mr. Hartley. I'll see what I can do, and then we can compare notes. I'll see you again—and thank you. It might be well to not mention our little talk to anyone?"

"I'll keep still," agreed Hashknife.

Sleepy was curious, and came over as soon as Colton left. Hashknife told him the conversation, and Sleepy said, "What's he tryin' to do—beat us out of our jobs?"

"Even a banker can make a mistake, pardner," smiled Hashknife.,

"He's shore mistaken if he thinks he can take our jobs over," declared Sleepy. "I like to draw money for loafin'."

———◦———

A double inquest was held next forenoon in Tomahawk Flats, and it seemed as though everybody in Dancing Devil Valley came to listen. Because they had been present at the shooting of Oren Blakely, both Hashknife and Sleepy were called to the stand to testify. Both Aunt Judy and Uncle Andy were there, and with them sat Ed Frawley and his daughter, Nell. Huddled together were Pete Morales and his wife, listening closely, but not understanding much of what was said. Frenchy Arnett was there, still half-drunk. Sam Hack and his one man, Gus Staley, were there, and Uncle Andy introduced Hashknife and Sleepy to Buck Nolan, who owned the Bar N.

There was no one to testify in the murder of Chiquita Morales. They put Pete Morales on the stand, but Pete either didn't understand, or had nothing to tell them. The jury in both cases brought in the only possible verdict—killed by a party or parties unknown.

Hashknife and Sleepy met the Davidsons on the street after the inquest, and were introduced to Nell Frawley and her father. Nell was a pretty, brunette, tall and willowy, but very sad over the plight of Johnny Davidson. Aunt Judy said, "Ed, you and Nell are comin' out to have supper with us, and I'm askin' Hashknife and Sleepy to come out with us."

"What are we waitin' for?" asked Sleepy quickly.

"But, Aunt Judy, we didn't intend—" began Ed Frawley.

"Don't lie to me, Ed Frawley," she said. "I saw that hunger-for-sour-milk-biscuits in your eye, when I mentioned supper."

"Well, I—uh—shore," agreed Frawley, while Sleepy remarked:

"Speakin' about love—I ain't et a sour-milk biscuit since ol' Settin' Bull got up and leaned against a tree."

"As Sleepy said," remarked Uncle Andy, "what are we waitin' for, folks?"

"It isn't noon yet," said Ed Frawley.

"Don't you folks eat at noon?" asked Sleepy soberly.

"Let's go out to the ranch," said Aunt Judy. "I've got to fill him up, before he starves on our hands."

The ranch-house and buildings at the AD were well-kept, the grounds clean. Uncle Andy admitted to Hashknife that Aunt Judy was responsible for the appearance of the place.

They met Ted Evans and Eddie Connors, the two cowpokes.

"I've allus wanted to see what you looked like, Hartley," remarked Connors.

"Wanted to see what I looked like?" queried Hashknife.

"Yeah, that's right. I heard about you up on the Wind River, and then I heard more about yuh in Colorado, and the last feller to speak about yuh was from the Thunder River country."

"I didn't know I was worth talkin' about," said Hashknife.

"Well, I'm tellin' yuh," grinned Connors. "If yo're half as good as the lies I've heard—yo're a ring-tailed wonder."

"I'm not, Connors," assured Hashknife.

"Men will lie, yuh know."

"Then I shore ran into several, Hartley—and they all lied about the same things." "What's this all about?" demanded Aunt Judy.

"Somebody tryin' to ruin my reputation, Aunt Judy."

"Ruin it!" exclaimed Connors. "Lemme tell yuh what—"

"Don't repeat it—there's ladies present," interrupted Hashknife, and went into the house with the others.

Nell volunteered to help Aunt Judy in the kitchen, and two ranch owners sat down with Hashknife and Sleepy in the main room. There was plenty of food for conversation, but no one seemed inclined to start it, until Ed Frawley, his pipe drawing well, said, "Andy, have you talked with Tom Colton?"

"Not for a couple of days, Ed."

"I talked with him this mornin'. It seems that he's representin' a land-buying syndicate, and they'd like to buy the Rafter F—if they can get it cheap enough."

"Yea-a-ah? The buzzards are already wingin' in, eh?"

"That's what I told him."

"I can see his angle," said Uncle Andy. "We owe money to the bank, which don't exist now. Him bein' the owner of the bank, wants his money out of the deal."

"And we can't pay him," said Frawley flatly. "If we get any kind of a decent offer, we'll have to sell."

Uncle Andy turned to Hashknife, "Sorry to talk about somethin' you don't know about," he said. "I'll tell yuh how I'm fixed. I owe the bank twelve thousand dollars. Not long ago I sold a lot of beef, and I put twenty-eight thousand dollars on deposit. I wanted to pay off that mortgage right now, but Colton said— Oh, I don't understand bankin', Hashknife. Somethin' about havin' to pay a lot of interest and a bonus if I took it up now; so I let it lay. Well, the twenty-eight thousand dollars is gone—and I can't pay the mortgage."

"I'm in the same boat," said Frawley. "My mortgage was due two days after the robbery. I owed Colton ten thousand, and I had—well, I had enough in there to pay it off and not mind."

"Tough deal," murmured Hashknife. "Just how was this robbery pulled off?"

"I can tell yuh what Weed said," replied Uncle Andy. "Weed is a bachelor, livin' alone. Been here years. He said he went to bed, but he don't know what time—maybe nine o'clock, and went to sleep. He don't know what time he woke up, but the lamp was lighted and three masked men was around him. They told him they wanted the key to the bank and the combination of the vault.

"One of them told him that he'd either do what they want, or they'd kill him, take the keys to the bank and bust it with dynamite. They got the keys and the combination, tied Weed up tight, and pulled out. They had all night to do the job—and they shore done a complete job."

"And he saw that turquoise ring, eh?" said Hashknife.

And Davidson nodded slowly. "He says he saw it plain."

"Weed is honest, eh?"

"Honest as a dollar," sighed Uncle Andy. "I've talked with him several times, and he's just about sick. Weed is pretty old, and he ain't got any job. Everythin' he owned was in the bank, too."

"I told him," said Frawley quietly, "that if things got too tough he could come out and live with us."

"I told him the same thing," said Uncle Andy, "and so did Buck Nolan. Buck didn't owe the bank anythin', but he lost every dollar he had in there."

"Seems like we're askin' Weed to join us in the poor-house," said Frawley dryly. "I know I can't keep goin'. I've got a couple good cowpokes out at my place, but I can't afford to keep 'em more'n a couple weeks longer."

"This looks like a mighty good range," remarked Sleepy.

"There ain't any better," declared Uncle Andy warmly.

"Maybe they'll offer yuh a *good* price."

"Why should they?" asked Frawley. "Colton didn't suggest any price. He said they'd naturally buy as cheap as possible, and he said for me to figure out my lowest price. He'll prob'ly make you the same proposition, Andy."

Uncle Andy stared thoughtfully at the carpet for several moments, before he said quietly:

"We've been here a long time, Ed. It ain't just like sellin' a piece of property—it's home. Yuh can't tear up roots that have gone as deep as ours, my friend. We ain't young men—me and you. Ed, I just can't sell the AD."

"I feel the same, Andy," replied Frawley.

"Will Nolan have to sell, too?" asked Hashknife.

"I dunno, Hashknife," replied Uncle Andy. "It hit him hard, but he don't owe the bank anythin'."

"What about Sam Hack?"

"I don't believe he had much in the bank. Yuh see, he's only had the Circle H a little over a year. He bought out the NK from a feller named Kinney. The bank had to foreclose a mortgage on the NK, and I reckon Hack made a good deal for the spread. He's buildin' it up."

"How long," asked Hashknife, "has Colton owned the bank?"

"A little over two years," replied Frawley. "Weed worked for the bank for at least twenty years Harry Colton was in college when his father bought the bank, and has only been here about a year. He's no good. Drinks like a fish, and gambles like a fool. He had the gall to want Nell to marry him."

"That," declared Sleepy soberly, "don't take much gall."

"You know what I mean, Stevens," laughed Frawley.

Hashknife walked out into the kitchen. Aunt Judy was working at the stove, while Nell was on the back porch, talking with Eddie Connors, who went down the steps and headed for the bunkhouse. Hashknife went out on the shaded porch. Nell said, "Your ears must have burned, Mr. Hartley."

Hashknife smiled and Shook his head.

"I haven't felt 'em."

"We were talking about you."

"That's a pretty dry topic for conversation," he said soberly.

"Eddie didn't think so. Oh, I didn't want to be curious, but Uncle Andy talked about you—and Eddie—" She hesitated.

"That's the trouble," he said quietly. "Somethin' ordinary happens, and somebody with a big imagination spins a windy about it. The next feller enlarges it. Well, after it's been told several times, you've either got wings and one of them halos, or a forked tail and a pair of horns. But even with all the lies, the poor devil remains a tired ol' cowpoke, just gettin' along in his own dumb way, Ma'am."

"You're not so old," said Nell.

"I'm old enough to know better, Ma'am."

"I don't like to be called Ma'am. My name is Nell."

Hashknife smiled slowly. "I like that name. I'm Hashknife."

"Just a poor, old, tired cowpoke," she said slowly. "Johnny said you just looked at him, and he decided to tell the truth, but he wouldn't talk to anybody before that. How did you do it, Hashknife?"

Hashknife looked at her thoughtfully. "I just asked him, Nell."

"Do people always do what you ask?"

"Well," Hashknife grinned widely, "I don't ask—much. Did you know Chiquita Morales very well?"

"Are you practicing on me?" asked Nell quickly.

"No, I just wondered if yuh knew her pretty well."

"Not too well," replied Nell. "Chiquita was pretty, tiny, full of life. She liked to have a good time, wear pretty clothes. But the Morales are poor people. I don't believe they had much control over her. I liked her. She was very generous, sympathetic, but very emotional."

"Do you think she would have married Frenchy Arnett, Nell?"

"No, I don't, Hashknife. Frenchy was too slow for her. She went to that Mexican dance with Oren Blakely, and Frenchy didn't know it. If Chiquita wanted to go some place she'd ask most any man to take her—she didn't have any favorites, it seemed."

"The Morales' are pretty poor, eh?" remarked Hashknife.

"Yes, they are. I never could understand where Chiquita got money to buy fancy clothes, but she wore plenty."

"Maybe some cowpoke bought 'em," suggested Hashknife.

"At forty dollars a month?"

"No, that don't go far," admitted Hashknife. "Did you ever know her to go to dances with Harry Colton?"

"With the banker's son? You amaze me, Hashknife."

Hashknife smiled slowly. "I even amaze myself, at times, Nell."

"No, I never have seen them together," she said. "No reason why not. After all, Harry Colton isn't too good, in spite of his money. Now that his father is broke, I don't know what he will do."

Aunt Judy came out on the porch to cool off.

"Who are you folks plottin' against?" she asked.

"The forces of evil, Aunt Judy," replied Nell.

"Well, it must have been pleasant plotting—the way you've been smiling. Isn't she a sweet girl, Hashknife?"

"Aunt Judy!" protested Nell.

"I've been thinkin' that all along," grinned Hashknife.

"How come you never got married?" asked Aunt Judy.

"Well," replied Hashknife thoughtfully, "I don't reckon I've ever had time. My old Dad was a range-ridin' sky-pilot up on the Milk River in Montana. He had a houseful of kids, and mighty little money to take care of 'em. When I was still a sprout, I got a horse and a riding rig. I had itchin' feet. Dad said, 'Son, I've been watchin' yuh a long time—lookin' at them hills. You want to see what's on the other side. When you was born the good Lord put a wanderin' brand on yuh. I've seen that brand growin'. You'll never call any place home, never be held by any ties. I've tried to teach yuh to shoot square—it's the best I can do.'"

"And you started wandering," said Aunt Judy.

"All my life, Aunt Judy— Dad's prophecy was right. Sleepy is of the same breed—we can't stay put."

"Helping people," said Nell quietly.

"Who told you that?" he asked.

"Eddie Connors. I think it is wonderful. We need help, Hashknife."

Hashknife squinted thoughtfully across the hills. After a long pause he said, "Yeah, I reckon yuh do, Nell."

"Johnny and me were going to get married Christmas Eve."

"That ain't far away, Nell, and there ain't much to work on, but we'll hope that it's all written our way in the Big Book."

"Big Book?" queried Aunt Judy quickly.

"There is a big book, yuh know, Aunt Judy," said Hashknife.

"I've never heard of it before."

"I've never seen it," smiled Hashknife. "No mortal's eyes have ever seen it—but the finger of Fate writes in that book. It shows what we do, how we live, how we die—and when."

"That's fatalism!" exclaimed Aunt Judy. "You don't believe in that, do you, Hashknife?"

"I believe," replied Hashknife, "that you'll never die until your number is up on the board, Aunt Judy. Bein' careful is a human trait, but it won't save yuh. Men have gone through hell and high water all their lives, only to trip over a chair in the dark and break their neck. What's yore argument against it, Aunt Judy?"

"Well, I—when you started, I had several—but I guess I've forgotten what they were."

"School is dismissed," grinned Hashknife.

It was a wonderful supper. Aunt Judy was a fine cook, and Sleepy almost ate himself under the table. They got back to Tomahawk Flats about nine o'clock, and were standing in front of the Pasatiempo Saloon, when a horse and buggy drove up. A man had just come out of the saloon, and the driver called to him, asking directions for finding Thomas Colton's home. Then the buggy turned and went back up the street. The man had leaned out of the buggy, his face full in the lights of the saloon. Hashknife said quietly, "Did you see that feller, Sleepy?"

"No, I didn't pay any attention. Sort of a fat man, wasn't he?"

"Sort of—yeah. I've seen that face before, but I can't quite place him. C'mon."

"Are yuh goin' to try and run him down?" asked Sleepy.

"I hadn't thought of that—but I'm curious."

Thomas Colton's home was only two blocks off the main street, but there were no lights on the street, and the night was dark. They found the horse and buggy at Colton's front gate. There were lights in the house, but the windows were shaded. Sleepy wanted to know why they ever came down there, in the first place. Didn't Mr. Colton have any right to have a visitor.

Hashknife laughed. "That visitor," he said, "is a man we both knew in Wyomin', Sleepy. His name was Slim Regan. What it is now, who knows?"

"Slim Regan?" queried Sleepy. "I 'member him. He was a gambler and a promoter, wasn't he?"

"That's the person—I'm dead sure. Maybe he didn't recognize me—my back bein' to the light, and we ain't seen him for at least five years. Maybe he's livin' straight now—who knows?"

They started back, when they heard footsteps on the wooden sidewalk, coming from the opposite direction. The walker was wearing spurs. It was too dark for them to see him, but he turned in at Colton's gate and went to the house. There were no lights, when the door was opened, but they heard it close behind him.

"Maybe the Coltons are havin' a party," suggested Sleepy.

Hashknife didn't offer any suggestions, but started down the road, heading in the direction from which the spur-wearing person came. After a short distance they cut over to the sidewalk, and went on, until they found the horse, tied to a tree almost at the outskirts of town. It was a tall roan animal, and with the aid of a match they were able to decipher the Bar N brand on the animal. Sleepy said, "That's Buck Nolan's mark, Hashknife."

They sat down in the darkness and waited possibly fifteen minutes, but no one came along.

"Even if he did come for the horse, it's too dark to recognize him. Anyway, there ain't no law," said Sleepy.

"I reckon yo're right," agreed Hashknife.

"No use settin' here."

They were almost back at Colton's house, when they heard the rasp of buggy-wheels, as the vehicle was turned around. A few moments later the horse and buggy came past them, traveling fast, heading back toward where the horse was tied. The Colton house was dark.

"Well," remarked Sleepy, "what's funny about that?"

"I didn't say it was funny," replied Hashknife.

They went up to their room at the hotel and went to bed. Sleepy said, "Ain't we even goin' to try and get prices on ranches?"

"We'll let Colton see what he can do first. After all, he knows values better than we do."

They met Thomas Colton next morning, and he asked them if they had discussed prices with any of the ranchers.

"We're leavin' that to you, Mr. Colton," said Hashknife.

"Well, that is right, Mr. Hartley. No use of both of us working on the same idea. Are you leaving here soon?"

"I'll tell yuh," replied Hashknife soberly, "if we can buy at a good price, we might take over a spread ourselves."

This seemed to confuse Colton. He said, "Well, I—yes, of course. I had no idea you—well, why not?"

"If we got it cheap enough," said Hashknife. "We like this range. After all, a feller ought to settle down."

"Yes, I believe—we will talk about it again, Mr. Hartley."

Mr. Colton went on. Sleepy braced against a porch-post, looked inquiringly at Hashknife.

"Settlin' down, eh?" he remarked. "That's wonderful. Goin' to buy a ranch. Total assets about twenty-five dollars."

"If we could get it cheap enough—" said Hashknife.

Aunt Judy and Uncle Andy came to town before noon, and were talking with Hashknife and Sleepy in front of the sheriff's office, when Buck Nolan came riding up to the office. He nodded to them, started for the office doorway, when the sheriff came out.

"Nick, there's a buggy wrecked in Horseshoe Canyon," said Nolan. "I saw where it went over the rip-rap, and it's down there about a hundred feet below the grade. I was comin' down from Northgate and—"

"Yuh mean—a buggy and team went off the grade, Buck?"

"It sure looks like it, Nick. Yuh can see some of the buggy, all smashed up on the rocks down there."

"I'll get Frenchy. You take us back there, Buck. Maybe Hartley and Stevens will go with us; we'll need plenty help. I wonder who went off the grade."

Hashknife looked curiously at Buck Nolan, big, raw-boned, just a bit gray. Buck was riding a sorrel, bearing his own brand. Then Hashknife and Sleepy hurried to the stable to get their horses. Sleepy said, "I'm wonderin' a little, too, Gardner."

"We don't know the man—if its Regan," said Hashknife.

"I know what yuh mean," said Sleepy.

It was several miles out to Horseshoe Canyon. Frenchy went along, but showed little interest. He was sober, but his brown eyes were bloodshot from too much whiskey.

The coroner went in a spring-wagon, taking plenty ropes along. The wheel-marks on the edge of the grade were very plain, and they could see part of the smashed buggy. There was a trail into the canyon just above the wreck, and they went down on foot.

Slim Regan had been thrown clear of the buggy, but straight into a jumble of jagged rocks. The scent of whiskey still lingered on the dead man's clothes, and there was a smashed bottle in the bottom of the buggy. They took the body to open ground, where the coroner examined the pockets of his clothes, but all they found was a pocket-knife and a few dollars in silver coin. There was not a scrap of paper to identify him.

It was quite a task, getting the body back to the grade. The coroner said that there was no question of its being an accident. Hashknife made no comments. The coroner could be right, except that the wheel marks on the edge of the grade showed the buggy traveling south, instead of north. Sleepy had noticed that detail, too.

As they rode together off the grade, the latter said, "If Slim Regan wanted to pile his carcass into the canyon, why did he turn the buggy around and make the dive? It's just as fatal, goin' north as it is south."

Hashknife nodded grimly. He said, "Keep yore eyes open, pardner—there's brains workin' down here. They didn't want anybody to know that Regan was in Tomahawk Flats last night. Regan rode up in front of the Pasatiempo Saloon and asked a man where Tom Colton lived. Who was the man he asked, Sleepy?"

Sleepy scowled thoughtfully, and finally said, "Hashknife, I ain't exactly sure. Yuh see, I wasn't payin' much attention, but I kinda seem to remember that it was Gus Staley. I can't be sure—but I think it was. He works for that feller Hack."

"Yeah, that's right. Regan went to see Tom Colton, stayed there maybe half an hour, and then pulled out. Regan is a gambler."

"Was," corrected Sleepy, "until he hit bedrock. What do yuh make out of it?"

Hashknife didn't say. He thought it over and finally remarked, "Sleepy, I wish we knew who the man was who walked in the dark and wore spurs."

"And rode a Bar N roan," added Sleepy. "But what does it add up to?"

"I dunno. Doc Talbert said he'd make a complete examination of the body. That might help our case."

But Doctor Talbert's examination didn't help them any. Any evidence of foul play, except by gun-shot, would have been wiped out by the man's fall onto the rocks. Nick McGarvin asked that everybody take a look at the body, hoping that someone would identify him, but to no avail. The keeper of the livery-stable at Northgate had rented him the horse and buggy, but had no idea where the man was going. He gave the name of Jim Hendricks, paid in advance for the rig, and said he would be gone overnight. Asked about Hendrick's having any baggage, the stableman said he wasn't sure, but believed the man had a small valise.

Hashknife met Sam Hack and Gus Staley on the street and stopped to talk with them.

"Did you look at the dead man, Staley?" he asked.

"Yeah—sure, I seen him, Hartley. I don't—"

"Think back," said Hashknife. "Wasn't he the same man who drove up in front of the Pasatiempo that night and asked you how to find Thomas Colton's house?"

Gus Staley looked blankly at Hashknife. "I dunno what yuh mean," he replied. "I never seen the man before. You must mean somebody else. I never seen him in a buggy in my life."

"I see," murmured Hashknife. "Well, it don't matter."

"Didn't the man run off the grade *comin'* here?" asked Hack.

"Yeah, it looks thataway," replied Hashknife. "A couple hundred yards further along the grade is a place where he could turn his outfit around. Maybe he was comin' back—I dunno."

"You ain't sure he *ever* was down here, are yuh?" asked Hack.

"Him or his ghost."

"Ghost?" Staley spat viciously into the dusty street. "You don't believe in ghosts, do yuh, Hartley?"

"I know what I have seen," replied Hashknife seriously, "but I never try to impose my ideas on other people."

"That's all damn foolishment!" snorted Staley. "When yo're dead—yo're dead, and that's all there is to it."

"That's the best way to look at it," remarked Hashknife.

Hashknife and Sleepy did not go to the funeral of Chiquita Morales, but they heard that Frenchy Arnett paid most of the expenses. Thomas Colton had approached Uncle Andy regarding selling the AD, but Uncle Andy avoided making any definite price. He knew he would have to sell eventually, but held off. Hashknife talked with Johnny at the jail, but Johnny was little help. He stuck to his story that he'd traded the ring to Chiquita for a pinto horse, and that she didn't wear the ring to that dance in Mexico. Hashknife didn't tell Johnny that he'd found the ring in the Morale's buggy. Johnny said, "I'm stuck, Hashknife. If Chiquita had lived, she could have testified that I didn't own the ring."

"That," said Hashknife, "is why she died. Johnny, do yuh know of any man around here she liked well enough to give that ring?"

Johnny shook his head. "Chiquita, I believe, was a good girl. She liked a good time, and she didn't have to want for men to take her places. She wanted money, fine clothes and all that. Yuh see, a cowpoke's wages don't cover that, Hashknife."

"Where did she get her finery, Johnny. Pete Morales couldn't afford to buy things for her."

"Yeah, that's right—I never thought of that. Well, she never tried to get money from anybody—as far as I know."

"Johnny, did Harry Colton ever go out with her?"

Johnny leaned against the bars of his cell and thought it over. Finally he said quietly, "I'm just wonderin'."

Johnny might have said more, but Frenchy Arnett came in. He was sober, but grim-faced. Hashknife said, "Frenchy, wouldn't you like to know who shot Chiquita?"

Frenchy shut his eyes tightly for a moment and his jaw tightened. "Sure would," he said quietly, but firmly. "I know she went to a dance with Oren Blakely. That was right; Oren didn't do it. Damn right, I'd like to know, Hartley."

"Maybe you can help us find him, Frenchy. Did you ever give her money to buy clothes?"

"Give Chiquita money? No! Why do you ask that?"

"They say she wore nice clothes."

"Chiquita always looks nice—silk skirt, pretty shoes."

"Pete Morales didn't have money to buy them with, Frenchy."

Frenchy thought it over. Suddenly he faced Hashknife, his eyes hot. "You mean to say somebody gave her money—Chiquita?"

"Keep cool," advised Johnny. "Hashknife wants to help."

"She was my girl," said Frenchy huskily. "If she wanted money, I'd give it to her. Who gave her money? Oren Blakely didn't have money to give to women. Who gave her money?"

"You knew about Johnny tradin' her that ring for a pinto?"

"Sure—I heard that. That is all right—the pinto belonged to her."

"Frenchy, Chiquita loaned or sold that ring to the man who killed her. Johnny is in jail for a robbery, and the evidence is that ring he traded Chiquita. She could have told who had that ring. She didn't tell, because she didn't want that man in jail—but he didn't take a chance."

Frenchy shrugged his shoulders. "Chiquita go out with other men. Sometimes I warn not here—sometimes I have no money to spend. I am not her husband—I can't say no. Maybe she don't tell me. That is her business."

"Frenchy, did she ever go out with Harry Colton?" asked Hashknife.

Frenchy's lips shut to a thin line and he walked over to a barred window, but came back.

"I think she did," he said quietly. "I accuse her of it, but she just laughed at me. How did you know this, Hartley?"

"I didn't—I just wanted to find out what men she went out with. Chiquita is gone now, Frenchy. Nothing can change that. Our job is to find the man who did it."

"Sure, she's gone—now," breathed Frenchy and walked away, his eyes filled with tears. Hashknife looked at Johnny and shook his head. "I'll see yuh later," he told Johnny.

Hashknife met the sheriff and Sleepy in the office. Hashknife said, "Nick, I've had a talk with Johnny and Frenchy."

"Yeah? Did yuh find out anythin' yuh already didn't know?"

"If anybody asks yuh, Nick," replied Hashknife soberly, "you can tell 'em that Dancin' Devil is in for some surprisin' things—very soon. In fact, before Christmas."

Nick McGarvin's jaw sagged a trifle. "Yuh mean—yuh know somethin', Hashknife?"

"You'd be surprised, Nick."

Leaving the sheriff to think this over, Hashknife and Sleepy walked back toward the hotel.

"He'd be surprised, eh?" remarked Sleepy.

"That's what I told him, Sleepy."

"What'd he be surprised about?"

"The few things I know, pardner. Listen, will yuh? Our only chance to find out somethin' is to scare the guilty into doin' somethin'. It works, when brains fail—and I don't mind admittin' that mine have failed."

"I know what yuh mean," said Sleepy quietly. "We paint black circles around our heads, with a bull's-eye in the middle."

"That's right. Nick's human. He'll pass the word."

"Well, all I can say is that we better find a quiet, remote spot, where we can practice dodgin' bullets," said Sleepy. "Yuh know, I think I like it better than settin' around, pardner. This ain't our idea of a good time, anyway."

"But just remember, Sleepy; we ain't dealin' with dumb rustlers in this game—but I figure that even the smartest men will get scared and make a break—when they're scared, enough."

———◆———

Tomorrow night would be Christmas Eve. They brought a big fir tree for the little church, but it seemed that the Christmas spirit was lacking. Someone told Hashknife that Thomas Colton was going to be the Santa Claus for the church celebration. The Davidsons and the Frawleys were in town, and Uncle Andy told Hashknife that Colton had asked him to make a price on the AD.

"He wanted it in a hurry, too," declared Uncle Andy. "I told him it wasn't anythin' I could hurry with."

"Did he suggest any price?" asked Hashknife.

"Well," replied Uncle Andy grimly, "he said I'd be lucky to get much more than the cost of the mortgage."

"What about Frawley?"

"He's goin' to talk to Colton this afternoon, he said."

"Tell him to hold off makin' any deal, Uncle Andy."

The little cowman looked quizzically at the tall cowboy.

"What's time got to do with it, Hashknife?" he asked.

"Well, maybe a better price. Anyway, you've got plenty time, after the notice of foreclosure to redeem the property."

"Not with the mortgages from Colton. It specifies that when the bank shuts down on the mortgage—yo're through."

"I see. Mortgage expires—ranch gone, eh?"

"That's the only way he'll loan money, Hashknife."

A few minutes later he met Ed Frawley, who drew him aside.

"What's goin' on?" asked Frawley quietly. "A man over in the Pasatiempo told me that—well, he said somethin' was goin' to happen before Christmas—somethin' you said. At least, that's the rumor."

"I hope it's right, Frawley. Funny how things like that get in the wind."

"You mean—there's ain't anythin' to it, Hashknife?"

"*Quien sabe?*" replied Hashknife soberly. "A lot can be done in an hour—and Christmas ain't until day after tomorrow."

He found Sleepy in front of the hotel, and told him, "I reckon Nick McGarvin spread the word."

"I heard it," nodded Sleepy. "Frenchy Arnett cornered me, and wanted to know. He said, 'If yuh know who shot Chiquita—don't arrest him; just let me know who he is.' I said we would. Aw, I didn't mean it—but what else could I tell him? He ain't no deputy sheriff now—he's a wolf with the rabies, pardner."

The Davidsons and Frawleys stayed in town for supper. Hashknife and Sleepy stayed together, ate supper in a little Mexican restaurant, where they could sit against the wall. The Mexican who operated the restaurant, usually very voluble, was quiet, serving the enchiladas and frijoles hurriedly, one eye on the door.

"I wonder what he's thinkin'," remarked Sleepy.

"I wonder what he *knows*," said Hashknife. "They tell me he was Chiquita's uncle. Maybe he don't want his place messed up with us."

It was dark outside, as they paid their bill. With a hand on the knob, Hashknife drew back, turned and came back to the little counter, where the Mexican was at his cash-box.

"*Amigo*, is there a back door to this place?" he asked*

"Sure," nodded the Mexican. "Go t'rough the keetchen."

They went swiftly through the kitchen, redolent with spices and other odors, out through an old door and into the alley. There was a short, narrow alley, leading to the main street, and they could see the silhouette of a man, leaning against the right-hand wall, evidently watching for somebody. Hashknife kicked a wooden box aside, making a clatter, and the man moved quickly, stepping up on the wooden sidewalk.

Hashknife didn't hesitate, but led the way up the alley. The man had passed the little restaurant and was standing at the edge of the sidewalk just beyond. It was too dark for them to see what he looked like, except that he was tall. Finally he went on up the street toward the hotel.

"Do yuh think he was tryin' to dry gulch us?" asked Sleepy.

"Who knows? He was waitin' for somebody, but we scared him away from the alley. He could look through the window and see that we're gone."

They went slowly up the sidewalk, watching closely, until they were at the front of the hotel. Hashknife peered through the window, as he heard Frank Olds, the hotel man, speak sharply to someone. Olds was over near the foot of the stairs, looking up toward the hallway, when he suddenly lifted his arms, shaking his head and protesting, but began walking up the stairs, both hands up.

Hashknife jerked away from the window, whispered sharply:

"Stay here! Trouble in there," and ran down the alley toward the rear stairs of the hotel.

Sleepy moved over to the open doorway of the hotel. The sheriff was crossing the street, and Sleepy said, as he came up:

"Hold it, Nick—until we hear from Hashknife."

"What's wrong?" asked the big sheriff.

"I don't know, Nick. Hashknife saw somethin' through the window, and he ran around to the back stairs. He told me to—"

Sleepy stopped, when two, closely spaced shots rattled the windows beside them. Both men sprang through the doorway, into the hotel, as a figure staggered into view, sagged at the top of the steps and came pin-wheeling down into the lobby. Hashknife ran to the top of the stairs, gun in hand, stopped for a moment, but came on down. Behind him came the disheveled, excited hotel man, waving his arms.

The stranger was sprawled at the foot of the stairs, tall, gaunt, unkempt. Hashknife was looking down at him, as Sleepy and the sheriff came over. The excited hotel man was jabbering:

"He stuck me up, I tell yuh! Made me come up there, or he'd kill me. Hartley, how on earth did you ever beat him? He heard you comin' up the stairs. How did you beat him?"

"I didn't beat him—he missed me," said Hashknife coldly.

"That's Cass Trent!" exclaimed the sheriff. "Why he's— Hartley, there's a half-dozen rewards for this hombre. He's livin' across the border for over a year. He's a killer."

"Was," corrected Sleepy, and looked around at the crowd, swiftly gathering. The sheriff said:

"What was Cass Trent doin' here—stickin' up a hotel?"

"He wasn't stickin' me up," denied the hotel keeper. "He was goin' to bush somebody in that hallway. I came and peeked down the stairs and I seen him. I told him to git out of here, and I was goin' up and run him out—but I didn't. Man, the bore in his gun looked like a tunnel in a hill!"

"Goin' to bush somebody?" queried the sheriff. "Who?"

No one seemed to know. Nick McGarvin looked at Hashknife and found the tall, lean cowboy smiling a little. The sheriff said, "Oh," and waited for Doctor Talbert to arrive.

A search of Trent's pockets revealed five hundred dollars in currency, all in a packet, and the usual impediments carried by cowboys. They took the body to the doctor's place. Nick McGarvin said, "He got what was comin' to him. Hashknife—yore cleared—and congratulations. They say Cass Trent never missed."

"They all miss sometimes, Nick," said Hashknife soberly.

"But why would he try to bush you?" asked the sheriff. "You didn't even know him."

Hashknife shook his head. "No, I didn't, and I never heard of him, until now. He was hired to kill me, Nick."

"Hired? Good gosh! Who hired him, Hashknife?"

"I can't tell yuh—'cause I'm not sure."

<hr />

The excitement was mostly over, as soon as the body was removed, but there was still a lot of discussion going on. Trent's name was well-known down there. Hashknife and Sleepy went over to the Pasatiempo Saloon, listening to the gossip. Harry Colton was at the bar, already more than half-drunk. Hashknife shoved in beside him, and Colton resented it. However, he looked at Hashknife, and decided to give him room.

Hashknife was only at the bar a few moments when the sheriff came in. Men were asking him questions about the affair at the hotel, when Hashknife drew him aside, whispered a few words. The sheriff looked at him in amazement, but finally nodded. About a minute later the sheriff arrested Harry Colton, who tried to shove the law officer away, swearing indignantly. The incident brought a lot of attention, but the sheriff was firm.

"Harry, yuh better go peacefully," he said.

"You're crazy!" snarled the young man. "Why arrest me? What's the charge?"

"Murder," said the sheriff coldly. "You killed Chiquita Morales."

"That's a lie!"

"It's the truth, Harry. You've still got that turquoise ring. It's in yore pocket. Take it out—and deny it!"

The arrest had sobered Harry Colton. Swearing his innocence, he felt in his pocket and took out the turquoise ring. He took one good look at it and flung it at the back-bar. The next moment the big sheriff had crashed Colton against the bar and deftly handcuffed him. Harry Colton was not swearing nor protesting now, he seemed too stunned to even notice the crowd, as the sheriff led him outside. The bartender recovered the ring, and gave it to a man to give to the sheriff.

Word that Harry Colton had been arrested for the murder of Chiquita Morales spread swiftly. The sheriff was in a quandary as to what to do about Frenchy Arnett. Hashknife got Frenchy aside and explained to him that arrest didn't mean that Harry Colton was guilty. Frenchy laughed shortly, but promised to keep his trigger-finger under control.

"I think yo're wrong, Hashknife," confided the sheriff.

"Maybe I am," admitted Hashknife, "but it'll stir things up."

"It shore will, if a mob decides to lynch Colton."

Sleepy showed up, having been on a mission, and reported quietly, "Sam Hack went to tell Thomas Colton, but he's back at the Pasatiempo. I heard Colton tell him he'd be right up to the jail."

"You stay here and keep yore eyes open, pardner," ordered Hashknife, and went swiftly up the street.

Hashknife wasn't sure of anything. When he had dropped that turquoise ring into Harry Colton's pocket, he was acting on a vague sort of hunch; a hunch that this was the time to force the issue. There was a light in the living-room of the Colton home. Colton hadn't been to the jail. Hashknife came straight to the house, so it was evident that Thomas Colton was taking his own sweet time in reacting to the arrest of his son. Hashknife circled to the rear of the house, working along a low fence, when he heard a door close quiet. A moment later someone came toward the fence, climbed over it and headed south. The man was evidently carrying something, which he lifted over the fence.

Hashknife trailed him as close as he dared. The man crossed the street, far from any lights and walked swiftly down the road, which led south from Tomahawk Flats. But he only went a short distance and stopped off the road. A minute later, he was coming back. Hashknife dropped flat as the man went past him, panting a little. He saw him turn into the main street.

Hashknife saw the man was not carrying anything when he returned; so he went on in the darkness, just off the road, searching as well as he could in the darkness, and almost fell over a valise, which had been left behind a small clump of brush, only a dozen feet off the road. The heavy valise was locked, and Hashknife didn't bother to try and open it. He picked it up and went back to Colton's house, where he left the valise against the low fence.

There was a light in the house, but the blinds were down.

Hashknife tried the kitchen door and found it unlocked. Quietly he opened the door, and listened, but there was not a sound. He closed the door, moved ahead to the partly opened doorway, which opened into the living-room, stepped aside against the wall and waited for something to happen.

He had been there about ten minutes, when he faintly heard footsteps on the plank walk, which led from the street. There was a sharp knock at the front door, and then the door opened. He was unable to see who had come, but heard more than one come in. A voice called:

"Colton!"

When there was no reply, he heard a man swear bitterly, damning the Colton family back several generations.

"Where the devil did he go? He never came to the jail. Yuh don't suppose—?" a voice began.

"Suppose what?" asked another man.

"Never mind. Where did Hartley go? I seen Stevens there, but I didn't see that long-legged bloodhound. That damned Trent! He made a mess of the deal. Five hundred dollars, all shot!"

"Never mind the five hundred dollars," said the other nervously. "We've got to find Colton. Don't yuh realize that Harry will talk? He ain't got the guts of a cottontail. Let's head south."

"No, we won't head no place—not till we find Colton. Damn it, we've got to find Colton! Where did that ring come from?"

"That beats me. I threw it away, I tell yuh. I heard it hit the buggy—maybe that fool Harry found it. He's half-crazy, anyway. He should have been dumped into the canyon with Regan. We'd have been safe, that's a cinch."

"Regan got what was comin' to him. Askin' the Association to send a man down here to buy ranches! Said it'd look legitimate. Legitimate—hell! They sent Hashknife Hartley. He found it out, and lost his nerve. Scared to write or wire us—came down himself, and wanted to get out of the deal."

"Never mind what happened to Regan—what'll happen to us?"

"Nothin'!" snapped the man. "Maybe we're through here, but we can live like kings in Mexico. Yuh see—"

The man stopped short. Hashknife heard the door click shut, and Colton's voice saying, "Keep your hands where they are—both of you."

"What's eatin' you, Colton?" asked one of the men anxiously.

"What did you two do with that valise?"

"Are you crazy? What valise?"

"Don't lie to me—you got it. I cached it beside the road, got Harry's horse and saddle, and when I got back there—it was gone. I'll give you ten seconds to tell me where—"

There was the sound of a scuffle, the thud of a falling body, and a voice drawled:

"Jist set right there, my fine-feathered friend! Pick up his gun, before he gits any bright ideas. Standin' on a loose rug ain't safe, Mister Colton—not when I've got m' toe through a hole in one end of it. All right, all right! This gun's easy on the trigger, my friend. Start tellin' us where yuh put the money."

"Money!" panted Colton, his voice husky. "You fools, I want to know where *you* put it. Put that gun away. Listen; I couldn't leave the money here; so I cached it. along the road—in a valise—but it's gone, I tell you!"

"Ain't he a cute thing?" queried a voice sarcastically. "Why, you lyin' pup! Scared somebody'd find it! You was goin' to pull out with the money, and leave us to face the music. I've got a damn good notion to blow yore head off, Colton. Maybe I will. If you don't—"

"Sh-h-h-h-h!" hissed a voice. "Somebody comin'!"

"Git in that chair, Colton! Guns out of sight!"

Someone knocked on the door, and one of the men said, "Come in!"

Hashknife heard the door open, and a voice said, "Come in, Sheriff. Oh, Mr. Stevens, too!"

Hashknife stepped into the doorway, shoving the door wider. He could see Colton, white-faced, sitting in a chair, looking toward the doorway. He could also see part of one of the other men, and he held a gun behind him, and cocked.

"Colton, you didn't show up," Nick McGarvin said, "and—and we've got to tell yuh. Harry had a gun hidden on him some'ers—and he shot himself. No, he ain't dead, but—he-e-ey! What's this all about?"

"Set down!" rasped one of the men. "Keep yore hands in sight. All right, Colton—where's that money? Our money? Our only chance is to get out of here now—and we don't go without that money."

"I told you," husked Colton, "that somebody got it. If you two didn't—"

"You ain't lyin', Colton?"

"Would I lie—now? I'll hold these two. Get your horses, and we head for Mexico."

"Broke? Colton, I don't trust you—not a bit. Tell us where that money is, or I'll shoot yuh flat. If we can't get the money, why should we bother with you, you sneakin' coyote. Either you get that money—and we all go south—or you die here and we pull out together."

"He ain't givin' yuh much choice, Colton," said Sleepy. "Yuh might as well play square with 'em."

"Keep yore nose out of this, Stevens!" snapped one of the men. "One cinch, when we leave here—*you* won't be on our trail."

"Hashknife will," reminded Sleepy calmly. "And if yuh ask me, I don't believe yo're goin' any place. Yuh see, yuh don't know where he is."

"Hartley!" whispered Colton. "Maybe he followed me an'—"

"I'm gettin' out!" declared a man.

"Money be damned—my hide's worth more'n any money."

The man wasn't taking any chances with his partners. With his forty-five tensed at his hip, he began backing toward the doorway to the kitchen. The door was open just wide enough to let him through—but he didn't make it. A dull thud sounded, just as he was almost out of their sight, and he went right back, head down, shoulders sagging, buckled at the knees and sprawled flat onto his face, almost into the sheriff.

<hr>

For a moment it seemed that everyone except Sleepy was off guard. Sleepy shot out of his chair and dived into one of the men, blocking his gun-hand, and the force of his dive crashed over the table, knocking the lamp off, and plunging the room into darkness. A gun flashed twice, but the spurts of flame went straight toward the ceiling. Hashknife flung the door wide open, as a man came at top speed, but the tall cowpoke dropped to his knees and the man tripped, going into the air and coming down with a crash against the old kitchen stove.

Hashknife was on him like a flash, gathering in the man's two arms.

"Light somethin', will yuh?" Sleepy was yelling. "I think this hombre is petterfied, but I'd like to be sure."

The amazed and excited McGarvin managed to light matches. Sleepy was astride Sam Hack's back, his hands locked behind him, and Sam Hack was having trouble getting enough air. McGarvin quickly handcuffed him.

"When yuh get a little time on yore hands," Hashknife called, "I could use some rope or somethin'. Better find a lamp, Nick; you'll burn yore fingers with all them matches."

Sleepy came out with a rush, lighting matches, while the sheriff found and lighted a lamp. Thomas Colton had struck his head against his own stove and was in no shape to try a getaway. They dragged him into the living-room, and stood back, panting a little. Gus Staley groaned and sat up, trying to caress his aching head. He peered at the three men, who were looking at him, groaned dismally and lay down again.

Someone had heard the two shots, which knocked shingles off the roof, and in a few moments plenty of folks were running forward. Sleepy tried to keep them back, but it was no use. Uncle Andy and Ed Frawley were there, Buck Nolan, Frenchy Arnett, and most everybody else, who could get in. The sheriff was at a loss as to what to do next; so Hashknife took charge.

"Folks, will yuh give us room, please? Gus Staley! Gus, do yuh know what I'm sayin'?"

"To hell with you!" groaned Staley. "I don't talk."

"If you don't, one of the others will. And the man who talks first gets off easiest. Shall I wait for the others?"

Gus Staley, his eyes just a bit off center, looked at the faces around him and decided to talk. He said, "I didn't do it."

"All right," said Hashknife, "we'll start from the first, Gus. You and Hack and Harry held up the bank and took all the money."

"It wasn't stealin'," whined Staley. "Colton planned it. His idea was to break the county—and buy it back, cheap."

"And Harry wore that turquoise ring, eh?"

"He bought it from Chiquita—and forgot he had it on."

"You shot Oren Blakely, Gus."

"That's a lie!" husked Staley. "Hack killed him. He refused to go in on the deal, got scared and pulled out. Hack was afraid he'd talk. I liked Oren. Hell, I wouldn't have done it—myself."

"Why did you kill Chiquita Morales?"

"Hack got scared," whispered Staley. "Harry was a fool to wear that ring. Chiquita could have told who had it. Harry wanted to make Chiquita swear that he never had the ring, but Hack said the safest thing was to shut her mouth. I wasn't there—it was Hack and Harry. Yuh can't kill women and have yore luck last."

"Who hired Trent to shoot me tonight, Staley?"

"Colton. He paid him five hundred dollars."

"Gus, we know why and how you fellers killed Regan. Wasn't he usin' the name of James Morrison?"

"Yeah—he was the syndicate—the yaller pup."

"Folks," said Hashknife wearily, "you've heard the story. I can't tell yuh any more. In fact, if Gus hadn't been scared, I couldn't have told yuh half that much."

Uncle Andy and Ed Frawley shoved their way over to the sheriff, and Uncle Andy said, "It all came too fast, Nick. Does this mean that Johnny's free?"

"Why, shore he's free. Don't paw me around—go and paw Hashknife."

But Hashknife wasn't in sight. He and Sleepy had gone through the crowd and were outside, heading for the main street. Uncle Andy went galloping past them, intent only on finding Aunt Judy and Nell Frawley. They paid their bill at the hotel. The old hotel keeper said, "Some excitement, eh? I heard there was more trouble down at Tom Colton's home. What happened down there—or don't yuh know?"

"That's right," nodded Hashknife and they walked out, smack into Aunt Judy, Nell Frawley and Uncle Andy. Uncle Andy grabbed Hashknife by the sleeve and turned him around, while Aunt Judy planted a kiss on his cheek. Not a word had been said, until Hashknife said, "Aw, gee!" He turned Aunt Judy around, facing the lights of the hotel, and she was crying.

"I thought that kiss kinda ran a little," he said. "When yuh see Nick, Uncle Andy, you tell him that valise-full of money is jist outside Colton's south fence."

"No, yuh don't!" whispered Uncle Andy. "No, yuh don't. Eddie Connors said that you two allus pull out on folks. You've got yore war-sacks with yuh—but yuh ain't goin'. Nossir, yuh ain't. This time, yuh don't go. Hashknife Hartley, tomorrow night is Christmas Eve—and you brought peace to Dancin' Devil. Johnny's free to marry Nell t'morrow night—we get our money back—and you just *try* to leave here!"

"You won't go—will you?" asked Nell, her voice choked. "You can't even think of it, Hashknife—not this time."

"Well," said Hashknife quietly, "I reckon we *can* stay."

"Can stay!" snorted Uncle Andy. "You'll stay, if I have to hog-tie yuh. You ain't the right size nor the right shape, but if Sandy Claus ever came to Dancin' Devil Valley, yo're him."

"Let's go get Johnny," said Aunt Judy quietly. "The sheriff just went down there."

Hashknife and Sleepy, still holding to their war-bags, stood in the hotel doorway. Frenchy Arnett came past, stopped and looked at them. Sleepy said, "How'r yuh comin', Frenchy?"

"I'm all right," replied Frenchy. "Everythin' is all right. Yuh see, Chiquita *sold* that ring; she wasn't tradin' it. Yeah, I reckon it's all right."

Frenchy went on. Sleepy said, "Well, yuh can't run away from everythin'. Maybe they'll make you best man. But tell me somethin', Tall-Feller; how'd you manage to suspect Tom Colton?"

"'Member the first time he talked with me, Sleepy. He had a telegram from James Morrison, who turned out to be Regan. After we took this job, Regan didn't have time to get a letter about us, and the telegram didn't mention who we were. But Colton said, 'After all, the Cattlemens' Association wouldn't recommend a man who wasn't capable.' How would he know who recommended us, unless he had another wire ahead of the one I read?"

"That wasn't much to go on," said Sleepy.

"It was enough," smiled Hashknife. "Maybe I better send a telegram to Bob Marsh, and tell him the ranches ain't for sale."

"Yeah, that's a good idea, pardner; and when yuh write it—give him my regards, will yuh?"

They grinned at each other, went back and registered again